D1141300

Aberdeenshire Library and Information Service
www.aberdeenshire.gov.uk/libraries
Renewals Hotline 01224 661511

DEVIL TO PAY

DEVIL
TO PAY

ROSS KEMP

ISIS
LARGE PRINT
Oxford

First published in Great Britain 2011
by
Arrow Books
A company within
The Random House Group Limited

Published in Large Print 2012 by ISIS Publishing Ltd.,
7 Centremead, Osney Mead, Oxford OX2 0ES
by arrangement with
The Random House Group Limited

British Library Cataloguing in Publication Data
Kemp, Ross, 1964–
    Devil to pay.
    1. Soldiers - - Fiction.
    2. Suspense fiction.
    3. Large type books.
    I. Title
    823.9'2–dc23

LP

ISBN 978–0–7531–8976–4 (hb)
ISBN 978–0–7531–8977–1 (pb)

Printed and bound in Great Britain by
T. J. International Ltd., Padstow, Cornwall

Aside from Kabul, all locations in Afghanistan in this novel are fictitious.

CHAPTER
ONE

Ben MacDonald did not kill himself. I knew the man and was certain of that, whatever anyone said.

Ben was a man who valued life — his own and that of his friends — and I should know because I owe him mine.

It was back in 2008, during the Battle of Basra in Iraq, and we were out in a team of four, identifying mortar positions and calling in the Yanks in their AC-130 Spectre gunships with the Iraqi army steaming in behind us, trying to get rid of the insurgent nutters from the Mahdi army. These boys were serious opponents — fanatical, well armed, plenty of them and with a local knowledge no outsider could hope to match. Still, they had to go, which was why we were there.

We'd kept a low profile on the way in, we were good at that in the SRR — the Special Reconnaissance Regiment — and we'd made it to our observation position without attracting attention. Well, much attention.

Basra's a sniper's dream — higgledy-piggledy blocky buildings that have had convenient gun holes blown into them by a series of wars — death holes we call them because it can be almost impossible to see a rifle inside one. The city's got flat roofs, balconies and a tight maze of streets to run through for a quick change of position. You can add to that a fierce sun and bright white walls so that anyone moving stands out like a rat on a wedding cake.

We had a few close calls — the odd bullet wasp past the ear — but nothing to get too excited about. The same narrow streets that are useful to the snipers are pretty useful to anyone trying to dodge them, if you know what you're doing. Mines were a big problem, though. The place was full of them and the going was slow.

We were playing things by the book — plenty of cover, constant observation. We always played things by the book because there's a name for a maverick when you're involved in street-to-street fighting: dead. So that's how I can say that we were doing things properly and professionally to the best standards of our training, despite the disaster that was to come.

We took out a couple of snipers. I got one. He was defending the main street in. First rule of sniping: move often. He didn't. Probably thought he was well concealed operating out of no more than a tiny hole in a wall. His muzzle flashed twice and I stuck an LASM into him — light anti-structure missile, a single-shot weapon. That was the end of him, and most of the side of the house where he was hiding. Ben got the other. We kept them honest with suppressing fire while Ben flanked them. With all the noise they never heard him coming. A grenade later we were moving on.

2

We'd made it very far into the city and had remained pretty much unseen. I identified the mortar position from a roof — it was behind a water tank on a high building and well concealed. I called in the big Spectre and watched as it came lumbering in above us, cutting a lazy circle around, dropping flares as it did as a precaution against anti-aircraft fire. Essentially, the Spectre is a variant of the Hercules transport plane but, where the Hercules carries people, this thing carries guns. Lots of them. More than virtually anything else in the sky.

As it turned in towards us I talked the pilot in.

"You see the communications mast south-east of the water tower?"

"Affirmative."

"Target that."

"Roger that. Heads down."

That's the sort of advice you do well to follow. I got flat to the roof and put my fingers in my ears. The ground shook and debris came pattering down on me. When I looked up again, there was no water tower, no mortar and not much left of the building it had stood on.

"Next target?" said Ben.

I nodded.

We made the street. I was first through the door, Gary and Ian next, Ben last man, covering each other all the way. Like I said, we were doing the whole thing by the book. You could have used our operation as a training film.

However, in a situation where people are throwing high explosives about and shooting at you from every nook and cranny you have to accept that, no matter what you do, sometimes it just goes wrong. As it did that day.

The motorbike came through at speed, the pillion with an RPG on his back. Ian took them down with a burst from his G3 assault rifle but what happened next, I don't know.

One second I was standing under a doorway, the next — nothing. We think it was an IED, although it could have been that one of the lads on the bike was wired up as a suicide bomber. Whatever it was it had a devastating effect. Ben got blown back into the house, Gary and Ian died where they stood and I was knocked cold in the street.

It turned out later that I had a smashed leg, fractured skull, broken jaw and dislocated shoulder, but I was spark out so it wasn't worrying me at the time.

Ben was the only man of the patrol who was conscious and relatively unhurt. He checked the street and saw that Ian and Gary had been killed and that I was lying by the side of the building, probably dead too. He had every right to think only of himself, every right to just get out and try to disappear. But he didn't.

The Mahdi lads were pouring into the end of the street, shouting and screaming and shooting up everything that moved and a lot that didn't. Ben spent ten minutes encouraging them to stay where they were with a combination of his grenade launcher and automatic fire and radioed in our position and status.

4

Then he got some smoke into the street and dragged me back into the house, though a bullet grazed his leg. Despite that, he got a line in me. Sod's Law says that all the air support will be needed elsewhere at moments like these and he had to hold his position until it turned up — fifteen minutes later. That may not sound like a long time but, believe me, in a fire fight it's an age.

Eventually an Apache came in and lit the street up with 113mm fire, giving enough cover for him to carry me out of there. Despite his injured leg.

Now, Ben didn't have to do that. He could have just run and he'd probably have made it — lost himself in the warren of streets. He had every right to assume I was dead anyway. That didn't matter to Ben. There was a chance I was still alive so I was his responsibility and he came through for me. I owe him everything. Everything. And it's a debt I take very seriously indeed.

I respected Ben more than I did any man alive — not just because he was a good soldier but because he was a good bloke, a proper, decent human being. I can remember his delight when he came to find me awake and recovering in the medical centre. And I can remember what the death of his friends Gary and Ian meant to him. Ben loved life, mine, his own and anyone's that he cared for — not least his wife and kids. So, like I say, he didn't kill himself. I know that like I know my own name.

It was late summer when I found out he was dead, one of those bright blue days you dream about — the sun warm on the water, pretty girls everywhere and a light offshore breeze ruffling the sails of the yachts.

I was in Cowes, the harbour town on the Isle of Wight, having brought over a bunch of property developer types on the little yacht I'd started to run when I left the army.

They were meant to be on a team-building exercise learning to sail, but were clearly more interested in getting pissed and watching the rugby so I docked early and took them to a boozer — not a classy place but expensive, big, new flat screens in every corner but with a nice balcony looking out on the bay.

I love the sea, it's always been my escape, right from being a kid. My best mate's dad had a little sailing boat and we used to spend hours tearing around the coast on it. I feel safe on a boat. Life can't touch you on the water.

To tell the truth, I'd wanted to catch the rugby myself — England vs Scotland in the opening match of the Six Nations. Strangely, I was actually thinking about Ben that afternoon because we often used to watch this fixture together. He was Scots — an Aberdeen boy more interested in football than rugby but he came along anyway — not wanting to miss the chance of calling me an English bampot for eighty minutes. Not that he stopped after eighty. Last I heard from him he was over in Afghanistan, doing the contractor bit like a lot of ex-soldiers do. CP — close protection, convoys. Tough stuff even for a guy of his experience.

I'd been out of the army six months and was doing OK for myself. I'd done in my leg properly in Basra — it was more than a year's recovery before I could stand on it again, another eight months before it was anything like normal. Two years after the injury, I thought I was match fit but the medics disagreed. I was offered a desk job. Not really me, I'm afraid.

And, to be honest, all that time out of the firing line had changed me.

In the months of my recovery Rachel, my ex, allowed me access to my beautiful daughter Chloe again and I was concentrating on repairing my relationship with my kid. With one thing and another I'd spent a long time away, a long time undercover. I really wanted to make that up to her, to give her back the dad she'd missed out on. There were people asking me to go out to work in Afghan and Iraq but I wasn't interested. I was enjoying the easy life doing not much for a month or two. Then the boat offer came up and I jumped at it.

One of the officers in my unit put me in touch with a mate of his. The deal was that I'd clean and maintain the boat and, all the time he didn't want to use it, it was mine to rent out to people who wanted to learn to sail, hen and stag parties, couples getting married, anyone who'd pay, really.

It was never going to make me a millionaire but it suited me right then, I even slept on the boat to keep my living costs down. I was loving it, the odd arsehole client aside.

The trip with the property boys starts OK. All of them are over thirty but they're still like kids, messing around, throwing things at each other, talking about the car or house they'd bought, how much they've made,

7

how much "Charles" they consumed at a mate's wedding, fights they've been in, deals they'd done. I had been trying to do my best to look impressed but it is starting to wear a bit thin.

When we get to the island and into the pub, though, their behaviour goes from childish to horrible. It's not that their chief team-building exercise seems to be going to the toilet together, wiping their noses and taking the piss out of the locals. No, it's a lot worse than that and something that I take very personally.

Just before the rugby, there's a news bulletin. Third item up — after a piece about some tax-dodging billionaire scab on the face of society who's bought his way into the government, and another about school buildings collapsing because they can't afford to repair them — the newsreader says: "A British soldier has been killed by an improvised explosive device in Afghanistan."

I feel a lump in my throat. How many times did I hear that news when I was out there? How many more times am I going to hear it?

"The soldier, from the Royal Anglian Regiment, was serving in Helmand Province."

My old regiment, back before I moved to the Det.

"His family have been told."

Five short words. I've never been unlucky enough to have to go and tell someone's wife or mother that their son is dead but I've visited the houses of mates who have been killed. There's a stillness to those rooms that you get nowhere else.

"Idiot."

It's one of the property boys talking, a big doughy-looking tosser with the sort of public-school accent you don't acquire for under eight grand a term.

"Me?"

"No, the soldier. He's an idiot getting killed like that."

I'm trying to say something reasonable, trying to remember that I'm in the leisure industry now and this man is my client, that I'm supposed to just smile and say "That's right, sir." Every part of me wants to smack him in the mouth but I'm not going to.

My old man gave me two things in life — the ability to take a punch and the ability to hand one out. Make that three — a bad temper. What the fat git doesn't know is that it's only because I was the sort of stupid wanker who joins the army that I've got the discipline not to nut him right now. If I hadn't learned self-control he'd be shitting his teeth tomorrow morning and I'd be in a cell — so we'd both be losers.

"They get paid less than they would if they worked at McDonald's," says another of them, a red-faced fool who looks prime for a stroke by the time he's forty.

"Why would anyone do that? I mean, what goes through their heads?" says another one.

"Shrapnel!" says the first guy. They all laugh.

"I was in the army," I say.

They go quiet. In fact, everyone around us goes quiet. The barmaid looks nervous, the man at the bar next to me moves away. All eyes are turned towards us now, but they needn't worry. I won't be wasting the effort, not today.

The big doughy guy shrugs. I can read him, the way he leans forward slightly and then back. He wants to back down, wants to apologise, and maybe he would if he didn't have a beak full of coke. But he's the big man here, the alpha male. He has to keep face in front of his mates.

"Which regiment were you in?" He says it like he doesn't believe I'm telling the truth, like he has a right to question me.

"Same as the bloke who died."

That's true, to an extent and as much as I'd ever tell anyone. I was in the Royal Anglian from the age of seventeen — five years out of a twenty-year career. After that it was 14 Company aka the Det — or the Special Reconnaissance Regiment as it later became — undercover stuff in Serbia, Iraq, Afghan, all that madness.

"How long were you in for?"

"Twenty years."

"Did it make you rich?"

"No."

"Well then you're an idiot too," he guffaws.

I don't react. If I valued his opinion I'd probably be annoyed. As it is, an insult from a bloke like that amounts to a compliment. I don't care what he says about me. It's what he said about the dead soldier that makes my blood boil. Still, I keep a lid on it. It's what I've been trained to do.

"Steady, Josh!"

It's one of his friends pulling his arm back. Is he thinking of hitting me? I can't believe he is. I've only been polite to him, he's got no reason to think he's been insulted by me — not unless he's a mind reader.

Josh stands up tall. He's a big bloke — a head above me.

"Just remember who's paying for the boat and who's getting paid sod all to drive it," he says, "then consider who's winning here."

He's in my face now but I'm still prepared to back down. So an arsehole has an arsehole's opinion. What a surprise. It's deeply annoying and offensive and no one would blame me for chinning him but I've spent twenty years learning self-control. I'm not going to chuck it away for a no-mark like this.

But then he goes to push me, raises his hands. You can say what you like to me, no problem. Sticks and stones and all that. But put your hands on me and we're heading somewhere else. I give him a look and he knows what it means. He takes a pace backwards. For a second I want him to come on, to put him straight the old-fashioned way about all those blokes who died, blokes whose boots he's not fit to lace. But no.

"I'll watch the rugby somewhere else," I say. "I'll be at the boat for seven."

I walk outside and wander a few metres down by the harbour. I'm not in the mood for the rugby now. I've let myself down. For a second I was my old man in there, wanting it to kick off. I light a cigarette. This makes me feel worse. I control everything in my life. I'm obsessive about it — too obsessive, according to my ex. I'm the kind of bloke who organises the socks in his drawer by colour, I plan my day to the last second when I can, I even have to have the tea bags stacked straight in the box. But I can't control this. Is that a bit of my dad coming out? Maybe, but I'm different to my dad. I was looking for an excuse to batter him; my dad never needed one.

I call my Chloe, dialling her number from memory. I nearly brought her with me on this trip but when I heard it was all lads I decided not to. My phone's the very cheapest Tesco can provide but it does the job. I finished with expensive mobile phones when yet another of mine got kicked into the drink. Third one in six months I've managed to soak.

She's not picking up but it's good to hear her voice. "This is Chloe, leave a lovely message, you lovely person." She sounds so grown-up — ten years old. I still think of her as five when I'm away from her. Rachel left me back then, said it was either her or the army. We were up to our necks in it in Iraq, fighting the insurgents close up. I couldn't leave the boys to that. I never thought she'd go, let alone stop me seeing Chloe. She said I wasn't good for her. And maybe I wasn't. Being in a war zone does things to your head and your relationships. The only guy in our unit who seemed to hold his marriage together was Ben.

"It's Dad, just calling to say I love you. Be good for your mum."

I sit for a while, watching the water — a white sail catches the sunset, turning it to burning bronze. Like I said, there's nothing like the water to make you chill out. My phone rings. Number withheld. I reject it, probably someone asking me if I'm 100 per cent convinced my life insurance is up to scratch. Actually, it isn't. I could never get any when I was in a war zone. Which is fair enough. I wouldn't have insured me, to be honest.

It rings again. I reject it. It rings once more. This time I answer it.

"Nick?"

"Yeah."

"Nick Kane?"

I recognise the voice. "Yes, John, it's me, what do you want? And more to the point, how did you get my number, you spooky bastard? I only bought this phone yesterday and I didn't register it."

"Ways and means," says John, "you bought it with your debit card, didn't you?"

John Fardy is an old mate of mine, a Black Country kid from Walsall, dragged up by his single mum in a one-bedroom flat. He's about the brightest bloke I know. Got his accountancy qualifications in the Pay Corps but transferred to the Det when he was about twenty-eight. Now he works for SOCA — the Serious Organised Crime Agency. He's not a copper, exactly, but he might as well be. He specialises in spooky stuff: surveillance, financial tracking, finding people who don't want to be found. He also specialises in cutting to the chase. This time, though, he doesn't. There's a silence and for a while he says nothing.

"John?"

More silence. I'm about to hang up, thinking the phone's gone dead, when: "Ben's dead."

At first I don't take in the words properly, they take time to register. Stupid thoughts go through my head. "The guy who died was Royal Anglian. Ben's a contractor, it can't be him." Of course, the fact that contractor deaths don't make the news doesn't occur to me, nor the fact that it's very possible, if not certain, that more than one person could have died in Afghanistan that day.

"How?" It's like I'm not actually speaking, like I'm an outsider hearing my own voice.

"He committed suicide."

"What?" I can't believe what I'm hearing.

"He committed suicide."

"No, he didn't."

The words come out automatically. I don't think about them, just say them because there doesn't seem anything else I could say.

"It's hard to take, Nick, but I heard from Claire yesterday. She couldn't get hold of you and she asked me to try. He's dead, he shot himself."

He didn't, though, he just didn't, and I know he didn't like I know the street I grew up on.

When you say you know someone, you really know them, what does it mean?

It means you've seen them in every situation and mood — happy, sad, scared, elated, bored, interested — and you can say without thinking how they would react. It's possible to know someone in ordinary life, of course, to be so close that you can finish their sentences for them. Most people, though, don't really know their friends. They're like the property boys in the bar — just

14

exchanging monologues, going through their whole lives seeing each other in the same situations, doing the same things. They're not tested, by happiness, by despair, by much, really — a divorce, the death of a parent. Big stuff, but nothing like a war.

When I say I knew Ben, I knew him. For a start, I had actually experimented on him, tried to make him crack. Ben was a Para — a tough little Scots bastard with an insane appetite for danger. That, if anything, was his weakness. He applied for 14 Company — and we were sceptical he was going to make it. We needed brave men — and women too — in the Det. We didn't need gratuitous risk-takers.

Not many people have heard of the Det. We were a special forces unit established during the Troubles in Northern Ireland to carry out surveillance work — we worked hand in hand with the SAS but had a slightly different skill set. Everyone in the unit had to be able to handle arms to an extremely high level but there was also all the undercover stuff to learn on top. I caught the end of that but, to be honest, it was all winding down by then. Where it really kicked off for us was the former Yugoslavia, during the madness over there and, after it, hunting Serb war criminals in Serbia. The former Yugoslavia provided us with a lot of our experience and we were still digging dirty little murderers out of Serbia well into the new century.

You had to be able to do the lot in the Det — burgle, hide, take photographs, bug people, drive and, if it came to it, fight with whatever weapon you had available, from a grenade launcher to a chair leg.

I'd been working in the unit for a couple of years and had been earmarked as a trainer. I didn't really want to go down that route but I was interested in becoming an interrogator so I agreed to help handle the mock interrogation of applicants to the company.

I enjoyed the psychological challenge of getting inside someone's head. I interrogated Ben over a period of about four days. The psychologist who was part of the assessment reported that Ben was "psychologically sound". I had a shorter appraisal of his mental state. "Unfuckablewith" just about summed him up.

For a few seconds neither me nor John say anything on the phone. It's me who breaks the silence.

"How did he die?" I ask.

"He shot himself. I just told you that."

"Yeah." Not thinking straight. Calm down. Sort yourself out. What's the most likely explanation? Somebody who didn't like him in his close protection unit? Argument with another contractor?

"Is a coroner going to look at him over here?"

"What do you mean?"

"When the body's flown back in, will a British coroner look at him? Presumably only the Afghans have seen him so far."

"He didn't die in Afghan, Nick, he died over here."

I pause a second, breathe. OK, that's the fact. Now deal with it.

"I thought he was in Afghan."

"He'd been back over here for three weeks, according to Claire."

Claire. Oh God, Ben's wife. Poor girl, Christ, what must she be feeling? Back in the country three weeks? This is getting more mental by the second. I got an email from him two weeks before but he sounded fine. No mention of him being back home. But while this is running through my mind John's used an interesting phrase: "From what I've been able to tell."

"You don't buy this either. You've been looking into it."

"I don't know, it just . . ." He tries to complete the sentence but I can hear his voice cracking and I guess he's trying to hold on to his emotions. ". . . it wasn't him, was it? Suicide. It wasn't something he'd have done. I've had a little dig around about it."

"So what have you found?"

"Nothing yet. I've ordered up the coroner's report. I can do some digging on his email account too. I might be able to find out where he was emailing from when he contacted you."

"How did you know he's contacted me?"

"I already hacked his Hotmail account."

"You don't hang around, do you? Anything?"

"No, not really — just that he had emailed you as if from Afghan when, by looking at a couple of the other emails, he was definitely over here."

That might mean nothing. For all I know he might have decided to get off the beer and didn't want me forcing him out to get pissed. Unlikely, but you never know. John clearly thinks something's up. Your first reaction when you find your mate's dead is to send his widow a bunch of flowers, not hack into his email.

"OK, look, I think I better go and talk to Claire, can you text me her number? How has she taken it?"

"I only talked to her on the phone. She can't believe it either. I can't imagine what her and the kids are going through."

"Yeah. Stay in touch, right."

"Yeah, I will."

It's then that I realise — Claire is in Shepherd's Bush up in London. I'm skint, bang up against my overdraft limit, and I haven't got any way of getting there.

Luckily a solution presents itself. Lumbering from the pub comes Big Twat. Like all bullies, having realised he can't intimidate me he's decided to try and make me his mate. Also, Brain of Britain has worked out he's relying on me for the trip home.

He sits down beside me, his fat arse squelching on to the bench like the sucker from a toy arrow hitting a window. He puts his arm around me and breathes in my ear.

"Are we cool, mate?"

"Yeah, we're cool."

He reaches inside his jacket pocket, which he's wearing despite the heat and the fact he's been indoors for a while. Obviously thinks he looks good in it — he's wrong.

"Smoke?"

"Ta."

I take a cigarette and he gives me a light.

"So we're cool?" he repeats.

"Yeah, we're cool."

"What time are we headed back?"

"I said seven but I can stay later if you like. Whatever time you like. I'll be on the boat all night, so if you want to go clubbing don't let me stop you."

"Cool. I think we will. You're missing the rugby."

"Yeah. What's the score?"

"Eight all. We should be murdering this lot by now we should be . . ."

He stops, clocks the way I'm looking at him. He probably thinks I'm trying to intimidate him. Actually, I'm reining it in, trying to be nice.

"I'll see you inside," he says.

"Yeah."

He goes in. I get up and walk down the quay.

I'm not someone who breaks the law lightly. If you start picking and choosing which laws you want to follow you can't start moaning when someone else does the same and comes and burgles your house or smacks you over the head with a length of iron railing. But I do break the law when I need to. I've been trained to do just that — burglary, fraud and even, as Doughboy probably won't even realise when he finds out his stuff is gone, pickpocketing. He has £1,500 quid in his wallet — a glory wad of fifty-pound notes and a variety of credit cards. He also has a set of Audi car keys — it's a TT, I know because I saw him pull up in it — and what look like the keys to his house. I pitch the house keys into the water and make my way to the boat.

Sometimes breaking the law is necessary — and this is one of those times. I feel a bit guilty about nicking the money but I look on it as a donation to fallen soldiers, whether he wanted to make it or not. I get back into the boat, cast off and head back to Southampton using the engine. There's a ferry for the property boys if they can get on it — it'll show them how the rest of the world lives.

As I cut out into the Solent, my head is spinning. I just can't take it all in. I'm sure of only one thing: Ben didn't shoot himself. So someone else did.

CHAPTER
TWO

It's still light by the time I get to West London — not too difficult a drive as I can cut off the A40 to where Claire lives without having to shove any further through the traffic into town.

The house is nothing special — a 1930s semi just on the edge of the White City Estate in Shepherd's Bush — an up-and-coming area that has never quite up and come. It has big bay windows redone in UPVC, a neat garden, pebble dashing. Millions of people lead decent, unremarkable lives in exactly this sort of house, which is what Ben and Claire planned to do when he left the army. The problem was that there's not an awful lot someone with Ben's skill set is cut out for. He could have become a private detective but the pay's rubbish. Beyond that there aren't too many options — and few that would pay the sort of cash he'd have been getting as a contractor team leader in Afghan.

I ditch the car in a back street in East Acton — no CCTV there, though I'm still careful to keep my head down. Plenty of householders have CCTV nowadays and you could get caught on that. Not that the police are going to go to the lengths of collecting it for a stolen car but I'm obsessive about this sort of thing. You do it right or don't do it at all is my view.

I've changed on the boat so I'm not wearing the same clothes the property boys saw me in, not even the shoes, and I've dug a greasy baseball cap out of the back of the cabin. The car park the Audi was in did have CCTV, so the cap and sunglasses were important there. Most CCTV gives a bad image, when it works at all, but you can't be too careful.

I give the car a quick wipe for my prints just in case and leave it with the key in. That'll keep the local hoodies from nicking the car of someone who doesn't deserve it at least, and hopefully it'll make it disappear off the map. I catch the Tube the remaining two stops and change again at the big McDonald's on Shepherd's Bush Green. Paranoid? Certainly, but it's an ingrained habit.

I make it to Ben's house and take a deep breath on the doorstep. I ring the bell. Claire knows I'm coming but we haven't said much on the phone. She's too upset when she hears my voice.

Claire's a remarkable woman — you have to be to be an army wife. Ben was gone a long time in their marriage but she stuck by him, brought up his kids and was looking forward to seeing more of her man once the mortgage was paid off and they had enough financial stability for Ben to take a lower-paid job.

There's barking inside — Ben's little Border terrier jumping at the glass of the door. Then more shapes appear — the kids, or two of them. Jim Leighton MacDonald, putting his hand against the glass, Alex —

22

as in Alex Ferguson McLeish MacDonald — pulling on the handle, blurred images like something half remembered.

The door opens and there's Claire — five foot two, dark, pale and pretty in that neat Scots way, with the youngest, Lara, just a baby on her hip. Claire's face is puffy. It's obvious that she's been doing a lot of crying.

"Hi," I say.

"Thanks for coming."

I give her a hug and her body is stiff with grief. I can't tell her it's going to be all right because it isn't. Words just aren't up to it in some situations and I just hold her, little Lara pulling at my collar.

"Come in," says Claire.

I follow her inside. The decorating's half done — the hall wallpaper stripped, the new wallpaper in rolls stacked in the hallway. Jim stretches out his hand towards me, pleased to see me, but Alex is looking at me with a trembling lip, a sort of defiance on his face. He wants me to go away, I can tell, not because he doesn't like me but because he doesn't want me to be visiting because his dad's dead, he wants me there like I used to be, swinging him around at a barbecue, letting him beat me up on the sofa, there with his dad.

I've been in some hard situations but there's nothing harder than this. What do you say to the kid? "Your dad was the most amazing man I ever knew and he ain't coming back. Sorry, life's shit like that." Of course not.

I just hold out my hand and his anger breaks and he runs up to me, hugs my leg and buries his face into it.

I swallow. It won't help things if I start crying so I don't but — believe me — I feel like it.

I pick him up and give him a hug. I still haven't got any words for him, nothing to say to make it better. There are no words that could do that, no actions.

"Hello, Uncle Ejit," he says and he smiles.

He's Ben's son all right, a tough little man.

We go into the living room. It's the sort you can find anywhere — big TV in the corner, white leather sofa, pale wooden floor, large windows looking out on to a garden that has a big enclosed trampoline on it. There's a shelf full of cheap trophies. Ben was a champion clay pigeon shooter — something he got from his dad. On the wall is a big photo of Ben with his family — one of those where they snap you mucking about on a white background in a studio somewhere.

He's grown his hair out a bit and he's smiling at the camera, holding Lara while the other kids have their arms around Claire. It can't be more than six months old and he doesn't have the expression of a man who's about to kill himself.

I sit down, Alex and Jim wrestling with each other, showing off to me really, before they lose interest and go and play on the trampoline. This is how it is with kids, I've found. One minute you think they're fine, the next . . . well. Let's not think about that.

Claire and I sit looking at each other. She offers me a brew. I don't feel like it but I have one anyway. It's part of the protocol when you visit a dead soldier's house. You have a brew. I don't know why — the psychologists came up with it, I think. It's just something you do.

24

She comes back and passes me my cup and then we sit looking at each other. She doesn't know what to say and neither do I.

"How are you?" I venture, finally.

She shrugs. Shit question, really.

"When did you hear?" I ask her.

"The day before yesterday."

We keep looking at each other. I can't say what I want to say. She says it for me.

"I can't take this in."

"No."

More silence. She shakes her head.

"I mean, Ben. Of all people. I knew, you know. I knew it might come to this one day and I'd prepared myself for it, as much as you can. But I thought it would be the army at my door, not coppers."

"Did the press bother you?"

"No."

"No journalists?"

"No."

Strange. You'd have thought someone shooting himself was a big enough story to make at least the local papers.

"What have the coppers told you?"

"He shot himself in the head."

"In Hammersmith."

"Yes."

Again, I can't say anything and again, I don't have to.

"I have no idea what he was doing there," she says.

"What have the police said?"

"Suicide."

I feel my eyes widen.

"I can't believe it," she says.

"No, neither can I." I pause for a moment, thinking. Perhaps Claire can offer me an explanation for something that's so inexplicable. "Why do you think he did it? There was no note?"

"Nothing."

Again, what to say? She's in enough distress already without suggesting that her husband might have been murdered.

"I don't know. Did he seem depressed?"

"He didn't seem himself last time he came back."

"In what way?"

"He seemed down. He was a bit, I don't know, angry. No, that's not quite right, not angry, just a bit snappy."

"Did he say why?"

"No."

More silence. This time a long one. I can't hide what I'm thinking for a second longer.

"Claire, I don't believe he killed himself."

She pushes out her chin, purses her lips. "Do you know something?"

"Nothing. I just know Ben."

She turns away, catching my implication. Digesting it. After a time she speaks. "I don't believe he would have killed himself either."

"The police were certain?"

"That's what they said. I told them that he was the last man on earth to do that."

"What did they say?"

"That you can't tell what's going on inside someone's head all the time. The most surprising people do it."

"Have you identified him yet?"

"No. I go down tomorrow."

"I'd like to see him."

She nods.

I think of the email he sent me, the one that was supposed to come from Afghan.

"Did he have a laptop or anything?"

"Aye, that was away out of the house so they didn't get that."

"I'm sorry?"

"We got burgled last week. Luckily we've got nothing to steal so they just had the DVD player. Twenty-one pounds from Asda, they're welcome to it."

"It must have been kids, even the junkies aren't stealing DVDs any more, there's no market in them."

"Probably. They took the PlayStation too."

"Definitely kids. Shitting themselves and grabbing the only thing they'd really want."

"More than likely."

"Can I have a look at the laptop?"

She brings it down and I power it up. Or rather, I don't. The battery's dead. Claire gets the lead and plugs it in by the side of the sofa.

"What's his password?"

"I don't know. That's his work one, I never touched it."

I try a few things. The kids' names. Claire's name. Alex Ferguson. 12th Man — the name of the Aberdeen crowd. Dandies, the team's nickname. Dandies1. Pittodrie, Aberdeen's ground. None of them work. I can't get into it but I know a man who might be able to.

"I can get someone to look at this if you like. Can I take it?"

"Have it, it's no use to me."

All the while we've been talking, something has been whirring in my head. I'm looking down at where the DVD is plugged in. I go to unplug the laptop but something's odd. The plug that's behind the telly is slightly discoloured. The one by the side of the sofa looks like new.

I kneel down by the sofa for a closer look. There's a faint black outline around the socket casing on the wall. It's old paint showing under the new stuff.

I put my fingers to my lips to indicate that Claire should say nothing but, just as I do, Alex comes into the room and asks to have the TV on.

"No," says Claire, "we've got a guest."

"Oh, don't mind me," I say and gesture with my eyes that she should turn it on.

She looks puzzled but she does, CBeebies — *Mister Maker*, nice and manic. I take the remote and turn it up.

"How about that cup of tea?" I say.

In the kitchen I put on the kettle and turn on the extractor fan.

"Have you changed the socket in the front room recently?" I say as low as I can for her to hear me.

She shakes her head.

Then, on the whiteboard "to do" list, I write: "Have you had any of the electric fittings replaced?"

She shakes her head.

I continue writing. "I think you might have a bug," I scrawl, then rub it out.

Her eyes widen.

"Have you got a screwdriver?" I write.

She goes to the bottom drawer in the kitchen. There are a couple of cheap crossheads in there. I take one.

"Can you take the kids in the garden but don't turn off the TV," I write.

Claire goes into the front room and scoops up Alex, who doesn't like it, but in a second he's in the garden with her and the sliding doors are closed.

I go to the socket and examine it. I don't want to disturb it if I don't have to. If someone is listening then they could hear me interfering with it and I'd prefer them not to know I've discovered it.

It is definitely new but I can't say for sure it's a listening device. Ben didn't notice it and he was a better counter-surveillance man than me. The plastic is chamfered at both top corners. An inspection of the DVD socket reveals it's a plain rectangle.

I now have to decide if it's worth risking undoing it. If anyone was under surveillance it was Ben, not Claire and the kids. But Ben's dead so why would they still be listening? It's doubtful they would.

I unscrew the first screw, then the second. Straight away, as the fascia comes off, I know it's a bug. It's too heavy to be a normal socket. Sure enough, there at the back is the chip and the circuitry. Gently I replace it and screw it back in.

My whole body is tingling with anger, rage and excitement. If ever I wanted something to back up my hunch about Ben's death this is it. I try to clear my thoughts. Firstly, it is quite a cheap bug, available in any spy shop or off the Internet. Secondly, it's been put in by a mug. It was clearly slightly smaller than the existing socket so it left a telltale line of unpainted board around the fascia. He should have realised that and just not put it in. A good operator would either have done his research first, gained access to the house somehow — a phoney market researcher offering vouchers, a subtle and unnoticeable break-in — or he would have carried at least a couple of devices to give him options.

So not military and certainly not British spooks. Who then? Who could want to bug Ben? The Serbs? They'd just walk through the door and kill him if they wanted to. Who? I'm racking my brains but I just can't think.

I look at the laptop. I pull up John's number on my phone and walk back into the kitchen. Here the plugs all look OK but I put the kettle on, turn on the radio just to be on the safe side. John answers.

"John," I say, "I think we should meet up and drown our sorrows tonight."

"Yeah," he says, "that's a good idea. Where?"

"I'll text you."

"Fine."

I text 21623163833273 1647.

It's a code we used to use occasionally — not a very sophisticated one but better than nothing. It refers to the position of the letters on a phone keypad. So A is signified by 21: 2 for the second key, 1 first letter. The code reverses every other word so, in the second group of numbers, M is 16. Letters are never repeated and you just have to work out any missing ones.

I look out into the garden to where Claire is playing with the kids and type in the code for Hammersmith.

CHAPTER
THREE

The Andover Arms is my kind of boozer — old-fashioned, wood and brass, no TVs, no fruit machines, just beer and a packet of Scampi Fries if you want to get fancy.

The river runs right past it and on summer's evenings, it's nice to sit outside, look out on the water and Hammersmith Bridge — a beautiful old Victorian suspension bridge in wrought iron, the sort of thing you can imagine Sherlock Holmes wandering across.

I'd stayed at Claire's the night before, kipping down on the sofa. I didn't think there was any point taking the bug out — why alert whoever was using it to the fact we were on to them?

My mind had been whirling. I'd been thinking about when I first met Ben — back when the Special Reconnaissance Regiment was still 14 Company. After that four-day interview session when I had interrogated him, I'd kept an eye on him in training and asked to have him in my detachment. It was the last of the Irish thing — though there was still work to be done against splinter groups from the IRA.

It's funny how you can get to know someone lying next to them under a bush for forty-eight hours in a rainstorm without ever saying anything, but you can.

We were involved in a bit of action together. Probably the biggest "off" we had was just after the main terrorist group — the Provisional IRA — had announced a ceasefire. Some of their colleagues didn't agree with this and a couple of splinter groups formed — hardliners, and few moderating voices. There was a roadblock set up on one of the main roads in Belfast — a show of strength from the boys who were still continuing their war.

We were fourth in line as they drove their cars across the traffic, ten of them, four carrying longs — old Armalite AR-18s — and the rest shorts — pistols of various sorts. We were in big trouble — we were in a queue of traffic and any attempt to turn back would have been met by an instant hail of gunfire.

We were actually on our way to another operation at the time and rule one is that you remain covert as long as possible. Plus, we knew if we engaged then innocent civilians were between us and the gunmen. Using human shields ain't British Army style.

I clicked the radio button concealed by my feet in the driver's footwell. "Roadblock green four junction with orange one. Contact likely." All the roads on our routes had code names according to a colour and number system.

The first two cars were waved through, allowed to drive around the truck blocking the street — the terrorists obviously knew the guys inside. Could we make it through that gap? Not at speed, it was deliberately set up to make it a very tight manoeuvre. The third was questioned, one balaclava at his window, another levelling the Armalite at him directly in front of the car. They were satisfied with what he had to say and let him drive on. It was down to us now. My Northern Irish accent is good for about half a sentence, after that it gets suspect. No chance of blagging it.

"I'll take the first one to the car, you engage targets to the right. Don't reload, just take my MP5 and keep firing. Don't get out of the car — I'm going to get out of here as soon as we give them something to chew on," I said to Ben. He nodded. His MP5 submachine gun was under his coat and a modified twenty-round automatic pistol under his leg. I had an MP5 under my leg, the twenty-rounder already in my right hand. I'd kill the guy at the window with the pistol. Ben would fire off his magazine at the guy in front of the car and then take my gun to the boys at the road-block while I hit the gas and went back the way we came. I was nervous, sweating. That alone told me there was going to be no chance of talking my way out of it. The terrorist would be looking for just such giveaways and, while they wouldn't make him shoot, they would certainly pique his curiosity.

He approached the window, balaclava over his face. The boys were being a bit careless. One terrorist was standing directly in front of us, pointing his Armalite into the car, the one approaching us had his weapon across his chest, the others were looking past us into the cars behind, more intent on posing with the guns than paying attention. Blokes are the same the world over — they like showing off. And that's what this was:

34

a show of strength to say to the locals that the terrorists still ran the neighbourhood.

Not here, though. Our cover was about to be blown; I had no other option. An attempt at an exit unsupported by gunfire was doomed. I double-tapped the guy approaching the car, putting two rounds into his chest at close range. Simultaneously Ben opened up with the MP5 on the guy in front of us, straight through the windscreen, semi-auto, bursts of three. That was the part that came back to me in my memory — the glass spraying out like water from a burst pipe. Then I floored it, swerving the car around in a violent U-turn, Ben motoring away at the terrorists with my MP5.

I'd like to say I said something profound as we floored it out of there towards the onrushing sirens of the Green Army who'd come to back us up. But I was blinking away the bits of windscreen that were blowing into my face and all I could come up with was "Fuck!"

"Yeah!" said Ben. "Fuck!"

We were laughing like idiots, not taking joy in the deaths of the terrorists — though we'd killed two of them and wounded two, it turned out — but in our own survival. Sure, we weren't weeping about the blokes we'd killed, but that was secondary to the fact we were still alive.

Could Ben's death be some hangover from those days? I couldn't see it. The Irish are the same as the Serbs — these boys don't bug you, they stick two pounds of Semtex under your car. And they let people know afterwards. They don't hide their killings, they're proud of them. Besides, it was such a long time ago. They'd have come earlier.

So that left me racking my brains but no one came to mind.

In the Andover Arms I passed John the laptop. He doesn't look like a former SF soldier, he looks like an accountant — wiry, big glasses, suit trousers, open-necked shirt, VDU tan — but he knows all there is to know about computers, financial tracking, finding people. He uses a wheelchair on account of him having no legs — courtesy of the Taliban. Me and Ben went to see him in the hospital. He was all tubes and wires. It broke my heart to see him like that. Ben's too. But what do you say? No use depressing him by crying about it. Also, John had a sick sense of humour. Ben knew how to cheer him up.

He leaned into him and said: "I suppose this is a bad time to ask but can I have your Nike Airs if you aren't going to be needing them?" John nearly pissed himself. The nurse thought he was having a seizure.

"His?" He looks at the laptop.

"Yeah."

He nods. "I'll see what I can do."

He drinks bitter, I drink Guinness — I enjoyed Ireland when they weren't shooting at me. He raises his glass.

"One effect of being an amputee," he says, "is that you get pissed quicker. Lower blood volume."

"Bollocks, you were always a lightweight," I say.

He smiles. "You know, I was told by the psychologists that one of the hardest things to handle for a soldier with this sort of injury is the sympathy. I said, 'Have you met my mates?' Cheers, it's good to see you, Nick."

"You too, Johnny Boy."

We clink glasses. A short silence.

"I found a bug in Claire's house." I say it quietly and close to his ear.

John's eyes widen but apart from that he betrays no surprise.

"We better talk on the move then."

"Yeah."

This sounds like we're overreacting but our mate is dead, he's been listened to at least, probably watched. That means me saying that I thought he didn't kill himself was heard. Would that matter? Would it put me in the firing line? Would they even have been listening in, given that Ben was now dead? Better safe than sorry is my viewpoint.

We finish our drinks and head out down the towpath going west. It's full of people out enjoying the late summer evening, cyclists carving through the walkers, soft amber lights on silver water. I push John along.

"What sort of bug?"

"Shit. Spy shop stuff — a fake electrical socket."

"Freelancers then."

"I suppose we can be thankful for that."

John glances around him, as do I. Instinctively we're looking to see anyone who might be following us or listening in. It's paranoia, sure — what reason have we to think anyone is interested in us? Only the fact that we're interested in them — which sooner or later they will find out. They were watching Ben. So they might be watching us and, more importantly, listening. So we adopt counter-surveillance measures — doubling back on ourselves suddenly and then again to see if anyone's following. You'd never flush out a decent team like that but not all teams are any good. To be honest, they'd have to be really rubbish not to be able to follow us while Ben's in the wheelchair and I'm pushing it, which is why we need some transport.

After a couple of passes up and down the riverfront we head for the traffic and I break into a jog, shoving John along. A taxi comes past and we flag it down. It takes ages to get the disabled ramp down, giving anyone who might be following us an age to readjust their game plan. Still, they're going to have to be better than they've shown themselves to be so far if they're going to listen in to us in a moving cab. It should give us the chance to talk properly.

We ask the cab to take us to Uxbridge and he sets off towards the Hammersmith Gyratory. The place is a surveillance team's nightmare — chocka with about eight exits, you're locked on the island and then suddenly you're free down an exit road. Someone two cars behind you can lose five minutes on you.

"What have you got?" I ask John.

He passes me a printout. It's the coroner's report.

"These boys don't hang around, do they? How did you get this?"

"I'm the police," he says. "Serious organised crime. Absolutely routine to request something like that."

I flick to the end.

"Deceased was killed by a single bullet wound to the right frontal lobe of the brain. The gun found at the scene — a Baikal IZH-79 tear-gas pistol modified to take a 9mm shell — matched the bullet found. Verdict — suicide."

I shrug. "What do you think?"

"A Baikal?"

"Yeah. Wrong, innit?"

Ben had been around guns all his life. He was a bloody clay pigeon club member and had free access to shotguns if he wanted them. They weren't long in their house in Shepherd's Bush but I know he planned on installing a gun safe in there eventually. All he had to do was walk into his club, take out his shotgun and do the business if he wanted to commit suicide. But a Baikal? That's a modified tear-gas gun — a criminal's gun imported from Eastern Europe. It fires 9mm slugs in its altered form and carries a magazine of eight shots. But why trust some dodgy workman to have sorted it out if you're going to blow your head off? You don't want it misfiring. Both barrels of a twelve-bore are a more certain way to go. Plus a Baikal would set you back over a grand even if you had the contacts to get hold of it, which Ben didn't. He was a soldier, not a gangster. In fact, the Baikal's probably the only gun he wouldn't have been able to get hold of if he'd tried.

Plus he'd just got back from Afghan. That country's full of guns — proper, reliable guns as well. So if you're going to commit suicide, why go from a country full of guns to one where — despite what the tabloids would tell you — they're very rare? Why then ignore the weapons you do have access to, to spend your kids' inheritance on a pistol that may or may not work?

"Did you —"

"Yes." He doesn't wait for me to finish my sentence, he knows what I'm going to ask.

He hands me another sheet. It's Ben's bank statement. It confirms that he did get back in the country three weeks ago — there's a cashpoint transaction at Heathrow — but there's no large cash withdrawal, certainly not £1,000 or more. His wages are all there — he started off in Afghan working for the big security firm Bulwark. Later he moved to an outfit called Sentinel, got headhunted according to his emails. There is, however, a large cash deposit: £30,000.

"Expenses?" I say.

"Seems a lot."

"Then what? A bonus?"

That would be logical. Ben was a good soldier and a meticulous planner. I've no doubt he saved lives out there and got his convoys through if it was at all possible.

"In cash?"

John has a point.

"This whole thing stinks," I say.

John nods. "Have a look through the rest of it," he says. "You might see something I haven't." He gives me a wodge of paper from his briefcase. I glance at it — police report, address history, ten years of bank statements, medical records, credit rating, travel history, army reports. It's amazing what these organised crime boys can get on you if they try. I look through it while John speaks to the cabbie and tells him to head back to Hammersmith.

I don't like looking through Ben's bank statements, it makes me feel like I'm prying but I do it anyway — we need all the information we can get. As far as I can make out there's nothing particularly suspicious in the rest of it — it's all as you would expect.

"You know where we need to go, don't you?" I say.

"I didn't think the choice of pub was a coincidence," says John.

It wasn't.

"The Albion Hotel, please," I say to the cab driver.

Eventually we pull into a quiet street just off the Chiswick road, full of big Victorian houses in varying states of repair. The one we stop outside is covered in scaffolding.

The Albion Hotel, proclaims the sign. This is where Ben died.

CHAPTER
FOUR

The Albion Hotel isn't exactly what you could call a hotel — it's a B&B under a great deal of repair, covered with a big scaffold outside.

There's a scrap of police tape across the front of the gate and not much else to indicate it's been a crime scene.

There's not any disabled access so I turn John backwards and wheel him up the steps. We get to the top and approach the door. We can see a dimly lit hallway inside, dirt on the window, a worn carpet. "Vacancies" says the sign. I bet there are.

I try the door. It's locked.

I ring the bell. No answer. It's clearly one of these B&Bs where the owner doesn't live on-site. Well, we do need to have a look, sooner rather than later. And if the owner's not here, he can't say "no" to us. I leave John at the front and go round to the side of the building. Security's pretty good — bolts on every window and the back door's solid and locked. You'd guess it would have to be like that in a reasonably dodgy area. I'd hoped a back door might be open and I could get in.

I come back to the front to have a look for an open window on one of the upper floors — the scaffolding provides a nice ladder up there. But as I'm looking a light comes on inside. Through the glass I can see a man — mid-thirties, scruffy-looking, baggy tracksuit pants and a hoodie — standard issue burglar's pyjamas as I call them.

He opens the door.

"Yeah?"

"I'm a friend of Ben MacDonald, the guy who died here the other day."

"Yeah?"

"I'd like to take a look at the room he died in."

"Why?"

"I'd just like to see it."

He looks me up and down. He has his hands in the pouch of his hoodie, like some seedy grey kangaroo.

"You can have a look if you're willing to rent it," he says. "Fifty pounds for the night, special rate."

"You're renting it already?"

"The police have gone and I've got a living to make."

I guess all that pizza, lager and porn can't come cheap. It sticks in my throat to pay this scruffy creep but I don't see we have much choice. I peel off a fifty-pound note from the wad, which is lighter than it was after I gave Claire five hundred. I'd have given her more but I've got a feeling I'm going to need the rest.

Inside the hallway's a greasy cream colour. There's a "no smoking" sign but the foyer smells of cigarette smoke and the only light is from an old bowl-shaped light shade flecked with the bodies of flies.

"I don't suppose you have a lift?" says John.

"What do you reckon?" says the owner.

"I reckon you don't."

"You reckon right."

"I'll carry you up," I say to John.

"Good idea."

I pick him out of the chair and put him across my shoulder and follow Mr Clean, making our way up the wide stairs, on to the first floor.

"There," says the bloke, pointing to a door, "they kept saying they were going to send a clean-up crew but they haven't come so I've had to do my best myself."

The keys are in the door. I'm hoping they're going to have cleaned up properly because it's one thing looking at bloodstains and another looking at your mate's bloodstains.

"'What time did he arrive?"

"I don't know. I was in bed."

"Late then?"

"S'pose."

"He was only here the one day?"

"Yeah."

"How did he get in?"

He looks at me with a deal of resentment, as if it really is too much of an effort to answer my questions.

"I left the key under a flowerpot for him."

"So he booked in advance?"

"Yeah, I never saw him."

"How did he pay?"

"Card. It's money up front here."

"Yeah," I say, looking at a large mould stain that extends over the wall like a map of Africa behind him. "Very wise. Was it his card?"

He shrugs. "I don't know, as long as the payment goes through I don't pay any notice to what's on the card."

"Would you have a record of it?"

"Somewhere."

"Well if you could find that, I'd be grateful," I say.

He looks blankly at me.

"Did you hear anything in the night?" says John.

He just shakes his head.

"You didn't hear the shot?"

"I was spliffed up. I don't hear nothing when I'm asleep."

Lovely bloke.

John and I go into the room and the owner remains in the hallway, looking at us with a slack-jawed curiosity. I close the door on him and lower John into a chair. We look around. It's like a room in a bad B&B anywhere — knackered double bed, sideboard with a little kettle on it but no coffee or tea bags. The wallpaper is a light stripe, though it might once have been a heavy one, and the oversized cupboard looks like it had a good war. There's a little loo in an en suite to the side with a tiny shower, mould at no extra charge.

A large, gaudy rug has been placed on the floor, a green candlewick affair.

I look at John. He looks at me. I pull back the rug and sure enough, there's a large, dark stain on the carpet with signs that parts of it have been cut away — forensics.

I gave John the bank statements back when we got out of the cab. He's looking through them now.

"No sign of any payment to this place," he points out, "or anything that looks like it might have been one."

The room begins to shake, there's a terrible noise and for a second I wonder what's going on. Then lights flash past the window and I understand. This room backs right on to the main Hammersmith and City Tube line. In fact, any nearer and it'd be *on* the Hammersmith and City Tube line.

"Do you think the cops missed anything?" says John.

"Well, I think they missed that someone shot him," I reply, "so it might be worth going over the place again. How are you on forensics?"

"Financial, fine. This side of the game, rubbish. I know nothing about it."

"Me neither. So our best bet's the laptop and finding out whoever paid the money in here. Let's start by asking shithead downstairs."

I bend down to pick John up. Then I see something.

"John."

"Yeah?"

"Have a look at the skirting board."

I pull the chair around to face it.

"It's clean," he says.

"Exactly," I say. I'm shaking now, fuming, angry. I've got an energy inside me that has nowhere to go. John stares down at the floor.

There is a patch of skirting board just below the window. What stands out about it is that, in this greasy fleapit of a hotel where every surface is stained or scuffed, every piece of white paintwork yellowed by age and grime, there is a section of skirting board about two feet wide that has been scrubbed back to whiteness. Someone has cleaned that and, given the state of the rest of the hotel, I'm betting it wasn't laughing boy downstairs.

This leads to the question of exactly why someone would have cleaned it. And why none of the cops noticed it. What it says to me is this: "there was something on that skirting board that someone thought worth scrubbing off, so much that they scraped away the top, aged layer of paint and left fresh stuff showing below. Not one inch of this hotel was thought worthy of a scrub apart from the piece of skirting board directly below where Ben was said to have killed himself. The thing is, suicide with a gun normally requires you to point your gun upwards. It's an unnatural movement to shoot down at yourself — your arms just aren't long enough to do it in any other way.

Then something else strikes me — the coroner's report said the bullet was still in Ben's brain. Even a relatively low-power gun like a Baikal would pack enough punch to send the slug through his head if shot from point blank. So what would reduce the velocity of the bullet? A silencer. You don't use one of those if you're going to top yourself — concern that their death will wake the neighbours doesn't feature very highly on most suicides' list of priorities.

Another train goes past, shaking the room to its foundations. You wouldn't choose this room for a suicide but it would be ideal for a murder.

"Let's go and get some information off him downstairs," I say.

All sorts of mad thoughts are in my head; how unjust it is that that louse downstairs is walking around alive just to waste himself sitting in front of daytime TV and running a B&B in a building approaching a condemned state while Ben is lying dead in a morgue. The bloke's attitude has got to me. Surely if someone says their friend has died you treat them with respect, you don't grunt at them, gawp at them and then fleece them.

"Yeah, let's but Nick . . ."

"What?"

"Keep your temper. This isn't his fault."

Was it that obvious? I'm light-headed and my mouth is dry, vision has contracted and focused to a tunnel as the adrenalin comes up in me. I've been taught to recognise these signs and deal with them. I exhale hard, force my breathing to be slower.

"You ready?" says John.

I've regained my cool. "Yeah," I say, "I'm ready."

"Then pick me up, you lazy sod."

I pick John up and we make our way downstairs. I'm certain I never want to be in that room again in my life.

It does occur to me to take this grubby landlord and shake him until I get the information I want but I can see John's right. No point. It's reckless, extravagant and self-indulgent behaviour and it risks drawing attention to the fact that our interest is beyond that of mourners wanting to see where their friend died.

There are other ways to find out his name. Once John has that he can find his bank accounts and discover who paid for this room. We could try to get the landlord to cough up the info but he doesn't exactly seem Mr Organised and, besides, there are ways and means of finding out what you need to know.

The American inventor Benjamin Franklin once said there's nothing certain in life but death and taxes. He'd clearly never heard of junk mail. The shelf in the hall's full of it. John takes a couple of envelopes as we go back into the street. Name, address, all you need.

"What now?"

"I'll head back to the office and try to get this open," says John, tapping the laptop, "and see whose card was used to pay for the room."

I look at my watch. It's 10.30 in the evening.

"I'll try to find out if we are being followed," I say.

"Is that likely?"

"Don't know. Probably not but I've got nothing else to do."

"OK, I'll call you tomorrow."

He takes a pen from his briefcase and scribbles something on a piece of paper. I take it from him and study it.

It has a phone number written on it.

"For the . . ." I gesture around with my eyes to indicate whoever might be following us.

"Yeah."

"Good."

I fold it up and put it into my pocket.

"Anything else? Could you do with a few quid?" John asks.

"Well . . . yeah."

We go to a hole in the wall and using a variety of cards he withdraws a grand and hands it to me.

Normally I'd be really grateful but neither of us says anything. This is for Ben and he knows it's crucial to the operation. John's just handing me a tool.

John gets in a cab and I'm left on my own in the street.

I enable Bluetooth on my phone. A list of names comes up, some in code, some actual ones.

I look up and down the street. There's a man with a dog walking towards me, none of the cars has anyone in them and there's a kid on a mountain bike cycling past. I make a mental note of the names on the list.

The phone could potentially pick anyone up within 100 metres, though, and it doesn't have to be line of sight. Will it tell me if someone's following me? Of course not, not for sure. But you use every tool at your disposal. If someone has Bluetooth enabled on his phone, on his MP3 player, on anything, it will pick it up and give me a code or a name. If that code or name keeps with me for too long, I'll know it's following me. And what if the person doesn't have Bluetooth enabled? Then it doesn't work but you've lost nothing. And, of course, I'll be doing it the old-fashioned way anyway, which mainly involves simply keeping your eyes peeled.

I set off, down towards the river again. To do a proper anti-surveillance drill it's preferable to have recced the route first. Then you can look for "choke" points — areas where it would be quite natural for you to stop and turn: shop windows, ATMs, pelican crossings. You can also find some areas that force the team following you to come out into the open a little. Narrow alleys are great for this — they have to follow you through. It's like fishing, though. If you get a nibble you don't snatch at the rod or you'll lose your fish. If you make it too hard to follow you then an experienced team will break off contact rather than come out into the open. That might be what you want, though not in this case. I want to know if someone is following me, how many of them there are and what they look like. If it's a professional team there could be a "box" around me — up to ten people communicating by hidden radio, some close by, some quite distant — 500 metres, maybe. They'll regularly hand me over to each other as I move on, reducing the chances of losing me or being spotted. Is this paranoid behaviour? Yes, a bit — but I am convinced someone shot my mate and if it's a choice between being paranoid and being dead then I'll go for paranoid every time.

I put a number into my mobile, pretend to make a call. Then I think better of it, or appear to. I make my way over to a phone box — thankfully one of the old "heritage" ones. This means I can leave the number inside and it won't blow away. Why would I use a payphone when I have a mobile? Mobiles are very insecure. Maybe I don't want someone eavesdropping on what I have to say.

I put in 20p and call the number — whoever follows me in has to find it on the phone. It rings, which surprises me. An answerphone says, "Not in right now. Please leave a message." It's a male voice, accentless, neutral. I dial two more random numbers to stop them pressing "last number redial". Why, when I want them to find the number? Because anyone can make a mistake and leave a piece of paper — which is what I'm going to do. Forgetting to cover my tracks twice seems very unlikely. I put the phone down and head out, leaving the number written on the piece of paper on the shelf. If someone's watching me, they'll be wanting to pick that up. I've clearly signalled the call's important enough not to risk using the mobile.

Then I'm off down towards the Hammersmith roundabout. I keep the mobile in my hand. Bluetooth is picking up quite a few people here.

Luckily, there's a pavement café just in front of me. I stop and sit with a reasonable view of the phone box. It's a long way away but just visible.

I order a coffee, double espresso as it's going to be a long night, and chat to the waiter. This gives me the chance to look past him, to observe the phone box without obviously staring.

Anti-surveillance, at least if you don't want the people following you to know you've cottoned on, is as subtle and time-consuming as surveillance itself. A kid goes into the phone box. Hmmm, easy enough to pay him a tenner and ask him to go in. Kids don't raise suspicions. Well, not in anyone who's never seen a dicker in Northern Ireland. Half the terrorists' spotters were under twelve.

He comes out again. If the team have got any sense they'll have advised him to copy the note on the paper. I've left it there specifically to see if it's been removed.

That won't necessarily prove I'm being followed but it'll start to build up a picture I can fill in with other evidence.

I look around at my fellow patrons. No one's joined the people outside since I arrived. I drink my coffee and smoke a cigarette. Then I pay up and wander back past the box. The paper's still in there, so it proves nothing. Still, worth a try.

I go to an off-licence and buy a packet of cigarettes. This has given me the excuse to reverse my direction. Nothing too demanding for the surveillance team yet and nothing to show I'm on to them. If they are there, of course.

Am I hoping that I'm just being paranoid? No, this will prove to me that there's more to Ben's death than the police have said.

I check Bluetooth. Three of the names that were there earlier are back on the "devices found" list. OK, the offy's not too far from where I started. Now, though, comes the long game.

I head towards the river again, through the grinding machine of the Hammersmith roundabout, a car mill that crunches them up and spits them out, down towards the bridge again. The moon's low above the suspension uprights and it's just the sort of evening on which someone might want to take a long walk. I cross the river and spend a while looking at the water. Targets who vary their pace are a nightmare for surveillance teams. Slow-moving, meandering targets are a sod to follow. I come off the bridge and walk down the towpath. Now they have a problem. This towpath goes on for miles and miles. It's ten feet wide at the most, backed by trees, gardens, sports fields and office buildings. Anyone following me has to look like they're following me — either that or get busy sending a motorcyclist, or team of motorcyclists, out to various exit points. Not going to happen, is it?

I walk. It's dark under the trees, but the moonlight through the leaves turns the path to a shifting ocean floor. There's no one behind me as far as I can see. I walk on a way, then a little further. I take out the phone again. Check the Bluetooth. One of the names from Hammersmith High Street is there. St John. Saint John? I'm being stalked by one of Jesus' mates?

It's too big a coincidence that he just happened to follow me down here. Somewhere, less than 100 metres away, is someone who can tell me something I don't know about Ben's death. They may have nothing to do with it — for all I know they may even have been trying to protect him — but what I do know is that they might be able to answer a few questions.

I walk on down the river.

If I can get out of range of the Bluetooth then I can establish for sure that it's behind me — as is my suspicion. The second I break contact I'll stop. Then, when it comes into contact again, my follower will be roughly 100 metres behind me. How quick can I do that? I might not be in the same shape I was in when I was selected for the Det but I reckon twelve seconds should do it.

He'll be surprised so that gives him perhaps six seconds to react. He'll have to get going which, even if he's a good sprinter, will put me within four seconds — thirty metres or less — of him. If he — or she, for that matter — isn't much of a runner, I can get hold of him.

I check my phone; St John is still on the list. I set off forward, head down. There are footsteps in front of me, coming towards me. I keep on walking. They might have guessed I'd go for the towpath but they'll want to keep in front of me if they can. I can't see anyone.

The footsteps are quick, assured. In the darkness I can see a bloke coming towards me with a strange way of walking. He's got his hands down by his sides, his head pecking forward like a rooster.

"You what, faggot?"

Following behind him are two of his mates, all three wearing angry expressions, all three coming towards me at a quick clip. It's only Charlie Chav in tuppenny sportswear. I'm being mugged! More than that, I'm being gay-bashed.

I can't believe this. I've been concentrating on winning a game played by one set of rules — subtle, stealthy — and now I'm about to lose the oldest contest in the book.

This is a good old-fashioned Southend-style mugging, like you used to get outside Talk of the South nightclub on a Saturday night — yes, they'll take my phone and any money I've got but that's not what it's about. What it's about is too much testosterone, bad education, bad parenting, and the all-round loserdom of three young men. They want to hand out a beating — which is what blokes of that age love to do. Well, as ye sow, so shall ye reap, saith the Lord, according to one of the school assemblies I was forced to sit through.

I can describe this in two ways. The first is how it appeared to me after the event.

Even though I'm taken by surprise I can see chav number one is going to hit me with his right hand, his entire weight is over that side and his arm is stiff. I put up my guard, ducking my chin into my shoulder, moving the left elbow up as far as it will go to cover my temple and my jaw. If he connects with my head now it's going to hurt him more than me. Simultaneously I duck and I feel his fist bounce off the top of my head. It's a hard punch and he feels it in his knuckles. He's a natural fighter, clearly, because that was quite a smack but he's no technician, he leaves his hand down by his bollocks instead of getting it back up where it might have a chance of blocking my counter. I don't know who he's used to fighting but maybe he expects me to go straight down and doesn't bother with defence.

I smack him with a left hook — open palm because I don't want to risk doing what he's just done, messing up my knuckles by hitting bone. I've no idea how long this fight might go on for and I'm going to need that hand. The movement's quick and tight, no more than five or six inches, but my weight's behind it and I back up the arm movement with a sharp twist of my upper body, engaging muscles from my legs to my back. It connects sweetly on the side of his chin, snapping his head sideways, twisting the jelly of his brain inside his head into a sudden acceleration. He goes down like a sack of shite and I leap forward at the couple behind him. This is clearly "lightweight club" because these two were content for their mate to put me down before joining in. If you've got three of you in an attack, use three of you. It ain't *Enter the Dragon* where everyone obligingly lines up one at a time to attack one bloke. But this lot obviously think it is. Mind you, it might be the old "mugging as a spectator sport" thing — we watch our hard mate batter Johnny Office Worker on his way home and then join in right at the end when any conceivable danger's gone out of it. Arseholes.

The guy's got his hand out wide anticipating I'm going to come in with a swinging haymaker but I come in low, my guard tight for any upcoming kicks, and I headbutt him, really hard, a full body movement, exploding up from the legs to drive the crown of the head right into the mouth and nose. As Ben used to say, there's something about putting someone down with a headbutt that really says "wrong guy" to any remaining opponent. It's surprisingly hard to head-butt properly but, if you can do it, it's a beautiful move, you can feel the crunch of teeth on the top of your head. The final chav leaps at me — full credit to him, he's just seen two of his mates get the treatment but he's game enough to come forward. I admire that. He comes in with a looping punch but I step inside, envelop his arm, sweep him and take him to the ground, landing on his ribs and jaw with my knees. A quick twist and his arm's dislocated. You'd think I'd set fire to him for the noise he makes. Not so tough after all, it seems.

Then it's back on my feet as the first two are getting up again. Mr "You what, faggot?" gets a straightforward Johnny Wilkinson conversion-style kick right under the chin as he comes up on to all fours. The ground's a bit slippy and I fall on my arse. As I get up Mr Headbutt jumps me. I block the incoming kick with both my arms and find myself virtually climbing up him, getting in as close as I can to avoid him hitting me. We grapple standing for a bit and he's surprisingly strong. He forces my head down and gets his arms around my waist, looping them over my body to try to pick me up. Ta very much. I trap his hands so he can't let go and stand up, effectively wearing him like a backpack — his legs up in the air. Then I just fall backwards, our combined weights coming down on his head. For those of you who are interested, that one's known as the Co-op throw, after the well-known firm of quality undertakers. I wouldn't have done that if we'd been on concrete because it would have killed him but here the chances are he'll get away without a permanent injury. Probably. Anyway, as they say on the football, his contribution is at an end.

I step forward to the one who started it. He's looking like a very sorry bunny indeed, lying on his back, his legs wide apart. My 2003 World Cup-winning punt on his head has knocked him gaga. I give him a good one in the bollocks and stamp on his knee as hard as I can. He and his mates have learned a valuable lesson. Open the box marked "mindless violence" and you can find it difficult to get the lid shut again.

58

OK, so that's the after-match analysis. At the time it just goes like this: "whoosh, smack, thump, swish, thump, crunch, bang, thud. There's faces looming at me, I feel my body snap, duck and twist and I only really know what I've done after I've done it. The details of the fight don't come to me until I'm taking their mobile phones.

Even as I do, I can almost hear Ben talking to me, laughing at the victim selection policy of these three lowlifes. The Det close-quarters course is reckoned to be the best in the army. It has to be — as an undercover agent you'll often have to defend yourself with no weapons other than your hands. I've spent years training for this sort of situation and with fit, hard bastards who know what they're doing too — not the puff and Special Brew brigade like these. Add that to the fact that my dad gave me the best preparation a fighter can have — and made me hate him — by giving me regular and sustained beatings and you can see why three West London representatives of the PlayStation generation don't bother me. If a full-grown man punches you as hard as he can when you're nine years old then it's fair to say any other smack in the teeth comes as something of an anticlimax. Would I treat a son of mine like that, to toughen him up? Of course I wouldn't because I'm not an idiot and I'd want half a chance of my kid growing up respecting and loving me. If you want to toughen up your kids the best thing you can do is grow up yourself. The most important thing for a kid is to be happy, not tough.

I rifle through their pockets. This is a matter of practicality — I could do with a few spare mobiles and a bit of cash. If they've done this to me then they've probably done it before. You go around shitting all over people and you can't start grizzling when someone does the same to you. They're not unconscious but the fight's gone right out of them and they're either sitting there groaning or lying curled up in a ball, expecting some more. Why did they choose me to attack? We've got two explanations. One is that they're in some way related to whoever has been following me, whoever was bugging Ben. The other is simpler. God hates them. I'd go for the second. I don't believe in karma or any of that bollocks but I'll say this: having trained in violence most of my life, it's weird how often I come across it in my leisure time. Ben used to say it was like buying an unusual car and then seeing them everywhere. They were there all along, you just weren't looking for them. That may be right but it seems that for years I've had a trouble magnet attached to my back.

None of the phones have Bluetooth enabled and one is clearly nicked. There's no way a no-mark like that could afford a top-drawer smartphone like the one I've liberated from him. And he wouldn't have been likely to have had it engraved with "Carrie, you mean the world to me", either — as I can see when I reach the light of the bridge. I spark up Bluetooth on all of them as I walk — I don't recognise any of the names. As for St John, well — he's gone.

There's a bleep. My own phone. It's a text from John. It just says "call — have news".

I hit reply and wait as the phone rings.

"Get to a secure line," he says, "the phone box, I'll call you there."

I go across the bridge and back to the call box. I get a half-funny look off someone because my shirt's been ripped and, from the way my chest feels, there's a large claw mark across it where the bastards tried to grab me. But this is London. There's doubtless a weirder sight just around the corner so no one pays me much mind.

I wait in the smell of piss and cigarette smoke in the phone box. Now everyone has a mobile I wonder why they keep offering payphones. A secure line is a service to drug dealers, maybe. Hey, it's an inclusive society. The note's still there but it's been moved. Proves nothing so I put it from my mind.

I'm shaking from the fight. All that adrenalin still banging around the body. No matter who you are and how used you get to it, fighting has a major effect on your nervous system — it fires it up like nothing else. It's what you're designed to do, to an extent. That's not an excuse for going around acting like a fool — you're also designed to work as part of a social group, to behave nicely to people and to put the concerns of others above yourself. That's why human beings have built cities, sent people to the moon and discovered cures for all sorts of stuff while solitary fighters such as tigers have — to sum up the plight of this magnificent beast — been fucked over.

That said, there is nothing like the thrill of winning a fight with another bloke — no drug, no drink, no sport. So I have to calm myself and concentrate on the task at hand. The feeling can make you vulnerable — perhaps not on the Chiswick Road — but certainly in any war situation. You have to recognise it and deal with it, just like you have to deal with other difficult emotions as a soldier — fear, grief, even boredom.

Five deep breaths. I can feel the sweat starting to cool on me. The phone rings.

"Yeah."

It's John.

"Nick, I've got some interesting stuff off the laptop."

"Already? How did you get round the password so quick?"

"Luck. It wasn't too complicated. Aberdeen 1983 — their best year."

"How did you find that out?"

"I guessed — second time right."

So I'd been on the right track, I just didn't get lucky.

"So what did you find?"

"Two calendar entries. 'Jeanette — six thirty p.m.', two days after he returned and the same woman's name marked in at seven p.m. a week ago."

"Who's that do you reckon?"

"Affair?"

"I don't think Ben rolled that way, did he?"

Ben was a one-woman man, and that woman was Claire.

He doesn't answer. "Is there a number?"

"Yeah."

"Have you tried it?"

"It's eleven thirty at night. I've traced it to an address in Barnes, though."

Barnes — I could walk that. However, turning up at past midnight isn't probably going to be on.

John speaks again: "Have you been running?"

"Don't ask."

"Also, the number was called again, from that box."

"So we've got a tail?"

"Yeah, looks like it."

"Right, well, I better lose them then."

"Be careful, Nick."

I look down at the phone. St John is back.

"Yeah," I say to myself, "I will be."

CHAPTER
FIVE

The fact we've got a tail means I'm going to have to use some proper anti-surveillance methods. I also need to break off contact with Claire immediately. Nothing's going to keep me from Ben's funeral but apart from that I need to distance myself from her in short order. If someone's following me then I might be putting her in danger.

So it's another B&B for the night — slightly more salubrious than the one Ben died in but not much more. The next morning I'm up first thing and note that the mugger's smartphone has been unlocked to a pay-as-you-go account. I head back to Hammersmith and into the entrance to the Tube where I buy a grey hoodie to replace the ripped one I've got on. It'll be good for keeping a low profile on the CCTV.

I want to make a call where there's a very heavy volume of phone traffic. That way there'll be less chance of them listening in on me. Why not use a payphone? I did last night. Because now I'm serious about anti-surveillance. I don't know who's on my case and it's not beyond the bounds of possibility they could read what numbers have been dialled on it. It's OK for John to call me on a secure line but not for me to call anyone else. I won't put Claire in harm's way and I can't really do that to a total stranger either. The mobile's not exactly secure either but, in a part of London this busy, it's the lesser of two evils. These are precautionary measures, of course. For all I know the surveillance could be from the police. Unlikely, but you can't jump to conclusions.

I dial the number. It rings, and an answerphone starts up. "Hello, this is Jeanette. I'm not —"

"Jeanette Davies." She's picked up.

No point beating about the bush, I get straight to the point.

"Hello, I wonder if you can help me. I'm a friend of Ben MacDonald and I was wondering if I could ask you a couple of questions."

"Of who?"

"Ben MacDonald."

There's a silence.

"You knew him?"

More silence then finally she speaks. Her tone is guarded. "I'm not trying to be obstructive but you'll understand that — given the nature of my business — it's an absolute policy to neither confirm nor deny any information about people we do or do not see. Please don't take that as an indication I know him. If you asked me if I knew Barack Obama or Groucho Marx you'd get the same response."

"OK. Can I ask what your business is?"

Another pause. I can tell she's thinking about her answer.

"Yes. I'm a counsellor."

Wow. A counsellor. I'd have been less surprised if she'd told me she was training him as a mime artist. A counsellor. Ben? Now, there's nothing wrong with counselling but Ben wasn't the sort to go in for that.

"What do you specialise in?"

"Counselling."

"Any particular sort?"

She doesn't reply again. Her reticence would tell me Ben had been there even if it wasn't written in his diary.

"Post-traumatic stress," she says eventually.

Now it's me who pauses — I need to catch my breath. PTSD can happen to anyone, anyone at all. It's happened to me, for God's sake. But it makes me wonder if I've been barking up the wrong tree here. No — the Baikal, the bug, St John following me. That's a point. I find Bluetooth on the phone. There he is. Somewhere, less than 100 metres away, someone is watching me.

"Look, Jeanette, Ben is dead. And the circumstances are suspicious. I need to know if he gave you any information that might lead us to who did it."

"I really can't help you. Please don't call here again."

Her voice is shaking. She puts down the phone. She knows something, I'm sure of it.

I could go over there and try to reason with her. But is there a point in a confrontation?

First I have to lose St John and whoever's with him. There's no place for that quite like the London Underground — especially when you've got all day. Any team that's on me needs to get in close — very close — or risk losing me. It's hard enough to follow someone when they aren't trying to lose you. If they are, it becomes very difficult indeed. Not impossible, though.

I head into Hammersmith, which is a good start because it's a busy station underneath a big shopping mall. I buy an Oyster Card because the quick access makes it nightmarish to follow me through the gates if you haven't had that foresight and have bought a standard ticket. There's also a bit of form filling to do, which gives me the chance to clock anyone who's around me. Then I go quickly to the gates and trot down the escalator. At the bottom I turn and pretend to be studying a little Tube map. One thing is sure, whoever is following me is on that escalator. They must be or they'll lose me. I make a mental note of the faces — as much as you can note the faces of hundred or so people. You'd be surprised, actually, the human brain has a great capacity to recall faces and you have a reasonable chance of recognising someone you've seen only for a second — if you were concentrating. I head for the Piccadilly line going east — into the centre of town.

I take it easy for a bit — read a *Metro* someone has left on the seat. I look at the phone. St John is here. Is he the young woman sitting opposite me reading *Grazia*? Is he the middle-aged black guy to my side? Is he the bearded tourist with a backpack? Unlikely — the beard would make him stand out. Is he even in the carriage or is he in the next one? No point thinking about it but plenty of point just memorising faces.

At Victoria the fun and games really begin. The station under the mall is one of the busiest in London and is served by three lines — Victoria, District and the Circle lines. I motor through the gate and rush to the District line. Excellent — a train's just leaving and I squeeze through the door at the last second. This is a good train — it goes into Earl's Court, where you have the option to change to a variety of lines.

I Bluetooth it — unfamiliar names come up; St John has gone. Am I satisfied I'm not being followed? No. But I am satisfied I've made things very hard for any team on my tail.

I keep on the train until Kew — there are too many direction options for me now for them to really bother trying to recontact me. At Kew I hop out and take a bus back round to Barnes, checking Google Streetview on the smartphone as I do. I can see the building Jeanette works in is a big old Victorian place, sash windows, three-storied. The address John's given me is on the riverfront. I need to see it to make a plan for this evening, so I have a scoot past. It's a pleasant house with a brass plaque on the door. It's up a short path but I can just make out the lettering — Jeanette Davies BACP, which I guess stands for something to do with counselling. Brass plate — nice touch — obviously wants to pick up on the authority with which doctors and solicitors are viewed. A little insecure about herself? Bound to be — counselling's seen as a bit Mickey Mouse compared to proper medicine — but there are some good people working in it, particularly in the NHS. In the private sector you take your chances. In my experience conmen are drawn to misery like rats to a takeaway dustbin.

It's not the only plate, unfortunately. There's another sign on there in plastic. I risk a quick trot up the path. It's for a dentist. I look at the bells. Jeanette's offices are on the ground floor, thank God.

I beat a retreat smartish because I don't want my face seen. It's still in my mind just to go up and impress on her the urgency of the situation. However, I know that's not going to work. Patient confidentiality and all that. Unfortunately I have to do this the old-fashioned way.

First thing I do is source a DIY store. Again, I'm thanking the chavs for their gift of the smartphone to let me find the nearest one. I get a good big screwdriver — the burglar's friend — a Stanley knife, and an automatic centre-punch — used for making marks in metal. Obviously I leave them all in their packaging. I won't open them until I'm about to use them. Walking around for hours with a big screw-driver sticking out of your back pocket is a good way to attract plod's attention. And the combination of centre-punch and screwdriver says one thing to any copper: "On the rob." Particularly because I combine it with a load of latex gloves — bought from Boots, not the 99p shop. You don't want your fingers coming through them. I also buy a reflective jacket and a hard hat. The sooner I can do this burglary and get out the better. The nights are light and the high-vis vest would seem like a counter-intuitive move. Not so. Anyone seeing me will assume I'm fixing the windows, not breaking in. The final thing I buy is a little penlight on a keyring. I'm going to need that, more than likely.

I've noted that the target building has sash windows at the front and that means a good chance they're at the back too. However, I'm going to cover myself for every eventuality.

I don't go back to Barnes until well after office closing hours, and bide my time sitting in a pub drinking coffee, then in a coffee shop drinking coffee, then in a betting shop going to the bog a lot and watching my horses lose. Still, £10 worth of bets covers a few hours and stops me looking like too much of a weirdo in there.

While I'm waiting I read the paper. I see that there's been a major offensive against the Taliban out in Afghan. Eighty fighters dead in a village in the Marjul area. Eighty's a large number at one go. And I thought the Taliban were under retreat in Marjul. The situation's unstable, sure, but that many fighters in one place makes you think they might have more in reserve. If eighty died, how many others are on the ground there?

At around eight with dusk coming down, I call the counsellor from one of the other mobiles. The answer-phone's on and the message plays to the end. Excellent.

I'm unaccountably nervous about doing this. I've broken into places many times, in training and for real. If you get caught doing it in Ireland you've got a chance of a bullet in the head. Serbia and it's a virtual certainty. Here I know I'm not going to die but my heart is thumping.

Why? Because you never really get used to this sort of pressure. Also, I know I'm closer to finding out the truth about Ben. I have no doubts that he didn't kill himself, none at all, but there's always Explanation B, the same Explanation B that all sorts of believers — religious sorts, alternative medicine-heads, New Agers — are confronted with. Explanation A is that you're right, you've seen a pattern in things that other people haven't. Explanation B is that you're a nutter. No, this is Explanation A stuff. I'm right, I know.

I take the stuff out of the packets and place it in my pockets.

There are no lights on inside and it's a gloomy enough building to require them now the sun's going down. I go up and ring the bell. No answer, good. So round the back.

There's an alarm up on the wall and a phone line exiting through a hole in the bottom of the window frame. The alarm's an old sort and I know they don't automatically trigger if the phone line goes down. I click out the blade of the Stanley knife and cut the phone line. Now the alarm can't call Jeanette or the police if I trip it.

The alarm's powered from the mains by the look of it. Even if I cut the line to the mains then the unit will go on under battery power and the loss of external power may even trigger it. Alarms go off all the time and no one pays any attention — at least not in

London. Still, caution pays so I have a very good look at the window.

I had thought the windows might be UPVC, which would have meant I could have centre-punched them cleanly and quickly. Councils often insist on original windows at the front but let you get away with what you like at the back. This is the sort of trainspotter stuff you learn when you've been trained in burglary. It's a proper sash, though. An examination reveals that the alarm contact has been removed — there's a bit of lighter paint where it used to be. The problem with these old sashes is that they "breathe" with the seasons. If the alarm's been put in in the winter then, by summer, the wood's drier, and the contacts on the sensor move apart. Next thing you know you've got false alarms every ten seconds, hence this one has been disabled. The only thing between me and getting in is a little sash clasp. I take off my coat and put the screwdriver inside it. Then I put the muffled end of the screwdriver to the window and give it a quick, clean tap. It punches a hole in the glass about the size of my fist. Yes, it's a bit noisy but this isn't a village, it's London. It'll need more than the tinkle of glass to get the neighbours round. I open the window and climb inside, pushing Venetian blinds out of the way.

I put them back in place and flick on the torch on my keyring. The room's as you'd expect it to be — stripped pine floorboards, big white fireplace, abstract art, a couple of chairs with a coffee table in between, a box of posh tissues on it. A consulting room, clearly.

This isn't the area I want. I'm looking for an office. I go out of the consulting room. To my right is the entrance and a set of big stairs that I assume go up to the dentist's.

To my left is a passageway. I walk down it. On the right is a small kitchen, cheap work surface, microwave, kettle, like you'd find in any workplace. On a clothes rack is a Belstaff jacket with a reflective belt around it and a crash helmet is hung next to it. In front of me is the office. I can see a light underneath the door. Shit. No one can have missed me coming through, can they? There can't be someone here, can there?

I open the door.

A woman is lying face down on the carpet in front of me. I feel a tightness in my stomach and I bend to look at her. I put my hand to her neck. No pulse. Shit. I'm thinking two hundred things at once. Breathe in. Can she be resuscitated? No, she's cold.

The office is untouched, apart from the PC. There's a monitor, a keyboard and a mouse but the main CPU is missing. There's also a handbag and the contents have been spread all over the desk. The woman on the floor is Jeanette Davis, no mistake.

It looks to me as if she's had her neck broken. On instinct I take out my phone to call the police. It's only when I see what's on it that I realise that's not a good idea. "Bluetooth devices connected:" reads the display. "Dave B. Nokia 3456, Jeanette Davies. St John."

There's a noise in the garden. Barking. A dog, and a big one. Flashing blue lights at the front of the house. Looks like the police are here.

CHAPTER
SIX

If the dog is at the back, then there's a fairly straightforward escape route — the front. There are ways of dealing with dogs but I like dogs and, besides, it's not practical to murder a German shepherd in the middle of Barnes High Street, twenty yards from a police station while its handlers and God knows how many more coppers come and dance on my head.

I take a quick look at the filing cabinet. Surprise, surprise, the whole "M" divider has been lifted. The computer's gone and there really is no more reason for me to be here. I open the desk drawers quickly, no keys. Out in the kitchen there are none in the Belstaff pockets either.

I go to the front door. Fan-sodding-tastic, it's been deadlocked from the inside. No one's going through that without a key. I could just come clean and tell them what's happened. It's never going to work, though, is it?

Bluff it? I could. I don't look like a burglar. I could go for the workman line but it would only take them to investigate and I'd have some tricky explaining to do.

No, there's only one way out here. I go back to the helmet and try to put it on. It's far too small. However, there's a stretchy silk balaclava thing inside that fits at a squeeze. It's tight as a nodder but it'll do, I don't want these cops recognising me.

Balaclava on, hard hat on, I go back into the consulting room. I pick up the chair and smash it through the front windows. There's a shout from the back of the house and I can hear the dog doing its nut coming round to the front. Now or never. I dash to the back window and throw myself out of it. Shit, there's still a copper there. He shouts and grabs me as I'm halfway out. There's no time for doing this nicely. I go for a front strangle, grabbing the lapels of his stab vest and driving my knuckles into the sides of his neck to cut off the blood supply to his head. There's a Japanese name for that, according to the close combat instructor who showed it to us, but I can't remember it now. Whatever it's called it does the job and in a second the cop's on his knees. It's like I've pressed an "off" switch on his head.

You'd think people would hit you or pepper spray you or something in that position but they don't. Their whole concentration goes on to getting your hands off their neck. No chance of that, though. In one second the little lights come on at the corner of your eyes, after two they've gone off again and you're blacking out. I shove him back against the gate, sealing it shut with both our weights. Four seconds, he's sparko. I bolt the gate, take out his cuffs and put them on him. Bang. His mate's kicking at the gate, the dog's going nuts. Brilliant, there's going to be a station full of coppers coming round here in exactly no seconds at all, I have to move fast. I take the pepper spray from the copper at my feet and give it a good squirt into the eyes of his mate as he tries to climb over the wall. He falls back shouting, the dog still going mental.

I jump the fence at the back and I run, up towards the side of the house behind. There's a gate there and it's locked. Lights are coming on in the back room of the house. A back door opens and there's a bloke standing in it.

"Police!" I say and he instinctively stands aside, despite the fact I'm wearing a balaclava and a hard hat.

I go in through the house. On a hook by the door is a car key and some house keys. I lift them both, deadlock the door behind me and make for the car — a Citroën Picasso. OK, it's not an Evo but it's going to have to do.

I turn right and, oh no. I've only come into the world's longest dead end, haven't I? Limes Avenue, for future reference, you're not an avenue, you're a close.

I swing the car around at the bottom and head back out.

There's a siren in the street and a cop car comes howling around the corner. I swerve around it and look around me. Left or right? But it's information overload, where to go, what to do? Indecision is final, as the Scottish Thunderbird on *Match of the Day* says. Right it is.

I head towards Hammersmith Bridge, although I can't go over it, the traffic's always diabolical down there. Great, the car's got me out of there but it's going to turn into a liability in about two minutes' time, as soon as they get a chopper airborne.

I can't see any cops in the mirror so I slow up. I hope they've gone the wrong way — this area's a warren of streets and it's easy to make a wrong turn. I need to change cars. Great, there's another car behind me. Only a panda so I might be able to drop him. I'm hammering through the Barnes High Street, up around traffic islands and out across Putney Common, the traffic unfolding in front of me in response to the siren behind, people at pavement cafés standing with their mouths gaping. There is absolutely nowhere to go here, nowhere at all.

Then I'm on a long straight road across a common, which means the cops can block it at any time. I need to get into some residential streets and lose them long enough to nick another car. I brake late and hard.

In the Det, the cars had switches to disable the brake lights — so you could pull up in the dark without attracting attention. They'd be useful here because they'd give the cop in the car behind less warning I was turning. As it is, I momentarily lose him, the rear-view mirror is clear. I immediately cut into some suburban streets. There's an entry at the side of some houses. I go down it, finding some garages at the back.

My first piece of luck of the day — one of the garages has its door open and nothing inside it. I park the Picasso in there.

I take the balaclava off, take the jacket off, make my way out of the garage and pull down the overhead door. It makes a sick amount of noise but what can you do?

I hear the sirens of the pursuing cop cars racing past me and breathe a sigh of relief.

There's an old Ford Escort parked up at the back of the entry, taxed, thank God, so it won't be registering on automatic number plate recognition. I centre-punch the window, which disintegrates. I bang out the ignition with the screwdriver and touch the wires. I take off my latex gloves, which in any case are ripped to shit. That's the sort of detail that might raise a copper's suspicions. I can wipe the car for prints later, though I'm careful to keep my head forward of the seat — don't want to leave any incriminating hairs. There's a baseball cap on the back seat so I put that on and put the hard hat, high-vis and balaclava under the seat. Not ideal to be taking them with me but I can't leave them for forensics to find. Then I'm away — feeling safer. I drive slowly out of the entry, indicate and pull away.

It's only then that I realise how much I'm sweating. Jesus, it's like someone's chucked a bucket of water over me. Still, two fights, a sprint and an impromptu touring car race, I suppose I have a right to be. I need some water. You have to keep hydrated to think straight. It sounds picky, but I am picky.

I take the car as far as I can through the suburban roads of West London, steering clear of the main routes. I don't want it appearing on CCTV anywhere if I can help it. I make it as far as Latimer Road and pull up in the quietest street I can find. It's a rough old joint around here, not 100 yards from the super-rich of Holland Park but a world away. There's a good crim count in this neck of the woods and I'm hoping one of them is going to nick the car and burn it out for me. Should confuse any forensic picture nicely. I take a plastic bag from the footwell at the back and shove the high-vis, balaclava and hard hat in there and give the steering wheel, gear stick and door handles a quick wipe with the baseball cap. Then I put the cap on, pull it low and make it out of the car.

I walk a good way from Latimer Road, up towards Notting Hill through the back streets. I ditch the balaclava in a skip. That's the most incriminating piece of evidence but it'll never be found there. Before I reach the Tube I shove the hard hat into the hedge of the garden of a run-down house and tie the high-vis in the plastic bag and drop it in a bin. My head clears as I walk along. So why did the counsellor die? She had notes on Ben. Someone was trying to shut him up, now someone's trying to shut her up. Who else might she have told? Husband, kids?

Shit, they're in the firing line now. I call John.

"Yeah?"

"It's got a bit tasty I'm afraid, mate." I'm not going to give too much detail because I'm calling on a mobile.

"Yeah, it's on the local news. Wasn't you who killed her, was it?"

"Don't be daft. Look, I think her husband might know what Ben told her."

"That makes him a target."

"Exactly."

I look around. This is a stolen mobile and no one can have tailed me during that escape. I can risk being a bit more open.

"Get me his address. The coppers will be with him until late but I need to get to him as soon as they've gone. We at least need to ask him a few questions and give him a warning."

"Right, I'm on it."

"One other thing, how were the police? I had to leave in a bit of a hurry."

"Just says they were assaulted, so no harm done by the look of it."

"Excellent."

This is the thing about choking people unconscious. It's not an exact science. Say you crush one of his arteries by mistake or give him some sort of fit. In fights people get hurt, worse. I respect the police and think they do a great job so I was glad there were no reports of serious injury.

"Do you want the address?"

I look around. I've phoned him on the mobile. There's no way anyone's following me after my hasty departure.

"Yeah, go on."

"Edgware," says John. "Twenty-four Whittaker Close, I'll text you the postcode."

"Right, I'm going there," I say, and already I'm on my way to the Tube.

CHAPTER
SEVEN

The Tube shunts me up through the Northern line, out to Edgware. I try to reflect and to plan. Well, it seems my hunch was correct — Ben didn't kill himself and someone is prepared to go to brutal lengths to cover up who did. Whoever did this scores highly on the mindless violence factor but nothing on the subtlety. Why are they being so high-profile, leaving a trail of bodies? That counsellor wasn't going to disclose the details of her talks with Ben to anyone. But why was Ben at a counsellor's? He had seen some bad stuff, very bad, but he'd seen that for years. Why would it affect him now, and not before? He had no problems with Claire that I was aware of, nothing else in his life to bother him. Combined with the fact of his death and these murders spells one thing: Ben had some information. It was something that someone was willing to kill him to prevent him from revealing whatever it was. Outside the Tube I get rid of the high-vis jacket in a clothes recycling bank.

I go out into the Edgware streets, past the bank, the rib takeaway, the LA Fitness, and down into suburbia — big Victorian houses, people carriers and SUVs in the drives, through this muted, safe, friendly world. I don't know what to think of it. Part of me envies this life, wants the cars, the big garden, the swimming pool you can only use for two months a year and which costs you a fortune the rest of the time, a big car to ferry your daughter between ballet and tennis. This is not wealth as such, not in terms of megabucks. It's rather what you might call comfortable. Yes, that's it — comfortable — and I can't tell if I love this place, this UK suburbia, or if I despise it, want to shake the people who live here and say "Is this it, is this all you're satisfied with?"

What else is there? Search me. Christ, if I was offered a place here, this lifestyle, I'd jump at it tomorrow. And yet there's a bit of me that finds it all so unreal. I can't work it out. Luckily I'm a soldier, because, if I was a philosopher I suspect I'd be a pretty shit one. It's just confusing. This is what we were meant to be fighting for, the wealth and security of these people, to protect these lives. Was it worth it, the blowing up, the dismemberment, the shattered bodies and lives just so these people could sit watching *Britain's Got Talent* untroubled by terrorists or hostile armies? The only answer I can come up with is "yes". It was, it is, though don't ask me to say why.

I head up through the poplar-lined avenues, and turn into a road heading up a hill. Then I walk past Whittaker Close. There's a police car parked down the way so I keep walking.

A couple of hours or so and a shit fried chicken later I walk past again. It's midnight. Actually, a trip to the takeaway hasn't been my only activity. I've binned the burglary tools and balaclava — in separate places, of course. I've also stopped at a big petrol garage. These places are amazing nowadays — you can get all manner of stuff in there. I keep the baseball cap pulled down and remind myself not to look for the CCTV. The chances of being traced here are slim but — as has become my motto these past couple of days — better safe than sorry. I buy a pair of tracksuit trousers, a Ferrari polo shirt, a trainspotter-style anorak, some CAT boots and a packet of Polos. Then I go to the local swimming baths and buy a pair of trunks from a dispensing machine on the way in and I hire a towel. Again, I'm aware that at some point soon I might be in the frame for a murder and it'll be a lot easier if the cops have nothing to go on. I follow the swim with a sauna so I'm squeaky clean when I come out. Or at least as clean as I'm going to be. I leave the trunks and my old clothes in the locker and head out into the suburban evening to score some fried rat from a takeaway.

I'm probably being paranoid but I make sure I get the spicy. If I've got any of the pepper spray still on me it'll provide a good excuse. Believe it or not it's exactly the same stuff in the spray as goes into your food, just a lot stronger in concentration.

By the time I make it back to Whittaker Close, it's midnight, the police car is gone. This is later than I'd want to be coming here but needs must. Jeanette's husband will be up, I'm certain of that. I go up the close. It's markedly more run-down than most of the roads around here, big 1930s semis, mock Tudor, with "how did they get planning permission for that?" extensions bolted on in cheap pale brick. Still, it's a sight more expensive than anything I've ever been able to afford.

I breathe in. I'm about to question a man who has just lost his wife in violent circumstances. I've got to tread carefully here. I'm going to pretend to be the police. Now that's a long shot for a start but I'm banking on him being so upset that he won't be thinking of how odd it is to have one copper turn up on his own after all the rest have gone. If he asks me for ID, what can I do? Not much. But there's no reason he should if I show him I know about the case.

Whatever happens, I need to treat this guy with kindness and respect. His kids have just been left without a mum, he's lost the woman he loves. A death, particularly the violent death of a young person, throws lives sideways, people sometimes never recover from them. I'm not going to forget that when I'm speaking to him. I need to keep a lid on my own haste and impatience for answers.

It's a big frosted glass door and I can see a light on down the hall. I knock the door gently. I don't want to wake the kids. There's movement and a shape in the glass. The door opens.

In front of me is a man in his mid-forties. He's wearing jeans and a T-shirt, has slightly unkempt curly brown hair shot with grey and from his red eyes I can tell he's been crying.

"Mr Davies?"

"Yeah?"

"DI White, Barnes CID. It's about Jeanette. We just had a few more questions."

"You're late."

"Yeah, it's kind of urgent."

"Yeah. Whatever, come in."

As I thought. His head is too shaken up by grief for him to even ask me for ID. One thing seems clear — he's not a suspect. The guy's been flattened by grief.

I go inside. It's the standard-issue artsy middle-class interior — books everywhere, a few art prints, a *New Yorker* cartoon cut out and framed, stripped floorboards, white walls. You'd think this sort of décor was mandatory with an arts degree.

We go through into the kitchen — a pine job, cork notice board full of kids' stuff, drawings, appointments. A fridge door covered in alphabet magnets with kids' paintings underneath them, on a shelf is a girl's award for gymnastics propped up against a stack of plates that clearly only get used for best. Just an average messy house. What was I saying about whether this was worth defending or not? Of course it is.

He sits down heavily at a large scrubbed oak table and I say the first thing that comes into my head.

"Cup of tea?"

"Yes, please."

Weird to be offering it to him in his own house but it seems right. I brew up and, out of nothing, he starts to talk.

"I thought it was the scooter at first."

"The scooter?"

"I didn't like her riding it, I thought it was dangerous."

"Yes." That explains the crash helmet.

"The kids have gone to my mother's." He's clearly not thinking in straight lines but that's fine. There are times and places that it's permissible to fall to bits and this is one of them.

"Are her parents still alive?"

"Yes. Up north. They're coming down tomorrow."

"I'm sorry," I say. "I promise you, personally, that I will find whoever has done this."

He nods. I want to tell him some other things. I want to tell him that it looks like whoever killed his wife killed my best mate, too. I want to tell him that I'm going to do all I can to make them face justice and go to prison for what they've done. And if I can't do that? Well. We'll see. There are ways and means.

Davies starts talking. He tells me about how they met, how she was so kind, always wanted to help people, that's why she became a counsellor, how it's killed her daughter, not literally, but since hearing the news the little girl can't speak. As soon as she was asleep in bed he had to come back to the house, just to sit in his wife's presence for an hour again. He says how he loved her, really loved her.

"Why kill her, though? Why kill her? She'd have given anyone money if they'd just asked. The bastards could have walked out of there with everything she owned. It's just stuff, just stuff. They could have taken it, there was no need to kill her."

"I might have an idea."

He looks at me, his eyes sick with grief.

"Did she speak to you about a man called Ben MacDonald?"

"I can't remember."

"Did she speak to you about many of her patients?"

"Sometimes. She took the confidentiality thing very seriously. And she wouldn't want to bring all that misery in here. So not many."

"He was a soldier. Back from Afghanistan."

"The mercenary?"

"Yes." I've never liked that term. It implies a lack of morals, that you'll fight for anyone for money. Maybe there are some people like that but most soldiers I've ever known have a strong sense of right and wrong bred into them. So, yes, they'll guard embassies or see medical convoys through, even arms if they're resupplying our boys. But there's no way most of them are going to turn round and fight for the other side, or for some dodgy moral hole of a public-school boy who wants to stage a coup in an oil state — believe me, it's happened. So instead I call Ben a consultant. It sounds like PC bollocks but I just don't like the connotations that "mercenary" brings. But it's his wife's death, his house, his word. I'm not going to argue with it.

"Yeah, she spoke about it."

"What did she say?"

"It wasn't her normal thing. He'd been involved in something out in Afghanistan. At Marjul."

He says the word badly but I get where. Marjul that was on the news. Where the Taliban died.

I say nothing, let him go on.

"He said some people died who shouldn't have and he was thinking of going public with it."

"That was the incident where they killed the Taliban."

"He said it wasn't the Taliban. He said it was another My Lai."

My skin seems to freeze. My Lai. The "how not to" of counter-insurgency. Five hundred women, children and old men raped, beaten and slaughtered in the Vietnam War when the American infantry lost it.

"This was the army?"

"His mercenary force."

"What was stopping him going to the press?"

"Loyalty to some guys he'd been with. They were still there. He said it would make life hard for them."

"Anything else?"

"No. Like I said, she rarely discussed her patients. She was just amazed at how they'd warped the news."

I nod.

"Why do you think he went to your wife in particular?"

"Why does anyone go to a counsellor? He just needed to speak to someone, I guess."

I look at the wall, the peeling paint, the retro kitchen clock.

"You might be in danger," I say.

"What?"

"If I've worked out your wife told you that then so can the people who killed her. They killed her to silence her. They could do the same to you."

"Jesus!"

He looks frightened, surprised.

I sip at my tea.

"What shall I do?"

"I suggest you go back to where your kids are. On your own here, you're vulnerable."

"But I've told you what I know. Surely there's no more damage I can do. If the police know."

"Yes. Make sure you tell the detective next time you're in contact with him."

"I've told you, isn't that enough?"

"I'm not from the police." He needs to know now. He must pass on the information. Once it's recorded then there's no point trying to contain it.

Davies' eyes widen.

"So where are you from?"

I don't know what to tell him, so I tell him the truth.

"I can't tell you that. But I am an interested party and I want to see your wife's killers face justice."

Now he does look scared.

"What are we caught up in?" he says.

"I don't know. But go to your computer now. Email the detective you spoke to today and tell him about this meeting. Then call and leave a message on his answerphone saying you've emailed him and confirming that it's about what your wife told you. Say it's all in the email. If the people who killed your wife are following you they'll hear that and realise there's no point in pursuing you."

He looks at me directly, gathers himself.

"I'm scared of you," he says.

I nod. "You've no need to be. I've offered you no harm and I will offer you no harm. If you like I'll even escort you to your kids."

"No, no. We'll leave my kids out of this."

"Just stay in a public place then, and don't be on your own for a few days. And mention this visit to the police. Have no secrets to keep."

"I wasn't aware I had."

"No."

"I'm going to go to my computer and do as you say but I'd rather you left the house first."

I shake my head. "I want to see you in your car and moving. But I'll wait down here so you know I'm not going to do anything."

"You're a mercenary too?"

"No. Just send the email, make the call and I'll see you on your way."

He goes upstairs. Five minutes later, he's in his car heading down the close. Will he survive? Probably. They may not even have wanted to kill his wife. She'd give up plenty of stuff but not her clients' notes. It's a giant-balls up that's killed her, basically. Still, the lack of professionalism is about tenth on my list of things I don't like about whoever did for the counsellor and Ben.

I step down the close. It's one in the morning, everything's wonderfully quiet on the still summer night and I'm pleased I've been able to offer the counsellor's husband some protection at least.

I take out my phone. Bluetooth reads "St John". It's then I see the blue lights coming towards me.

CHAPTER
EIGHT

They really aren't messing about this time. Two squad cars, one ARV, one riot van, the cops rolling out and levelling MP5s at me. "Get on the floor!" screams one of them. Nowhere to run this time.

I do as I'm told and lie down. I've got two strategies here. One is to bluff it — act the terrified innocent. The other is just to say nothing. They've got nothing on me and anything they do get is going to have to come out of my own mouth. Keeping schtum is my best bet.

I'm cuffed and pulled to my feet and told that I'm under arrest on suspicion of murder. Nice start.

They put me in the car and then drive me over to Paddington Green. Paddington Green! That's a terrorist police station — it's like a fort. It's also a normal nick, it turns out, and serves the area where Jeanette's body was found.

I'm bundled around the back of the station. It's a horrible 1960s affair, like an office block but sturdier looking. They take my phones, which worries me a bit, though there's nothing incriminating on them. John can look after himself if they question him.

They ask me if I want to make a call and I do — John. I tell him where I am and that's it. He'll know what to do with the rest. I give my name and my address — no fixed abode. I'm fingerprinted, DNA swabbed, they take my clothes and give me a paper suit, they try to take material from beneath my fingernails but of course there is none thanks to my swimming pool and sauna trip. Then they take my photo and I'm stuck in a cell that has, weirdly, a TV screen in the wall. It's about twelve foot by twelve and has a desk in it too. This is one of the terrorist cells where someone decided it was unfair to keep them locked up for extended periods without being able to watch *Jeremy Kyle*.

I'm locked in the cell for around an hour before the cops show up. It's a uniformed sergeant. He asks me if I'm tired. I say nothing.

"Come on, mate, this isn't the Gestapo. I just asked you if you were tired. We can't interview you if you're not up to it."

I say nothing.

"Be like that then."

"Do you have my solicitor here?"

"I was getting to that. Yes."

He leads me down a hallway to an interview room.

In it is a tall studious-looking chap. The cop leaves and the solicitor introduces himself as Andrew Holmes, a friend of John's. He says he normally works for the other side, prosecuting people, but he's stepped in at John's request. He asks me what's happened. It might put him in a dodgy position if I confess to being in the house and especially to beating up the cops. So I just say, "Mistaken identity, plain and simple."

"You went to see her husband."

"That's not illegal."

"But it is suspicious."

"I had my reasons for being there but I swear to you I didn't kill her."

He nods.

"Well, I suggest you continue to say nothing. If they charge you we'll develop a defence then."

"Yeah, I'm happy with that."

"Shall we, then?"

"Yes."

He presses a buzzer and a couple of detectives come in and identify themselves. DC Brandon and DI Philips.

"Righty-ho," says Brandon, who has Heseltine hair and looks more like a 1980s entrepreneur than a copper, a sharp face on which he's plastered a jolly smile which makes him look a bit sinister. Philips is short and bustling, probably became a copper so people had to take him seriously. Do I really think that? Not really, I've never spoken to the guy but forming quick opinions on him keeps my mind busy, far away. I don't want to even listen to what they're saying properly, that way I won't feel tempted to respond to it.

"I should congratulate you. Two uniform done with their own kit, two flat-out unconscious and one bitten by his mate's dog. You've given CID in West London a right good laugh."

I say nothing.

"Is that part of the interview?" asks the solicitor.

"Just an observation," says Brandon.

They sit down. It's the standard Bill-style desk, them facing me, the tape recorder whirring. I've been an interrogator myself, I've been interrogated under threat of death. The one thing I know is this: they wouldn't be asking you questions if they didn't need to. If they had everything they needed to go to court they wouldn't be interviewing me or, rather, they wouldn't need a confession. From the moment they begin and tell me I'm arrested under suspicion of murder this is clearly what they're after.

There are lots of different techniques you can use in interview. There's the behavioural — you look for clues that the person is lying, stammering, evading eye contact, failing to be able to relate the story when asked to go through it backwards. There's the accusatory — you confront the guy with what you suspect and make him explain why you're wrong. There's the exploratory — you ask open-ended questions, you beat around the bush, you establish rapport and see what emerges. They all have one thing in common. They are worth nothing if the interviewee doesn't open his mouth.

We go through the jolly approach Brandon first tried to the "what do you think is going to happen when forensics get down there?" to asking me to show him my hands — which as I chinned his mate with my palm don't show any bruises.

They get angry, telling me that a boot print has been found on the woman. Someone stamped on her and has left the imprint of his shoe. I know it's not mine so this actually relaxes me a bit.

We go on like this for a long time. Philips asks me when I'm going to start playing the game, reminds me that a court might interpret my silence as an admission of guilt. Brandon says if I want to play hardball they'll apply for a magistrate to keep me for four days, by which time they'll have the forensics to nail me. I say nothing. It's cheering that they spend so long. It means they haven't really got anything to go on. Eventually they give up, though they try again over the next couple of days. Each time I say nothing. In the end they do get their extension and they turn off the DVD in the cell to try to bore me into wanting to talk.

Then, on day four, I'm drawn back into the interview room. The solicitor's nowhere to be seen. Neither is anyone else. I wait there twenty minutes. Thirty. An hour. No one.

The door opens. It's a short man in a sharp suit. He's dark-haired, close-shaven, a dab too much aftershave for his age — forty-five, forty-six, but an old forty-six. When I say that I don't mean that he looks particularly old, just that he looks the sort of forty-six they had in the 1930s and '40s, when people weren't concerned about dressing younger, having their hair cut younger. He has an air of authority, I think that's what I'm trying to say.

He doesn't sit, just puts his fingertips on the table opposite, staring at me. I've been round soldiers all my life and I can tell that he's one. He's no copper. Greyness seeps into policemen after a few years — the grey of pavements, of interview rooms, of the dingy and horrible places they have to see, the low, squalid human sludge they have to wade through. They're set an unsolvable problem — stop badness. This guy isn't like that. He has something altogether more colourful about him. He's used to taking on the world and winning.

He's expressionless as he begins speaking.

"Nicholas Kane, born seventeenth of November 1972, educated at Westcliff Comprehensive, Southend, left June 1988 with eight GCSEs including, against expectations, French. Academic reports showed him a bright pupil rather given to settling his arguments with his fists. Family life 'difficult' at best. Father known to social services though children not thought to be in mortal danger. Talented rugby player who might have taken it further but preferred a military career. Joined Royal Anglians September '88, promoted to sergeant by '93. Joined special operations with 14 Company, the so-called Det, after passing selection course during the worst weather in living memory. Regarded as a model soldier. Saw action in Ireland, Serbia, Iraq and Afghanistan. Captured while in Serbia but managed to escape. Killed — well, well, well, Nick, coffin makers are never going to go out of business while you're around, are they? Expert in surveillance, advanced driving techniques, interrogation, close-quarters combat and most weapons systems. Burglary."

He dropped the word like a stone.

"Care to tell us what's been going on here, Nick? If you're leaving bodies all over our patch we have a right to know. We know you're working with SOCA. You'll be free to go in an hour but I think we'd all like an explanation, for curiosity's sake."

For the first time in days I feel like speaking but I bite it down. Who is this bastard? He may as well have "Military Intelligence" plastered all over him. I can't see the coppers pulling a stunt like this — no solicitor, breach of the rules, case thrown out. Still, silence is golden and I keep it zipped.

"Partner Rachel, twelve years, separated. Daughter Chloe, ten years old, address . . ."

"You leave my daughter out of this, you spook bastard."

He smiles and he knows he's got what he wanted, seen my weakness. Not so clever, is it? Man loves daughter. Congratulations, Einstein. Ten years ago I wouldn't have been such an easy mark. But I've spent a long time in war zones and it can start to get to you.

"I didn't threaten her, did I? Who have I threatened here? You seem a little jumpy, Nick."

"After four days accused of murder, I wonder why."

"Just tell me what's going on and you're free to go."

"You got that wrong. In forty-five minutes I'm free to go, no matter what I tell you. Someone killed my friend Ben MacDonald. Someone killed that poor woman in her office. Whoever it was wasn't me and I intend to find out exactly who." Shit, I've lost my temper. Bad, bad move, I'm telling him too much.

The man's eyes widen.

"So this is some sort of freelance operation? I didn't have you down for the melodramatic type. A little bit Hollywood, isn't it? Who are you, Steven Seagal?"

I clamp my jaw.

"We could help you, what's your evidence?"

"Come and see me when I'm not in a police cell. I'm sure you'll be able to find me."

"Yes, on the boat, maybe. Or with Claire. Or at that awful hotel you're in. My God, do you field soldiers get addicted to sleeping in shitholes? Yes, Nick, we might come and see you but let me warn you of something. There are things going on here that don't need some tearful squaddie stamping his big boots all over. Your mate died. He was a soldier. It's what we do. Get over it."

"What's going on?"

"Nothing that concerns you. Go back to your boat, drink and eat, get fat, breed with your ugly wife, have a few ugly kids and eventually die. Haven't you read the retired grunts, Guide to Life?"

"Have you anything else to say?"

"No, oh, but the policeman who you choked unconscious did ask me to pass this on."

He suddenly leaps forward and plants one on me. It's a good smack and he cracks a tooth at the side, I can virtually hear it split. White light fills my eyes and it feels as though his fist was a sledgehammer trying to drive me into the floor.

I smile back at him.

"A good one," I say, "make sure you hit the bloke who did attack your copper just as hard."

He smiles.

"Good luck outside," he says, "with your current attitude you are going to need it."

He knocks on the door and it's opened by a young copper. He looks shocked when he sees my face. The man in the suit smiles a curt smile and brushes past him.

"God," says the copper, "I'm to lead you back to your cell. You look awful, is there anything we can get you?"

"A dentist, mate. That'd be nice."

Four hours in casualty, one tooth lighter, I emerge into the Paddington day. I check my phone. A message from John. "Ben's funeral — today 2.30. Kensal Green Crem." It's twelve now.

I call him. "Get to a safe phone now," he says shortly before hanging up.

I go to a phone box and call him. He calls me back.

Before I can fill him in on my news he launches in: "I've got something to tell you as well. I passed on the information about what we saw in the room to the police. They weren't interested, said the case had been closed. Remember, this is information coming from SOCA, so they don't dismiss it lightly."

"What are you saying?"

"I got access to the case notes. There aren't any. All I got was this — it was classified as a military matter. I think the civilian police have been told to back off."

"You mean the army shot him?"

"Of course not, you dozy git. I think he was caught up in something, God knows what."

"Well, the counsellor's husband had a story to tell." I fill him in on what I learned in Edgware.

He whistles through his teeth. "You think Ben got involved in that?"

"Another My Lai? No way. No. Too good a soldier."

"What then?"

"Maybe he saw it. Maybe someone he cared about got involved or was implicated and he didn't want to drop them in the shit."

"What do you think?"

"I think we need to find out who was involved at Marjul."

"I'll get on it." And with that John rings off.

I hang up the phone; I have no intention to stop looking for Ben's killer. A good place to start might be the funeral. You never know who might turn up there and, if any of Ben's old work colleagues are there, I'm going to want a word.

CHAPTER
NINE

The cemetery entrance is through an enormous stone arch. I'll say this for the Victorians, they could turn out a mean monument. It's a cemetery just like you'd imagine — stone angels stained with moss, big avenues, wide and very green in the bright sun. I can hear birds singing, despite the muted roar of the traffic. Not a bad place to spend eternity. It makes sense to bury him here as opposed to Scotland. The kids have their lives in London now and they'll be able to visit if they want to. Besides, Ben didn't really care where he was buried — only that he was buried and not cremated. We had discussed it more than once.

"I should have thought you'd have wanted to be scattered on the waters of a loch," I said.

"And why would I want to foul the waterways?" he said "I'm from Aberdeen, I should be scattered over a chip shop. Never mind being cremated, I should be deep-fried."

Ben had this weird thing that he might one day be brought back to life if his DNA was still intact. He might be dug up and resurrected.

"Before or after Einstein, Churchill and Isaac Newton?" I'd asked.

"After them but before Wee Jimmy Krankie," he'd said.

This is the weird thing about some soldiers. Long parts of the job are very boring and it allows the mind to wander to some strange places.

Where would I want to be buried? To be honest I don't give a shit. I'll be dead, won't I? So it's hardly likely to bother me. Maybe they can sprinkle me off Southend pier.

I make my way to where he's being buried — a weird old place. It's the Dissenters' Chapel and it's at the end of what amounts to a dirt track. It's an old thing — built like a Greek temple, four big pillars at the front and an apexed roof. I'm a bit early so I walk among the graves. There's a bench and I sit down for a while.

I try to enjoy the summer — it certainly beats the stale air of the police cell. It suddenly hits me how tired I am. It's not so much lack of sleep — there's little else to do in a police cell other than sleep — it's the mental strain.

I phase out a little, lost in the sight of bees moving among the bright flowers.

"Nick."

A woman's voice.

I look up. Next to me is a face I haven't seen in five years.

"Beccy!"

It's Beccy Sorrenti, a girl I was in the Det with. 14 Company's the only special operations force in the UK that admits women — it has to because of its undercover work. I was her partner for a short time in

Iraq. She was a language expert who joined us from military intelligence. She was useful out there. You can get more out of the women with the right approach than you often can the men. Women tend to be saner than men, in my experience, less up for the fight and more willing to compromise. Soft, in military speak. Still, sometimes you can achieve more from a ten-minute talk to the right person than you can in two months of kicking in doors. Not that Beccy can't kick in doors if she has to. She might only be five foot six and as lithe as a whippet but how big do you need to be with an MP5 in your hand?

"Nice whistle," she says.

"Ninety-nine quid at Burtons," I say, "it'll do for the hour."

She smiles. "How are you, Nick? Up to your usual tricks again?"

She gestures to the bruise on my face.

I shrug. "You should see the other fella."

"Really?"

"I think he might have hurt his hand a bit."

"Didn't have me to fish you out of it for once?"

"Something like that."

She looks fantastic — she's got a kind, open face and doesn't look like a soldier at all, which I suppose is why she's useful on undercover stuff. Her parents were both Italian and she has that dark Mediterranean look to her. She can pass for an Arab with no problem at all and her language skills are good enough to let her do that.

Did I ever? No. Wouldn't have worked. Would I? Absolutely. If she'd let me.

"I'm fine. How about you?"

"Yeah. How's Claire taking it?"

"As well as you could expect. How did you hear?"

She smiles and says nothing. I smile too.

"Still at it?"

She looks away. Then: "How's the yacht?"

"How did you know about the yacht?"

"Julian told me."

Julian's the officer who sorted the whole thing out for me.

"Good as far as I know. I've been up here for a bit."

"Looking after Claire?"

"Sort of."

"Yes? You've got something you want to say, I think." She can read me pretty well.

"Yeah."

"So what is it?"

I'm aware I may be about to sound like a complete nutter but I think Beccy knows me well enough to know I wouldn't say something like this lightly.

"I don't think Ben killed himself."

Her eyes widen and she takes a fag packet from the pocket of her coat.

"Big statement. Why not?"

I look at her. Should I fill her in? At the front of the chapel Claire and the kids pull up in a big black car. I haven't got time to run her through the details now.

"I've got my reasons," I say.

"Which are?"

"Come on, there are a few old faces here," I say, "let's go and talk to them."

I meet Claire and apologise about the state of my eye.

"What happened?"

"There's not really time to go into it now. Look, I think our suspicions about Ben are right."

"Is that part of it?" She points to my eye.

"Maybe."

"You look after yourself, Nick."

"Yeah, well I was coming to that. I think the more people know about our suspicions the better. I'm going to say what I think at the funeral, if that's OK."

"Yeah," she says, "I think you should."

The chapel is beautiful — a lovely yellow interior with a wooden floor and 1920s-style pillars alongside the doors. It's not a formal military funeral, though you could be forgiven for thinking it was — there are a lot of people here in uniform. I feel slightly out of place in my cheap suit. Never mind, I'm here, that's what counts. The ceremony is awful, though, as in heartbreaking, as they so often are. There's Ben's favourite song, some stuff by Big Country that I always told him he only liked because they were Scottish. It still has me near to crying. John goes to the front and talks about Ben, Claire talks about him, and then she turns to me.

"Nick was Ben's best mate and would like to say a few words."

I stand up. I feel dizzy.

"OK," I say, "we all know what world Ben inhabited. He was a guy who liked to do the right thing and I think he joined the army to do some good in the world, the same reason he was over in Afghan until recently. Unfortunately, what we do brings us, by definition, into the sphere of some pretty bad people. So all I'm going to say is this: I don't believe Ben killed himself. Not for a second. I have confidence that it will one day come to light who did. Beyond that I'd like to say that Ben was the best friend I could have hoped for and I'll miss him for as long as I live."

As I take my seat there's an embarrassed murmur goes through the mourners. I look at Claire. She just nods back at me, so I think it was OK what I said. The vicar himself seems slightly discomposed as he leads the congregation through the end of the ceremony. We go outside for the burial bit and no one speaks to me, though I see everyone wants to.

As I throw the dirt on to the coffin I want to say "goodbye" or something profound but I can't. The words just don't seem to come. The only thing I can think of is my certainty that I'm going to get to the bottom of why he was killed.

Then it's over; we're off to a local pub, to honour Ben in the way he would have liked — by getting smash-eyed.

Some of the boys are there — a variety of SF types. I get plenty of questions about Ben and I do my best to answer them. The more people know what I know then the harder it becomes to kill them to shut them up. You can silence one person, ten is a bit more difficult. I don't mention the Afghan thing, though. I just say that we've been to look at the room and saw enough there to convince us that Ben didn't commit suicide. I'm hatching a plan and I don't want anyone finding out about it and trying to stop me. Claire listens, shaking her head. Then she goes and sits down, head in her hands. Beccy goes to her.

Five minutes later Claire's composed herself and is back fussing over whether everyone's got the sandwiches they want. She's a tough woman.

It's a bright day and there's a play area in the garden for the kids. Claire moves among us. I chat to her for a bit and she says she can't handle taking it all in right now, she just wants to get through the wake. Fair play, so we just talk about Ben and the daft things we all used to get up to together. She even manages a smile but I can see it's a front. She keeps glancing at the kids, clearly wishing that their dad was with them to push them on the swings, chase them around the climbing frame.

I watch Beccy and then I'm aware that I'm watching her so I try not to. I look at my phone. Bluetooth reveals St John is somewhere close by. John wheels up to me. For a mad second I think it might have been him who's been tracking me. I shake the thought out of my head.

"Sit down," he says. "No further problems from plod?"

"No, I don't think so."

"Holmes said they had nothing on you. Anyway, I've done a bit of digging on the Internet," he says.

"Oh yeah?"

"The village this happened in was supposed to be under Afghan Army control."

"So?"

"Well, this was an operation that was meant to involve British forces."

"Perhaps they were helping the Afghans."

"No, look, I put in a phone call to a contact at the Military Police. He put a call in for me. Eighty Taliban dead, that's all anyone's been told. They won't even say which unit was meant to be responsible. You'd think someone would want that on their battle honours, wouldn't you? On current deployments there shouldn't even be a British presence there. It's a calm zone now, relatively. Bit of smack dealing but that's how you know it's Afghanistan. Nothing special."

"But Ben was there?"

"Yes."

"So why?"

"Exactly. And who with?"

"What do you think?"

"No idea. Ben was a contractor. Could have been hired by anyone."

"We need to see Sentinel."

"You can't — they went bust a week ago. Everyone's gone home."

"Have you tried getting hold of them?"

"Yeah. No joy so far but I'll keep trying. The head office is located offshore. Makes it very difficult to get any information."

"Do you think some of those boys did it?"

"They're used in a defensive role. I don't think they go out hunting Terry."

"So?"

"So I don't know."

The plan that's been forming in my head finally comes to fruition. I look over. There in the corner nursing a pint is a big guy I recognise — Mick Wright, an SAS bloke from way back. He's not a tall bloke but he's powerfully built. He has the squashed look of a Rottweiler that's run into a wall. I wander over.

"You really think someone did for Ben?" he says.

"Yeah."

He nods. Mick's not a big talker.

"What are you up to now?" I say. I sort of know because Ben mentioned Mick in an email he sent to me.

"Close protection," he says, "for a firm called Corinthian. We're contracted to the Swedish embassy in Afghan."

"Good job?"

"Has its moments. Bit short of staff at the moment."

"Short or you being fussy?"

He shrugs. "Well, you know. I don't want to work with just anyone. I was only back in the country running the rule over a few blokes when I heard."

My phone buzzes in my pocket. A text.

"Excuse me," I say. I open the message.

"Love you." It's from Chloe.

I swallow. I can feel my palms sweating. I know what I should do. Have a good drink in Ben's name and go back to my life, look after my girl and get a tan on the water. I want to live to be there for my kid. But Ben wanted to be there for his kids too.

I go over to the bar and order a double of a single island malt, straight, no ice. I need to know what happened to Ben. There's no point Chloe having the sort of dad who hates himself, who thinks he's let his mates down, who can't look at himself in the mirror. I owe Ben, plain and simple. I should go away and think about this, but if I think about it I'll never do it. I down the whisky and walk back over to Mick.

My mouth is dry and I can feel the tension in my jaw as I speak. This is the end of the easy life, of days on the yacht, of being there for Chloe. Never mind. It has to be done.

"As it happens, Mick, I'm looking for work," I say. Afghanistan is where it all went wrong for Ben. So Afghanistan is where I'm going.

"Really? Well, if you're up for it you can be on the plane tomorrow morning."

I look at him directly. I don't want to mess him about.

"To be honest, I'm more looking just to get over there. How long do you need me for?"

"I've got three blokes covering an entire embassy. A week would be better than nothing. It'd give me some cover until I could get some full-time blokes out there. I'd do you the air fare for the week out there, plus grub and a grand a week after that if you want to stay on."

"You're on," I say. "How about I turn up, I'll do your week and we'll see how it goes?"

"Are you up to something, Nick?"

110

"Me?"

"Yeah, you."

There's no point bullshitting Mick and so I tell him what I've decided to do, that something went on with Ben down in Marjul and I intend to go up and have a sniff around. He tells me to be careful. There's all sorts going on down there and the road from Kabul is a tester. IEDs, bandits, craters, you name it. And, when I get there, the locals are hardly likely to throw down the red carpet after there was a massacre there a few weeks before.

What does he know about it? Only that it happened. He heard US Special Forces had given the Taliban a kicking, other people were saying contractors had done it.

"Do contractors have the firepower to take out eighty Taliban?"

"Do they crap," says Mick, "but that's the rumour if you care to hear it. There's others saying it wasn't Taliban at all but they always say that. You get the Taliban claiming the coalition's done peaceful villagers but what do you expect them to say? 'Yes, lads you kicked our arses fair and square'?"

Beccy is walking towards us. On instinct I say: "Thanks. Best keep all this between us, eh?"

"All what?" he says with a wink.

Then we're back into the hum of conversation. Beccy smiles as she slides by. Could that smile mean what I think it means?

"Got to go," she says, as if catching my thoughts. She passes me a card. "Call me sometime."

"Yeah, I will."

She turns and leaves and I feel a big thump in my ribs. It's Mick.

"You're in there, son," says Mick. He's clearly a bit pissed.

"Thanks, Mick," I say.

"I would, son, that's all I'm saying, I would."

"Yeah, Mick, I know you would. In fact, it might be easier if you just let me know when you wouldn't."

Mick, it has often been noted, has "inclusive" standards when it comes to women.

"When do you need me out there?"

"I'm at Heathrow tomorrow morning," he says. "Six thirty flight to Dubai. You'll have a ticket at the desk. If you want one."

"Visa?"

"No problem. What's your passport number?"

I tell him and he scribbles it down on a ripped-up beer mat.

"Kit?"

"I wouldn't come in that dodgy suit," he says, "but you'll have to provide your own basics. Where are you staying?"

"Shepherd's Bush." I'm going to stay back at Claire's tonight. I figure that now I've made it clear that I think Ben was killed, Claire and the kids are safe. Whoever it was who made it look like a suicide aren't going to draw attention to the fact that Ben was murdered by harming his family.

"Write me your address. I'll pick you up on the way in."

"Great."

I've got a fair wodge left in my pocket so it looks like a trip to Silverman's in the East End is in order.

I take out my phone. "Love you too," I text Chloe back. I hit send and then head off to get the kit I'm going to need to do this job.

CHAPTER
TEN

Next morning I'm out there. I've got a Goretex shell jacket with a cheap puffa jacket to go underneath, some bargain basement surplus fleeces, a pair of decent gloves, socks, thermals, walking trousers and some hiking boots as well as a Bergen, roll mat, Camel Pack, Israeli bandages, a Leatherman, a head torch, a torch compass and a few other bits including a couple of bottles of iodine — useful for water purification and for wounds. On top of that is a balaclava I can roll up into a hat. I'm left with £300 from the grand that John gave me.

Last night, I went back to Claire's and told her of my plans. She went nuts at me.

"Do you think it's going to help you getting killed too? Have you thought of your girl and your family? Do you want your Chloe growing up without a dad?"

"I've been there five times and come out alive," I pointed out.

"So your odds are shortening. Look, Nick, don't do this for us. Ben would have wanted you to live your life. You deserve it, you've been through enough."

"Ben was my mate, Claire," I had told her.

That was all I could say. He put his life on the line for me. I owe him my life. Someone had done him over. That makes it my responsibility to sort it out, no matter what the cost to me. I'd like to go back to my boat and my easy life but I expect he'd have liked to have done a runner when I was lying broken in the street in Basra. But he didn't. He lived up to his responsibilities. Now I'm going to live up to mine. But I left all that unsaid.

She shook her head. "Well, don't take any unnecessary risks," she said.

"I never have," I replied and I saw from her face that she knew I was telling her the truth.

Still, I've got a weird sense of foreboding about this one. I've seen this in blokes before, they think their number's up and it turns out to be so. I wouldn't say that I feel I'm going to die but this whole thing has a bad smell and it's making me wary. So what do you do about it? You get on with the job and you tell yourself, "It won't be me."

Mick picks me up when it's still dark. I leave £250 for Claire on the kitchen work surface. We make the airport and do the waiting around thing. I actually like airports. When you've spent as much of your life as I have staked out without so much as a pot to piss in, the idea that you can get everything within one building really appeals.

On the flight Mick immediately falls asleep. He's a soldier and has the ability to kip anywhere at any time. I kick back and relax for the first time since I heard the news of Ben's death. Paper, coffee, no one to bother me. And the plane isn't full, so we get a seat between us. Result.

The plane begins to taxi on the runway and the hostess makes an announcement about safety, asking us to turn off our mobile phones. I take out mine and go to click it off but, a moment before I do, I flick up the Bluetooth screen, out of superstition more than anything.

There's a fair old list of devices but there at the bottom is one I recognise. St John.

He's on the plane. For a second it occurs to me to check my smartphone. No, that's not registered as St John. Don't laugh: worse mistakes have been made. He's definitely here.

"Could you turn off your phone, sir?"

"Yeah."

He's here all right, and that means one thing. I have the chance to see him. I might not be able to identify him but I'll have his face in front of my eyes. How many people on a 747? It's 75 per cent full so three hundred or so? It'll give me a chance of recognising him if I see him again.

The plane hits the runway and begins its surge into the skies. I'm pushed back into the seat and note that Mick still hasn't woken up. I look around me as we climb, just letting my mind settle on faces, some frightened, some bored. There's no point in trying to remember these people, you just have to let their appearance sink into your subconscious.

The plane levels out, the seatbelt sign is off and the stewards start to come through with breakfast. I'm starving but have other things on my mind. I stand and walk to the loos — the ones right at the back. Who here looks like a spook or a private detective? Even if they're working freelance then it must be someone with basic surveillance training who's following me. It's a useless game I'm playing but, like I said, I'm in this for the long haul. Just like you might recognise someone from the plane if later you see them on the beach on holiday, it's possible to recognise people you've only really glanced at.

I go forward to the loos, up towards business class. On impulse I walk through it, up to the first-class curtain. Is this where St John is? I need to see everyone on the plane so that means having a butcher's in here.

Suddenly there's an air hostess at my arm.

"Can I help you, sir?"

"No, it's fine," I say, stepping through the curtain.

"Are you a first-class passenger?"

"Not exactly."

"Well, this area is restricted."

I look around the area — of course the seats all have their backs to me.

A man stands up from one of them. And up and up. He's about six foot six and meat was cheap when he was growing up by the look of him. He's enormous — 'roidy, I'd guess, banged out on anabolics. He's wearing combats and a tight-fitting black T-shirt, which he's nearly splitting with his muscles.

"Do you have a problem, ma'am?"

"It's all right, sir."

"The lady wants you to go back down the plane, buddy," he says, "these seats are for the haves. You are one of the have-nots." He has a mild accent. American? Canadian? Something like that.

I smile at him. If I meet this guy in a bar he will "have not" any teeth with an attitude like that. However, such unprofessional thoughts must go to the back of my mind. I'm after St John, and he's clearly not him. This guy isn't exactly tailor-made for undercover work — he's got about as much chance of blending into the background as the Angel of the North. I might have been out of the loop for six months but I'm not so rusty I'm not going to spot someone who looks like Arnie's big brother following me.

"Do you want to make something of it?" he says.

I look him in the eye.

"On a plane, endangering the lives of you, me and everyone on it?" I say very slowly so he can understand.

"Pussy."

"No, thank you, I've just put one out."

I can see the hostess is getting worried so I just wink at the Incredible Hulk and head back down the plane, drinking in the faces.

I pick up the paper as I sit down but I'm not really looking at it, still too excited by the idea that my tail is on the plane.

"What can I get you, sir?" says a voice.

"I'll have a —"

"Small world, isn't it?"

It's not the stewardess at all. I look up into the smiling face of Beccy Sorrenti.

118

CHAPTER
ELEVEN

"Is this a coincidence?" I say. My mind is racing. Is it her that's been following me? Is she St John? I thought she was still with the SRR. Mind you, she didn't actually tell me that, did she?

"Not really, I was meant to fly out tomorrow but I heard Mick offer you the job so I thought I'd keep you company. Do you mind if I sit?"

I slide across, next to the snoring buffalo that is Mick. She sits down.

"I didn't see you in the departure lounge."

"I got there late. Not keen like you."

"You're going to Afghan?"

"Yeah."

"Still . . ." I shrug, feeling slightly ridiculous. I know I'm not likely to get a straight answer.

"I'm a translator."

"For who?"

"The Taliban, who do you think, you daft fucker? I trim their beards as well. ISAF and the UN."

I nod. "Tough stuff?"

"Some. I'm back room now so not as tough as it was."

I look directly at her.

"Is it you who's been following me?"

"No." She replies straightforwardly, no sign of tension, no real deflection of the eyes. "Has someone been following you?"

"Yes."

"Who?" Is it worth revealing my Bluetooth tell? Probably, because I want to see if she registers surprise.

"St John. Do you know him?"

"I know St Michael — patron saint of quality underwear."

"You've never heard of him?"

"No. What do you know about him?"

"Only that's his call sign. Could be his name for all I know."

"Well, if you've fallen out with people who are mates with God, you might be in trouble."

"Am I in trouble?"

"Your face would suggest you were."

I'd forgotten the bruise. Christ knows how, it hurts like fuck, now I come to think of it, even through the painkillers the hospital left me with.

I can see no point in holding back information from her now. She's either the person who's been following me, in which case she knows it all already, or she isn't and so it can't hurt to tell her.

"We found a bug in Claire's house."

"What sort?"

"Not military. Two-bob stuff."

"I heard what you said about the hotel room. It wasn't exactly conclusive evidence."

120

"I think the body of the woman he'd confided in was more of a clue."

I fill her in on the fate of the counsellor, on the fact that someone has been tailing me ever since I started looking into Ben's death.

She orders a drink from the air hostess. I do too, London Pride in a shamefully small can. I take two.

"You have no clue why he died?"

Now, I don't know who Beccy knows in Afghan. She might be able to help me or she might set out to hinder me, for a variety of reasons. The main one might be for my own good. So I opt not to tell her about Ben's connection to whatever went on in Marjul.

"I was hoping a few people out there might be able to throw some light on it."

"Is that why you're here?"

"I'm working for Mick."

She nods. "Corinthian. They're a bit of a cowboy operation, you do know that?"

"Oh good, will I get a ten-gallon hat?"

"He's always moaning on about equipment and stuff. I tell him he should come and work for us."

"Who's us?"

"Bulwark," she says.

Now it's me who's wrong-footed. Why does that surprise me? Why does that feel wrong? I've just never liked that firm, and I know Ben had his misgivings and that's why he left to work for Sentinel.

Bulwark are a huge conglomerate that takes in all sorts of interests — arms manufacture, heavy industry and security work like Ben was doing. It's run by Sir

121

John Carlyle — a tax exile and political string-puller. He's clear in his principles: he has none. He backed the last government with his fortune and now he's backing this one. The man buys influence in bulk.

"You work for the same firm as Ben?"

"Yeah. Well, the one that he used to work for."

"Why didn't you tell me at the funeral?"

"Habit, I suppose." She touches my arm. "I suppose I didn't want any awkward questions."

"Well, here's some awkward questions now then. What do you know? What went on over there to make someone want to kill him?"

"It's a huge corporation," she says, "Ben was at the sharp end. I hardly ever leave Kabul."

"You must know something."

She shrugs. "I should have thought you would have known best. He was in contact with you, wasn't he?"

She sees by my eyes that I've read something into that.

"I presume he was in contact," she says, "even you have to have email nowadays, don't you?"

There's no point in denying it. "Yeah, I was in contact with him."

"And he never mentioned anything?"

"No."

"All I know is that he got the hump over something and left for England."

"What did he get the hump over?"

"He didn't think we were very professional."

"Aren't you?"

"It's a big company. A very big company. Standards vary. Unfortunate but true."

I sip at my beer. She's either a very powerful source of information or a potential enemy. I need to keep my counsel until I decide which. I have the strong sense she knows more than she's letting on but it's only a sense. She's revealed nothing, made no suspicious moves. She's told me about her connection to Ben — although I was always going to find that out. So why am I wary of her? She sure as shit didn't kill him. I know her, she was as loyal to the team as anyone when we were back in the Det. That won't have changed overnight. But it's too much of a coincidence that she's here.

"I should get some sleep," I say, "I only got an hour last night."

She smiles.

"I'll try to find out what I can," she says. "Look me up when you get settled. I'm at the Afghan International hotel."

"Isn't that just a passing-through place?"

"My guesthouse owner got shot," she says.

"I'm sorry to hear that."

"Yeah, he was a nice guy."

Beccy leaves and I sit back in the seat in the aisle, once again leaving a space between me and Mick's relentless snoring. I lean back. Beccy's given me a lot to think about — a lot. But even with my mind racing, my eyelids grow heavy and I fall into a deep, dark sleep.

CHAPTER
TWELVE

Out of Dubai, the passengers have a different look to them. In Bad Terminal (so called because it seems to fly to all the "bads": Hyderabad, Islamabad, anywhere with "bad" in the name) there's quite a few contractors of all sorts — old hands like myself in jeans and sweaters; flashier 'roidheads in combat trousers and shades even in the bright light of the airport terminal; few emaciated and fag-wasted journos; charity and agency workers in something like normal civvy clothes; suntanned builders and even a few businessmen in suits. The one thing there isn't a lot of is women. Beccy's one of only three on the flight and all of them have stuck headscarves on even in the plane, where there are only a couple of Afghanis.

I didn't catch a view of any of the first-class passengers disembarking — though I did try. I got up as soon as the plane hit the tarmac but it was a nonstarter. The hostess barred my way and told me to sit and, without decking her, which was clearly out of the question, there was no way I was going to get to the front of the plane. Then the seatbelt light came off and the place was jammed out. Sometimes you have to know when you're beat. And of course, there's no guarantee that St John was in first class. For all I know it could be Beccy.

The plane out of Dubai itself is a creaky 767 run by an Afghan airline. It's got garish seats, a broken tray, broken seat — it won't come up from the recline position — and Mick next to me has the seatbelt come off in his hand. I check my Bluetooth. St John has gone. Proves nothing. He or she could just have turned off his phone.

There's no way Beccy could have been involved in Ben's death. But as soon as that thought comes into my mind, I start making connections. Say things did go tits up in Marjul. Say someone knew the Bulwark boys were involved — Ben would have known them and might have heard. Say valuable contracts were jeopardised. Is it too far-fetched to think someone might want to defend those contracts, particularly a firm that runs its own private army? The trouble with that sort of thinking is that you can start putting things together that don't really belong. Just because something's logical and possible doesn't make it true. It was possible and logical that I slotted the counsellor. All the evidence pointed that way. The only problem with that point of view was it was bollocks.

Beccy's across the aisle from me, in a row of three with the two other women. They don't sit next to men on this flight. Just the way it is, so you have to live with it. One Afghani view is that if a bloke's left alone with any woman for more than a second then he'll make a pass at her. I look over at Mick. Actually, maybe they've got a point.

I pull down the tray in front of me and it comes off in my hand. Nothing to worry about but it does make you wonder if the maintenance schedule's up to snuff on the engines and wings. A fucked seat I can handle but I have to confess, when it comes to stuff like ailerons and undercarriage I do get fussy. The one thing to be said about military aircraft, though some of them can be a bit old, at least you're sure someone who knows what he's doing has run a spanner over them.

Mick grins at me as we creak through the sky.

"Makes you realise why this lot aren't allowed in European airspace, don't it?" he says.

"Aren't they?"

"No way, safety record's shite."

"Great," I say. On the other side of the aisle a bloke in a business suit is rocking back and forth, clearly praying. "Put in a word for me will you, son," I say, but he doesn't understand. He's a Pashtun, by the look of him, and he's been in the sun of Dubai. Still manages to look pale.

Every time I've ever flown in to Afghanistan, Kabul never fails to impress me from the air. It's sunrise when we come in and the snow-capped mountains light up in a gleaming bronze. The whole landscape is a burned brown colour — stretching out like the stubble of some monstrous parched wheat field beneath the towering walls of rock that surround it. It's more like you imagine Mars than anything on earth. It's amazing just how close the mountains are to the city. They're all around it and even within it. The Hindu Kush. I don't think anyone who's ever read his bit of Kipling can

126

come here and be immune to the romance of the place, and just for a second forget the reality of the awful war that's going on beneath and think back to the Great Game, the Victorian wars out here, the Hussars and the Highlanders storming through the Khyber Pass, Sherlock Holmes's Dr Watson taking his bullet from one of the long Afghani Jezail rifles. It's easy to forget that all that was a bloodbath too. I wonder if some soldier will be flying in here in a hundred years' time looking back on what's going on now through rose-coloured glasses. Probably.

We circle the city, above the mountain where the masts of the TV station look down on the valley known as Sniper Alley. I don't know if there was ever a huge lake where Kabul was but it reminds me of a dried-up seabed, Sniper Alley running off it like a dead river. The land looks drained, petrified, drab but still curiously beautiful. And of course, much of the city is in ruins, something that's visible even from the air.

The plane makes its swift dive into the city. It's a smooth landing and we're quickly on the tarmac. I've got no luggage to collect but I go to make my way through the terminal building. Mick tells me not to bother. He knows the guys on security so it won't be a problem going straight through. He leads me out through a chain-link gate to where a bulky-looking armoured Nissan is parked. It's good to know the Swedes have this sort of kit at their disposal. There's a local driver at the wheel — a guy called Arnan. He greets me in that friendly Afghan way, making the tiny gesture with his hand to his chest that indicates we should be friends.

The early-morning air is cold and I'm glad of my fleece but there's already the sense of heat building behind it. I remember the Afghan summer. It can be blazing by day but at night the temperature can leave you shivering beneath a good coat.

"Hey!" It's Beccy calling, running towards us.

"You can give me a lift," she says, "I need the male company until I get to the Afghan International."

Arnan looks perplexed as she comes forward but Beccy just says, "Tell him I'm your whore."

"What?"

"*Khor*," she says, "say I'm your *khor*."

"Bit presumptuous," I say.

"It means 'sister'," she explains, "he won't understand how I can be travelling with you otherwise."

Mick cracks a big grin and points at Beccy.

"This is my whore, Arnan," he says, "my who-er."

I roll my eyes, Beccy rolls here eyes, even Arnan rolls his eyes. Still, I reflect, Pashto would be a lot more popular with schoolboys in England if they knew it enabled you to go around shouting "whore" at your sister without any fear of a comeback.

Arnan nods. "It's OK," he says, to me and Beccy, "we're not all country boys. I have been in England myself so I know your customs aren't ours. And, Mick, your pronunciation is rubbish."

"You were in England?" I say. "Why did you come back?"

128

"To help my country," he replies. "Now, please, get in and I will drive you."

We're off through the streets of Kabul. It's like a circus out here. The locals are cutting up the road in their pickups, there are people herding goats, pushing wheelbarrows containing all manner of stuff and with first light building is already underway. The streets are teeming with people, some in traditional dress and turbans, some in dusty Western-style clothing. The buildings are all battered and broken and people have made tents and temporary shelters out of whatever they can find. There's also the smell of the streets: sewage, smoke, roasting meat from stalls at the roadside, the choking fumes of the fucked-up engines. Kabul is shattered but it has a buzz to it, an intensity that you just don't get in the west. Life is lived on the edge here: nothing is easy, nothing taken for granted. I realise that in a weird way I've missed this country. I don't miss being shot at, I don't miss the nagging fear that at any moment you might cop an IED or an RPG, but I do miss the people. They're like the mountains that surround them — they were here before we arrived and they'll be here after we're gone and, whatever happens, they will endure.

"Afghan International, Arnan," says Mick.

The hotel looks like it's been dropped out of some nightmare about Torremolinos in the 1970s. It's like a medium-sized office block in concrete with a row of shabby-looking shops along the bottom. Inside it's worse — the walls painted a shocking pink and the furniture in every dayglo colour available. Still, it's an interesting place, they have satellite TV and a lot of Westerners, so you can always catch up on the news from around the town.

We drop Beccy off and I help her in with her bags. She checks in while I wait in the lobby. Suddenly there's a big commotion and five blokes are running towards me. All are heavily armed, in combats, and the one at the front is wearing only his body armour on his top part over a tight-clinging T-shirt. There are a couple of grenades attached to straps on the front of the body armour. He's like the bloke on the plane — about six foot four, slabs of muscle attached to his arms like polystyrene. He has a radio headset on — the sort that Madonna favoured in the nineties — and he's barking into it. "Subject on the move! Subject on the move!" In the centre of the group is a frightened-looking middle-aged man who is clutching a voice recorder. He's bundled along at the trot with the big guy at the front screaming, "Stand aside, security!"

As the group come level with me, the main guy shoves me in the back, knocking me forwards into the desk.

A huge armoured Humvee screeches up outside and the middle-aged man is bundled in. Then the vehicle screeches off with two of the meatheads leaning out of the window, one covering the street with an HK416 ultracompact, the other — unbelievably — with a Desert Eagle. A Desert Eagle is a huge hand-held cannon that can literally stop an elephant, as various men with small penises have proved down the years. If someone fires on you while you're in a moving car it

130

has about as much chance of laying down meaningful covering fire in response as if you were throwing cotton buds at them. In fact, throwing cotton buds would be better because a cotton bud isn't going to miss and blow some kid's head off. The gun has a real snap on it, so you have to have a very good grip — not always possible when you're fighting for your life — and it's impossible to conceal. It's not a bodyguard's weapon. That said, it looks great — so at least your corpse will look cool.

"Who was that?" I say to Beccy.

"Sorry," she says, "our boys. Bulwark. We protect some of the businessmen around here."

"And that was protecting him, was it?" I observe. "I'm surprised the businessman would allow it."

She shrugs. "Some would, some wouldn't. It's Brad Anderson's call. He's the big guy with the plastic arms. He's in charge and that, as he would say, is how he rolls."

"He'll be rolling in a fucking ditch with his head blown off if he carries on like that," I point out. "He may as well carry a sign on the top of his car with 'important person inside, please assassinate' written on it.

When you're working CP — close protection — your main aim is to avoid drawing any sort of attention to yourself. In the old regiment parlance, you have to be the grey man. Ideally, you move your subject around the place completely anonymously. And if your subject is anonymous, then you're invisible.

If I were doing this Brad Anderson's job, I'd wear my armour under my coat, use a small pistol, which I can keep in an ankle holster, and maybe go for a short-version MP5 on a sling, again inside my coat. No passer-by could tell you were armed.

"What's his background?" I say.

"US military."

"Special Forces?"

"Logistics as far as I know. Came over here as a manager but decided he liked to get his hands dirty."

"I think he'll get his wish if he carries on like that. Surely someone's going to chin him."

"Maybe. He has a lot of big guys around him if anyone tries." Beccy smiles at me, her eyes warm and inviting. Once again I'm struck by how attractive she is. If I thought I was in her league . . . I force the idea out of my head. Talk about wrong time, wrong place.

"Thanks for seeing me inside." I could be imagining it, but the way she says it, it's almost as if she's thanking me for seeing her to her door after a date.

"No problem. If you need an escort out on the town let me know."

"I just might do that."

I give her a kiss on the cheek. Outside I rejoin Mick in the Land Cruiser.

We make the embassy and I'm pleased to see it's a big compound with only one well-defended gate into it. There's a couple of Afghan guys there and they come out to question Mick, which is a bit of a waste of time since they clearly recognise him. Still, it's good to see he's drilled the routine into them. As we pull in we hear a voice.

"All right, boss?"

From nowhere an armed man has appeared. He's nondescript, apart from the bulky coat that conceals his body armour and, of course, the M1 carbine in his hands.

"Billy," Mick nods at him.

We do the introductions. Billy Fuller, a former marine aged around twenty-six, looks as fit as a butcher's dog and, if his low profile so far has been anything to go by, is someone who has his head in the right place.

Mick shows me round, introducing me to the rest of the boys and briefing me on the movements of embassy staff, restaurants inside compounds where they're allowed to eat because of good security, restaurants that are forbidden to them, who has to be collected from guesthouses in the morning, routes to take to the embassy, the whole kaboodle.

After that I get issued with my armour and weapons. There's Paraclete body armour, which is good, light stuff, an HK416C ultracompact like the bloke in the jeep had. It's ideal for concealing under a jacket, which is good. And a Walther P99 — a small gun that fits very well into a jacket pocket or waistband and is easily hidden.

Then I have my duties assigned. It's a heavy-looking schedule for the week ahead. Mick's certainly getting his money's worth, and I can see that any investigation into Ben's death will have to wait until I've fulfilled my obligations.

I'm expected on duty that afternoon, but before I change into the uniform Mick gave me, I take a shower and think through my investigations into Ben's death. I want a chat with Brad the lad. I'm not surprised he's a Green Army guy rather than Special Forces or undercover. Part of the selection for any Special Force group is to identify trappy sorts. You don't want to stand out during selection, you don't want to be either first or last in the physical tests, you don't want to buddy up with the assessors, start cracking jokes or, God forbid, show off. Any of those things will make the unit determined to fail you and, if they want to fail you, believe me they will.

Brad Anderson, though, is flash, which indicates a weakness. One thing's for sure. If Bulwark do have any secrets out here, he's not the man to keep them.

CHAPTER
THIRTEEN

It's not until early Saturday afternoon when I get my first time off so I make my way over to the Afghan International. It's popular with NGOs and journos. I thought I'd look in on the off chance that Brad Anderson might be there. I've been told he drinks at the Afghan and I can see why — as it's not a military drinker it's much more likely that there will be women there. And since Braddy boy looks like a bit of a poseur to me, chances are that he'd like to bolster his ego with the adoring attention of some ladies. I know his type, ferried plenty of them around on my boat. Presuming they're straight, any guy who spends that long bulking out his arms is insecure about women — I'm all for going to the gym but you're not going to bother putting on that level of muscle if you've actually got a girlfriend, are you? In any case, not many women fancy the Incredible Hulk look, at least, not in my experience.

I'm knackered. When Mick said I was working for a week, he wasn't joking. I have eight hours' kip a night, the rest of the time I'm ferrying embassy staff about, guarding the compound, recceing areas the ambassador wants to visit and identifying threats.

I've surprised myself at how comfortable I feel doing this, how natural it seems. I'd always thought I'd avoid becoming a contractor, going on the circuit as it's called. I'd done my twenty years of adventure and thought I owed myself a soft retirement. It's enjoyable, though, to feel a buzz of excitement again and to do something I'm good at.

Mick fronts me a bit of money at the end of the week and I agree that, with one evening off, I'll work at least one more. The dining area in this hotel is like something devised by the CIA to break suspects — bright pink walls, bright yellow tablecloths. It sends my eyes funny just walking through the place.

That said, I like this place. The owner is a good guy, funny with — improbably for an Afghan — a Texas accent. He's hosting one of his kebab nights out on the terrace when I arrive.

The bar's got a couple of computers set up for punters to use. I check the Internet and draft an email to John, telling him where I am. The slippery sod set up a new Gmail account when I came out here, which we share. All I do is write a message and keep it in the drafts folder. He then logs on to the same email address with the same password and he can see it without it ever having to be sent. That way there's no record of emails sent and received, no way for anyone to intercept them. I ask him to check out anything he can on Marjul, the village and the people who live there. I want maps, local culture, military situation, what day they do their washing, if he's got it. It won't replace local information, which I intend to discover for myself, but I need as much background as possible. Preparation is the key to success in any mission and, if I'm going up to this village, I need to brief myself as well as I can.

As I log out of the email account, I suffer a bit of a pang. Just to be on the safe side I clear the computer's history. Email's not that secure but there comes a point you just have to work with what you've got.

Whoever is following me, whoever killed Ben and Jeanette the counsellor, now knows I'm here. I'm a target and much easier to kill than I was in the UK. We're moving from the surveillance phase to open warfare and I will have to watch my arse very closely while I'm over here.

Inside the bar there's a throng of people hitting the beer. I've only got the night off so it's soft drinks all the way for me. There's no way I'm going on an operation with a hangover.

I recognise the middle-aged guy who was being bundled about by Brad. He's sitting at a table nursing a whisky and a cigarette while a couple of the meat-heads sit either side of him — cut-off T-shirts, combat trousers and conspicuous guns on their thighs.

"Hi," I say to the guy, "I thought you were being abducted."

"Back away, sir," says the bodyguard.

"Jimmy, this guy isn't Taliban, try relaxing for a second." The man's voice is American, educated — New York, I'd say.

"I'm the security consultant, sir, the risk assessment is in my hands."

"Jimmy, give it a rest," says the man. "Brad's upcountry for a fortnight so acting like an asshole is no longer mandatory."

"Seems like it's still an option, though," I say, winking at GI Joe.

The man nods towards his bodyguard.

"You know what, I had hopes of getting laid on this trip. You try meeting a girl who's going to let these guys do a security check on her panties before you take her to bed."

"Hey, I'm always available for work like that," I say.

"Back away, buddy," the meathead says.

I just flash him a smirk and he puts his face into mine, an inch away. We do that staring at each other for a bit but the business guy just gets up and walks out, meaning the bodyguards have to follow him.

"Bye, girls," I say. So much for inconspicuous.

So that's that: Brad's not here after all.

I take a powdery-tasting orange juice and sit next to a group of reporters. We get chatting and they're a decent enough crew — just coming off embeds in the south.

There's a documentary crew — young-ish blokes, camera, sound and reporter — who've been down in the south. They've seen a bit of the action and are clearly relieved to be out of it for a while. The three of them are smoking as if someone's going to take their cigarettes away, and banging back the beers as if prohibition starts tomorrow.

They're a good source of information because they like to keep their ears to the ground. We get chatting for a while and I tell them I'm on CP work. They haven't got anyone doing that for them in Kabul but they're experienced guys who are only in town for a day or two. It's the Afghan International and then home for the lot of them.

One of them, a guy called Dan, a thin bloke with a sunburned face and frizzy hair, tells me all about his embed, though he doesn't mention the unit as he says he's been asked not to.

Eventually we get round to the question I've been wanting to ask.

"What do you think went on up at Marjul the other day?"

"Special forces, I think," he says, "had to be."

"Why?"

"It's got to be inside information. That village had been cleared of Taliban for a couple of months — the whole area around it, too. Someone must have got word that the boys were in town and come for them."

"You've been to the village?"

"No, but I've been in the area. Nice people. Not extremists. They're traditional but they don't like the Taliban. They probably tipped the coalition off and 'bang!' "

"So what were the Taliban doing there?"

"What are they ever doing? Extracting support, collecting a bit of cash, that sort of thing, probably."

"But if the area's been cleared . . ."

He shrugs. "How clear is it ever? They only have to hide their weapons and they're invisible again."

"True enough," I concede.

I get up and head for the gents. As I do, I see there's a disturbance at the front door, a lot of shouting. I look round. There are two big Afghan guys in turbans trying to get in. The man on the reception desk is arguing with them, clearly telling them they can't come in. It's a scene you might see in any bar in the UK on any night, the only difference here is that the receptionist carries a Glock. Can't see what the fuss is about, they'll have been through a roadblock on the entrance and would have had to leave any guns outside.

Not my business, so I get a couple of drinks and go back to the journos.

"What's that about?" I ask Dan.

"Don't know. I think they're a bit careful about who they let in after what happened last month."

"What was that?"

Dan takes a pull on his beer. "A couple of Pashtun guys came to see some contractors who were staying here. There was a bit of a falling-out and the Afghans finished up dead. One of the contractors was quite badly wounded."

"That happen a lot? How did they get the guns in?"

"Contractors can bring them in here. The Afghans? God knows. Someone fucked up. Funnily enough, the Pashtuns were from Marjul."

This piques my interest. "And the contractors?"

"Geordie boys."

"Who were they working for?"

"Biofuels International, I think. They're a weird bunch who set up odd factories in deprived areas —

more a charity than a business. The contractors were engineers — former army guys."

"Right. And where are the engineers now?" I ask.

"The Mir prison."

That takes me aback. "Why?"

"The Afghans don't accept they acted in self-defence. They've been nicked."

"Really?"

"Hey, whatever else happens in life you can at least be glad you're not them."

"Too right."

There are worse things that can happen to you than lying wounded in an Afghan nick facing a life sentence but I'd struggle to think of them.

"Has anyone been to see them?"

"No idea. My beat's the infantry regiment."

"So much for the spirit of investigative reporting," I say. "If it was left to the likes of you President Nixon'd still be in the White House."

"Hey, it's a job."

I nod. I look at my watch: 3.30p.m. Is that too late for a visit?

"Come on, newshound," I say, "you're coming with me. Have you got a secret camera?"

"No."

"Well, you better rely on just remembering what you see then."

"Where are we going?"

"The Mir prison. But first we need to see if the hotel has a photo printer. And to call a mate of mine."

CHAPTER
FOURTEEN

Half an hour later Arnan pulls up in the Land Cruiser outside the prison. It is not a welcoming building, it has to be said. It's on the outskirts of Kabul and is a huge compound — high stone and cement walls with a watchtower like you might see on a castle, complete with battlements at every corner. It's in the middle of nowhere, a long dusty stretch from the nearest buildings.

It's been a quick trip down the Asian highway and as we approach the gates we can see guards — in something approaching a uniform, a bizarre combination of combat trousers, olive green shirts and flip-flops — coming out with AK47s, screaming at us to get away. The risk of suicide bombers around here is huge.

Arnan, though, is undaunted. He shouts at them and gestures to us, putting his hands above his head. Slowly a guard comes forward, jabbing his Kalashnikov at us. It does make me a bit nervous. Guns have been known to go off accidentally, especially cheap-as-chips Chinese copies that aren't maintained properly.

Arnan, though, comes through for us. He explains we're Western journalists who would like to talk to the prison director. There's a lot of arguing and inspecting of the Land Cruiser but no one looks to search me. I'm still pale enough and Dan's blond enough to convince them we are who we say we are. Luckily I didn't bring the 416 with me and only have the P99 stuffed in my pocket. Even if they find it, it won't cause comment. The basic Afghan attitude to weapons is that, if you can afford one, you have one and you carry it with you wherever you go. I'm surprised the Afghanistan national football team don't play with AKs strapped to their backs.

We're led up to the gates by a couple of the guards and I'm quite surprised by the lack of security. There's a barrier like you might see on a car park across the gates and wire barricading the entrance but no real anti-suicide bomb stuff, no checkpoint well away from the gates. There are a bunch of relatives out front, all with food and stuff like that, trying to get in.

This is how a bad Afghan prison works. All the money that is paid to the prison for salaries, food etc., goes to the director: he nicks the lot. The guards get paid by arresting people and ransoming them back to their families. The meals inside consist of precisely sod all. If you've got no relatives to come and give you food, then you'll starve to death. End of.

As we go in there I see a couple of big fit-looking guys in military uniform coming out. I recognise the dagger they have for an arm badge — it's the Korps

Commandotroepen, Dutch Special Forces — a private and a corporal.

I give them a nod and the guys say hello and ask us what we're doing there. I explain we've come to see the Bulwark boys.

"Yeah," says the corporal, "we've looked in on them."

"How are they?"

"About as well as you'd expect," he says in excellent English, "we've done what we can for them. At least the guards know we have an interest in them, that's some protection."

"What are you guys doing here?"

"We've come to see if there's any prisoners who might be of interest to us."

"Are there?"

"A few. Listen, watch these guards, some of them aren't very good at holding on to their tempers. Any problems, give us a call." He takes out a pencil and a small notepad from his pocket, scrawls down his name — Mattias De Vries, I note — and number and passes it to me.

"Cheers," I say.

The guards take us down a passageway and into what passes for an office — an old Formica desk, a few plastic chairs and a sort-of bed. There's also a set of barbells in the corner. We're introduced to the prisoner director who greets us with great smiles. He doesn't seem like a psycho, but an open and friendly guy. For some reason, though, he's pulled on a knackered-looking ballistic vest and is clearly flexing his arm muscles.

144

"Friends," he says, "how are you?" His English isn't bad. "What can we do for you here? I'm afraid visiting has to be arranged."

I explain that we'd like to see the Bulwark engineers and his face immediately darkens.

"That will not be possible," he says, "these are dangerous men, we cannot allow that."

I smile.

"OK," I say, "that's fine. Perhaps we could see them another time. But, as a token of our thanks for taking the time to see us, please accept this gift." I pass him a big envelope with the printouts from the Afghan International in it. It's stacked with some porn I printed out from a website named "Hot and Willing", though to my eyes the girls look a bit cold and reluctant. There's also a wodge of cash in there.

He looks inside and smiles a big smile.

"Ah, the Internet, I wish we had it here. Perhaps you might see these men after all."

He leads us out of his office, taking one of the guards that escorted us in with him. There are prisoners milling about there — exercise time for some of the luckier ones, I guess. As we cross the courtyard, he suddenly turns to one of the prisoners.

"What are you looking at, you bastard?" he says in English. The man stands expressionless. It's clear that he knows that no matter what he says or does the outcome will be the same. The prison director walks up to him and hammers him as hard as he can in the guts. The prisoner falls to the ground, where he gets a boot driven into his neck. The fallen man doesn't make a noise, doesn't cry out. The prison director catches the look on Dan's face.

"Don't worry, my good friend," he says. "He is a drug dealer and without connections."

Dan says nothing but I can tell he wishes he'd stayed in the bar. Even in the evening sun the place is boiling and buzzing with flies.

We enter one of the cellblocks. It stinks even worse than the outside. We're led down a corridor to a solid wooden door.

"Western prisoners get special treatment," he says, "they have their own cell."

He opens the door. It's a narrow room, more of a closet, really — no more than four feet wide and about the length of an average man. There's no toilet, nothing to lie down on, no bedding. There's a plastic bottle and a buzz of flies swarm around it. I guess the guys have to piss in the bottle and throw it through the bars on the cells. Same with the shit. Not a place to be a sick man. Luckily the boys are less badly off than I'd been led to believe, not that they're in what you'd call the peak of health. Both are sitting against the wall. One is a tall pale man in boxers and a T-shirt, which is torn and covered in blood. Next to him is the other guy, similarly dressed. He's in better nick, but not much. He's dirty and thin and looks up with hollow, fearful eyes.

"Shit," says Dan. He whips out his mobile and takes a couple of snaps.

"Who are you?" says the second guy.

"Press," says Dan, "I'm from International News Network."

"I don't know them."

"We supply material to all the broadcasters."

The engineer squints up at me. "And you?"

"Me? I'm security."

"You're not from Biofuels, are you?"

"No."

"Thought not. We've heard nothing from them since we've been in here."

"They're not trying to get you out?" There's an incredulous note to Dan's voice.

"No. The embassy's been in touch but they say it's very difficult. We're in the Afghan legal system so it's up to Afghans what happens to us."

"Did you do it?" I ask.

"Aye, after one of the bastards tried to put a bullet in Phil here." He nods to the bloke next to him. Phil says nothing.

"What's your name, mate?" I ask the engineer.

"Paul," he says with a sigh.

"Why did they target you?" Dan's busy with his mobile phone, taking photos, so it's up to me to ask the questions.

"They said it was about Marjul."

"What about it?"

"Retaliation."

Bingo. "For what?"

"The killing there."

"Were you involved in that?"

"We just saw it. I'm here as an engineer."

"With a gun?" says Dan, who is clearly greener than he looks.

"We're both former Royal Engineers. You need a gun out here."

The prison director comes back in. "My friends, time is short in here, you can't bother the prisoners, they are both sick men."

By the way the engineer flinches I can tell he isn't pleased to see him.

"Were you with Ben MacDonald?" I ask.

"He was our security. Nothing was meant to happen there, it's a peaceful area."

"What did happen?"

"Enough!" The prison director can't possibly know what we've been talking about. Paul has a thick Geordie accent for a start and the director's been out of the cell for most of the conversation. It's just his way of exercising his power. He takes my arm, trying to pull me out of the cell.

I stand my ground. "Look," I say, "I swear I'll do all I can to sort this out for you. I'll send someone along with some food if I can."

They both nod.

"How about your mate?" Paul asks. "I thought he was the reporter."

But Dan isn't there. He's outside the cell being sick. At least it won't add to the stench.

CHAPTER
FIFTEEN

Arnan is waiting for us when we leave the prison and drives Dan and me back to the Afghan International. Dan and I sit together in silence. He's still got the pale-green, slightly sweaty look on his face, and I can tell that he's trying hard to keep himself together.

"Get you a drink, mate?" I ask Dan after Arnan drops us at the hotel's entrance.

"Yeah," says Dan, passing a hand through his unruly mop of hair. "I need one after that."

He's not the only one. I won't be getting drunk — not when I'm working tomorrow — but a whisky to settle the nerves and help send me to sleep is just the thing.

Having left Dan slumped in a chair, I'm standing at the bar waiting for the drinks to be poured when I feel a tap on my shoulder.

"Buy you a drink, soldier?"

I turn round. Beccy. God, she looks good. Smells good, too — clean and fresh. How she manages it in the heat and dust of Kabul I'll never know. I smile down at her.

"Can I get you something?" I say.

"No thanks, just passing through. Surprised to see you here though. How's the work at the embassy going?"

I shrug. "It's fine. But listen — I've just been to the Mir prison," and just like that the atmosphere shifts. The smile on Beccy's face fades and her expression darkens. I know she knows where I'm heading with this. "And the engineers are in pretty bad shape."

Her eyes drop to the floor and she nods. She doesn't need to be told what kind of hell they're facing in there.

"Any chance you could get some food to them? Some medicine? Can you swing something with your contacts?"

Beccy sighs. "I'll try, Nick. I really will. But you know what the internal politics are like here. I have to be careful what I ask for and God knows I don't want to inadvertently make it worse for them. But yes, I'll see what I can do."

"Thanks, Beccy."

She gives me a sad smile and turns to leave as the bartender comes over with my drinks.

"Look after yourself," I say to her.

She turns back to me with an odd look on her face that I can't quite read. "You too, Nick. You too."

I hit the sack at the embassy late. I've agreed with Mick to carry on in my post, which means another week of working my arse off, though I do manage to meet the Korps Commandotroepen guys and give them some food to take to the boys in prison, along with some medical supplies and a packet of wet wipes. I also stick

150

in a few calls to the British embassy but nothing comes of it.

Gathering the information for my trip to Marjul takes time. Arnan says he can get hold of a 4×4 and is willing to drive me up there. It shouldn't be too much of a problem, he says. I love Afghans like Arnan — he's a generous, straightforward, hard-working guy, but one thing you can't rely on is his assessment of danger. This is a macho culture that has survived years of vicious conflict. He wouldn't admit something was dangerous, he's almost blind even to the possibility something might be unsafe. It's not that he's playing the hard man, though there's a bit of that. It's just his head has been recalibrated by all the brutality he has seen. His idea of "not too much of a problem" might be mine of "near certain death".

Eventually I assemble the necessary maps and get an assessment of the lie of the land from as many locals as I can. The general view accords with Mick's. It's hairy but what isn't in Afghanistan?

This is supplemented by a trawl of the ANSO reports on the Internet. ANSO stands for Afghan Non-Governmental Organisation Safety Office, which gets information from NGO employees working around the country. It says that convoys have been attacked in Marjul and also at Afghan police checkpoints. There have been a few abductions — mainly Afghans and a school attack by the Taliban, which left a teacher dead. Ironic that Taliban means "students" when they seem so down on education.

The trip is a relatively short one to Marjul, maybe eight hours if we go flat out — which Afghan drivers always do — down Highway 1, Afghanistan's giant ring road that connects its major cities. Bridges have been blown recently but Arnan is confident they're intact most of the way down. After that it's off road up to Priand Asad — where the massacre took place. My research tells me this is one of the poorest areas in Afghanistan. About one in ten of the villages don't allow the Taliban, though no one seems to know why some manage to resist while others fall under the Taliban's sway. There's a sixty-four-kilometre border with Pakistan and the population has been described as "semi-rebellious".

Highway 1 is at least paved but I decide to stop checking the Internet when I find a 2008 article from the *Asia Times* with the headline "Death Stalks the Highway to Hell". Yeah, I've got the picture.

It's not just the Taliban we have to worry about. Straightforward, old-fashioned bandits are thick on the ground here, too. Ideally I'd like to assemble a bigger convoy to put them off attacking us, but it's a case of working with what we've got.

As we set out near dawn, I look down at my mobile. It can't make any calls out here but the Bluetooth is still a useful indicator. I've not had a sniff of St John in a fortnight. I decide to take that as a good sign.

We travel south-west out of the city in an old Toyota Hilux. It's not armoured but it's what the locals drive so it blends in. Arnan is driving and his cousin Pamir — who must be all of sixteen — has agreed to come along for extra security. At first I told him I wasn't taking him but Arnan said the kid could look after himself and that he'd be personally responsible for him. Pamir's got an AK47 and watches fascinated as I strip it and clean it for him. Arnan carries a 9mm Makarov automatic, which is a decent side arm. I've had to leave the embassy guns behind. If we're searched by the Taliban we can't be found with Western weapons. Afghans all use old Russian stuff, so it's an AK from the arms bazaar for me. It's always good to have top kit but you can get too hung up on guns. The AK's an excellent, practical weapon and it'll do the job.

We run through what we do if we're attacked. Plan A is turn the car around and get out of there. Plan B is, as ever in an ambush, to get to cover and take the fight to them as quickly as possible. I consider driving myself but I decide I'd rather be able to assess the situation from the passenger seat because I'll miss less that way. I assign Arnan's cousin one side of the road to watch and I'll look at the other. It's not ideal giving a job like that to a kid and it's not ideal travelling alone like this but I don't have any other option. I haven't got the money to pay for a second — or ideally third — vehicle and I need to get up to Priand Asad to see if I can find out what's happened.

We're well prepared for the journey — two billycans of fuel, a small amount of food and I've been growing my beard since I got here and am now dark enough to pass for a local, at least, without close inspection. I haven't gone the full turban but I've picked up some traditional clothes at a market in an effort to blend in more — a flat hat and the dishdash, which is a combination of pants and a long dress-like shirt. I've also taken a risk and concealed some of my kit in the back as best I can — which isn't very well. I had to bring boots and socks because I might be out and about on rough terrain and my soft Western feet just aren't up to the battering they'll take. To be convincing I have to wear flip-flops and I've brought a few sachets of instant coffee to stain my feet brown. Don't laugh: it's the best you can do in these circumstances. It might pass; it might not. Let's hope it does.

The sky is pink and the mountains are just cardboard cut-out shadows as we hit Highway 1 out of Kabul, jostling with the bikes, wheelbarrows, motorbikes and brightly decorated trucks that are our companions on the road, passing through the battered buildings, the impromptu stalls and shelters. It never fails to amaze me just how much cargo can be loaded on to one truck. The one in front of us has sacks piled up to the height of a house — the suspension is completely bottomed out but still it goes on down the pitted and bumpy road.

Mick's been informed of my trip and I'm in contact by satellite phone — one of the perks of working for the embassy is we get some decent kit. This allows me to take latitude and longitude readings once in a while and text them back to him. The important thing is that someone knows where we are and when we're expected back. The sat phone will go under the seat if we get searched and if it's found Arnan is just going to have to say he's nicked it.

We head out down Highway 1. Arnan sticks on a tape of some Afghani music and it starts to feel like quite an adventure. Everything goes smoothly for the first part of the journey and I could almost say I'm enjoying myself. Arnan's cousin has some almonds and raisins with him and I crack open a bottle of Coke, which seems to delight the kid. If I wanted to get New Agey about it I could say that Highway 1 is a symbol of Afghanistan's freedom. It's certainly crucial to its future. The Taliban don't like Highway 1 — it enables Afghanis to move around, to meet people from outside their area and to exchange ideas. According to the Taliban, ideas should only travel one way — from them to the people.

The land around the road is wide scrub and there are plenty of bridges and culverts for anyone looking to secrete an IED without the bother of digging. At a couple of points we have to wait while the traffic files around craters.

We stop at a police roadblock and pay a couple of US dollars to be allowed through. The Afghan National Police officer who takes the money is the politest extortionist I've ever met, a genuinely friendly robber. The police have a quick look around the car but they can see we're not Taliban. The Afghans can spot them just by looking at them, even when they're not obligingly wearing their black turbans. God knows how.

It's a chance to test my disguise and it seems to hold. The cop doesn't speak to me and takes no notice of me. Good stuff.

We head off down the highway and I'm pleased to be in a good flow of traffic, even if it does resemble an old-fashioned demolition derby, with the battered cars and trucks racing each other down the highway at frightening speeds. I tell Arnan he should be wearing his seatbelt and he laughs at me.

"When God decides my time is up, my time will be up — no seatbelt will make a difference to that," he says, "only a coward would need one."

"It's a view," I say, but I still wear mine. My view is that it's no good being the bravest bloke in the cemetery.

In the rockier areas we come across a couple of diversions. The road has been IEDed to bits and there is a hand-painted sign with an arrow on it. The diversion takes the route out of view of the main highway. This is a standard bandit trick. Still, we're protected to an extent by the dilapidated state of our car and its lack of cargo. There's no real way of checking out to see if we're being set up for an ambush. The other traffic is emerging back on the main highway, so we keep going, trust to luck.

We head on down through Ghazni province — big ramshackle compounds sprawling away from the highway, on the flat plain between the road and the mountains. We stop at a shop to fuel up from cans and use an air line to blow the filters clean.

I look around me. Sitting on a small motorbike about fifty yards away is a thin man in a black turban.

"Taliban?" I say to Arnan.

"Yeah." He quickly kills the music that's still blaring from the car.

They're all over the place down here, it has to be said. So why don't the ISAF or ANA just go in and lift them? Because the Taliban simply disappear as soon as they arrive. This whole war is about drawing them into a proper battle. There they can be defeated. But of course, the Taliban know that. They're quite happy planting IEDs and doing hit-and-run ambushes. There's a forty-mile border with Pakistan here, should the insurgents want to use it.

The guy's looking at us, but then he's looking at everyone. That's what they want — to make you feel like you're under their surveillance. Arnan decides to bin the Coke at this stop.

"They don't like Coke?" I ask.

"I don't know what they like," he says, "but you can't be too careful."

We kick on, climbing up into the mountains. We go through the sprawling Ghanzi town — a wide scrubland with a background of mountains populated with mud buildings, oil depots, big areas of parked cars. Away to our right a big hill — it resembles a mound of heaped earth — rises suddenly and steeply behind ancient mud-brick walls. The place is crumbling but still imposing and magnificent. Again, I'm reminded of something I've seen from a science-fiction movie. You wouldn't be surprised to see Luke Skywalker wandering around on the back of a bantha round here.

"Genghis Khan sacked this place," says Arnan.

157

To be honest it looks like they didn't bother doing it up afterwards. Life's hard here, resources are few, there's been a war going on for generations. No wonder the place is shattered. You have to feel for these people. They've taken one of the biggest and most sustained kickings in history.

"You'll get a good sheepskin coat here," he says, "like the hippies wear."

Peace and love isn't really my style. On a crowded bus one rainy day, I sat next to a bloke who was wearing one and, after three washes, I could still smell the sheep on the jeans I was wearing. Eventually I gave up and chucked them away.

Out of Ghazni we're pushing hard for Marjul. Then, as the traffic begins to thin a little we see something ominous up ahead. The road is completely blocked. Three big trucks are across it. I check my weapon. The AK's on the back seat so it doesn't threaten anyone. I won't be touching it unless I intend to use it.

Arnan smiles at me.

"It'll be OK," he says.

I wonder if that's an Afghan "OK" or an "OK" in the way the rest of the world understands it. Arnan ejects the cassette from the player and puts it under the seat.

We pull up at the stop and it's definitely Taliban — about twenty of them armed with AKs and RPGs. I breathe deeply, trying to remain calm. I kick the satellite phone further under the seat for luck. I don't know why. It's in a bag, so they'll either see it and ignore it or they'll open it. Shoving it backwards isn't really going to help.

Arnan waves as we pull up and gets out of the car. He goes to talk to them and they seem friendly enough. Then they approach the car. Arnan speaks to me in Pashto and I can't understand a single word he says.

I guess he's asking me to get out. I do, his cousin crawling out after me. A couple of Taliban look through the car.

One of the Taliban reaches forward and picks up the bag. Another one has wandered over to me and the boy. He's looking us up and down closely. The Taliban takes out my AK and looks at it. It's in good nick for an Afghan weapon, that's why I chose it. We've also got ten clips back there.

He nods appreciatively at the gun. Then he tosses it into the car.

Then he looks beneath the seat. Thank God it's on Arnan's side. He emerges with the cassette. His whole expression changes and he looks furious. Arnan begins talking twenty to the dozen, holding up his hands and protesting; his cousin looks as though he's going to cry.

The Taliban shoulders his AK and forces Arnan to his knees. He puts the gun into his mouth. If he clicks off the safety I'm going to take him no matter what. I'll die, but I have to try something. But he doesn't click off the safety. He just kicks Arnan hard in the chest, sending him sprawling back into the dirt. Then he takes the tape and throws it on the ground and stamps on it. It's almost comical because he's only wearing flip-flops and the tape doesn't break. In the end he gets a rock and smashes it. Then he breaks the aerial off the car and rips out the stereo, throwing that to the side of the road too.

He says something more to Arnan and gabbles at us. Arnan jumps back into the car. His cousin leaps in too and I do the same. Arnan pulls around the roadblock and boots it down the highway, wiping blood away from his lips.

"I told you it would be all right," he says.

"Yeah," I say, "thank God, eh?"

The threat of execution and a kick in the chest, a smashed stereo and a potential gun battle. Like I say, the Afghan idea of "OK" is different to most.

I text in our position to Mick and mention the roadblock. He can inform ISAF, though it'll very likely be gone before anything's done about it.

We push on further. There are police stops and more diversions before we turn off the highway up towards our destination. Here the road is just a dirt track, winding between some pleasant orchards and across little streams, which we occasionally have to cross.

According to my intelligence, this is IED hell, but I'm hopeful we can avoid trouble. We climb up and up on a road through the mountains. There are a lot of tight bends and perilous drops but Arnan keeps going at quite a pace. Around any corner could be an ambush. At one point we see two men at the side of the road with AKs. No choice, we keep going and they look at us blankly. Stoned, very likely.

We pass various earth-walled compounds. The people here are as poor as dirt but they are friendly — as most Afghans are — and wave at us as we pass.

It's a long day and we won't make where we're going before nightfall. We have a choice: pull in at a village or risk the open road. Neither option is safe. In the end I opt for a small area just off the road that's shielded from the main highway by a big bank of earth. We plot up there as night falls, finish what food we have and kip as best we can in the truck. It's freezing and cramped but at least no one's shooting at us.

The next morning we make our way back on to the road. As luck would have it there's an ANA convoy coming along — three big armoured trucks and a Toyota pickup with a Dushka heavy machine gun mounted on it at the back. We've come out behind them and Arnan pulls back. Driving up the arse of a military convoy is an excellent way to get shot. Get too close and they'll suspect you're a suicide bomber.

It's a call whether we follow them or give them a really good head start. In the end we let them go for a couple of hours. They're a magnet for insurgents and it's best for us to leave them to fight them on their own.

Sure enough, after travelling for three hours at a painfully slow pace on the unpaved road, we hear a big bang ahead and the sound of the Dushka chewing away.

When the shooting subsides we continue. When we finally catch up, one of the trucks is in bits on the road and a chunk of earth is missing. The bodies are already gone. The Afghans bury their dead very quickly.

We stop at a small collection of buildings to buy some food. There's a small stall selling flatbread to locals. A nearby householder brings us yoghurt and tea.

161

I feel curiously moved by that. These people are desperately poor — you only have to look at their scraggy animals, their crumbling houses, the lack of cars to see that — but they would give you the shirt off their backs rather than be thought bad hosts. I'm aware, though, that I might have a different reception if they thought I was a Westerner. The Taliban have put a $30,000 bounty on Westerners around here. I reckon that's more than two hundred years' worth of wages for some of them.

We stop climbing on a wide plateau. It really is incredibly beautiful here — the yellow earth of the floodplain dotted with bright green trees, which I think are some sort of bushy pine. There are pink rhododendrons, pomegranates, mulberry and peach trees. Purple mountains hem in around the winding plain. Surrounded by nature it all its glory, it's impossible to think that there's a full-on war going on, that if you go off certain well-marked paths you're going to encounter landmines going back to the Soviet era.

There is a forward operating base of the ANA up here — the aptly titled FoB Lonely. It's been left to the ANA because most of the Western troops have pulled out for a push in Helmand.

We push on to the base as a long lilac dusk falls over the mountains. The village is only ten kilometres from here but we won't make it before dark. The base is an old mud-brick fort that looks like it was built in the nineteenth century, which it probably was. We report there because we want the Afghan Army to know we are in the area, not go mistaking us for outside agitators. Again, the hospitality is first rate and we take tea outside with the ANA, me keeping quiet again, pretending to be some sort of idiot or mute.

When Arnan tells the commander that he has a cousin in Priand he'd like to visit, the atmosphere takes a turn for the worse.

The ANA commander shakes his head and I can see he's saying that won't be possible. I need to talk to Arnan, to find out what's happening.

There's some chat and we're led inside the fort. There's a sleeping room at the back — a dormitory for about fifty soldiers, basic but clean and with sleeping rolls on the floor. We're directed to some spare beds. The ANA doesn't have the best attendance record in the world and I guess some soldiers might have awarded themselves a bit of leave.

Whatever happens, I'm here for the night, so I bed down. Later on we're invited to a meal of some surprisingly good stew of unknown meat served on bread plates. Afterwards I go outside as if to piss. Arnan follows me. The night is incredible, millions of stars and a big bright full moon hang in a firmament coloured a deep navy blue. Afghan night skies are the best.

I do what I have to do and Arnan approaches me.

"We can't go to Priand," he says.

"Why not?"

"Westerners. That's all he'll say."

"What sort of Westerners?"

Arnan shakes his head. "He said no more. Just no. We have to head back tomorrow."

"Right."

I do a quick calculation in my head. I know the village is south-west. I have a map, courtesy of the NGO site. Ten kilometres equals six miles. At a run I reckon that's an hour and a half in the dark, having to navigate in an unfamiliar area. I could run it in under forty minutes on a road in Britain but this isn't a road and it isn't Britain.

So double my time. Eighty minutes there, less back as I'll know my way. Say a total of three hours' travel time, to be safe. That gives me a decent amount of time at the site. It won't be difficult slipping away. The boys were whipping out a hookah and it's a fair guess they might put something in the fruit-flavoured tobacco to give it a bit of poke.

"I'm going up there to have a look tonight," I tell Arnan.

He nods. "What shall I say if they notice you're gone?"

"You've told them I'm simple?"

"Yeah," he grins ruefully.

"Stick to that. Just tell them I've wandered off."

He smiles at me. "I can't work you out," he says.

"Why not?"

"You won't travel in a car without wearing a seatbelt but now you're going crawling around in the night where the best you can hope for is that a farmer shoots you."

I could talk to him about avoidable and unavoidable risk. However, I just put my arm around his shoulder.

164

"If I don't come back, contact Mick. If I'm not back at the end of forty-eight hours, assume I've been kidnapped and try to break the news to the Rocksteady Crew in there," I say.

"They won't be happy I've lied."

I take out a hundred dollars and pass it to him.

"Is that enough?" I say. Arnan nods and I sense I can trust him.

"Good luck," he says, "I'll tell the sentries you're watching the car." He gives me the keys.

"Good job."

I embrace him. My guess is that they won't notice I'm missing. The sentries' job is to guard the fort. I'm not a threat so I can do pretty much what I like. The sentries aren't watching me anyway, just chatting to each other.

I go to the car and retrieve the AK and my socks and boots. I take my coat too, along with the other few bits and bobs I'd chanced it to bring — the map, the compass torch and a cheap digital watch. A quick glance confirms that I'd guessed the right way out of there, around the back of the fort. I stick all the kit, including the boots, into a drawstring bag and start to make my way around the building.

There's no guarantee these guys would shoot someone for just walking near the fort after dark but there's no guarantee they wouldn't, either. To be fair, if I was them I probably would. It's not like the locals don't know it's a military facility. I walk around casually. There's no door at the back of the building but there are sentries on the roof who have a Dushka —

something that would reduce me to a pink mist if they decided to open up with it.

There's no real cover for a long way. The moon is bright but my clothes are drab. I think that if I can put two hundred yards between me and the fort I can keep to the shadows of the deserted compound that stretches away from it and not be seen. Suddenly I hear voices behind me. Arnan is shouting up to the roof. There's the sound of laughter. I don't know what he's saying but he's got the guys' attention momentarily. Good man.

I'm moving towards the track. I haven't been seen, as the lack of Dushka rounds up my jacksie indicates. Once out of sight I put on the boots and put the flip-flops in the bag. Now I can really go for it. My heart is thumping and I'm moving as quick as I can. I'm certain I'm near to the spot where Ben's life changed for ever, the tipping point that sent him spiralling down towards the floor of a Hammersmith shitpit with a bullet in his head.

CHAPTER
SIXTEEN

The going is not easy along the track — it's dry but it's rutted and you could easily turn an ankle in the dark. However, I am wary of sticking to a main road. Ideally I'd like to go cross-country but time is short and I have to take the risk of meeting someone.

The advantage is that this road leads directly to the village. So I chance it. The problem with chancing it is that sometimes that chance doesn't pay off.

I'm making good progress at the jog and I estimate I've done about seven kilometres and have passed a couple of turn-offs when I hear a truck coming towards me. Shit. I've come off the plateau where the fort is and I'm now heading up around a mountain track. The drop is steep but not vertical, so that's what I'm going to have to go for.

I get off the side of the road and cling to the slope, flat as I can to the shadows. It's not at all an ideal hiding spot. There are a few bushes but no major cover.

The vehicles draw level and I hear them go past and turn off at one of the tracks that goes down to the valley, avoiding the fort. I don't see what the convoy's made of but the engines didn't sound like Afghan trucks and there's not the usual pall of diesel smoke behind them. I just catch the back of the last vehicle's profile against the moon. It's got a rocket launcher on the top and its shape's unusual.

If I had to identify it as anything I'd say it was a Mowag Eagle IV — the Swiss version of a Humvee. It's an impressive bit of kit and I wonder whose it is. The Yanks don't use them. I thought only the Danes had them in any number over here, and I know there aren't any Danish troops nearby. That decides it: I can no longer have the luxury of sticking to the road; I need to go cross-country.

The slope up is not as hard as the slope down so I make my way along that. This makes progress slow. The moon is bright but I can't risk slipping so I have to make my way forward very carefully. After another hour — it's now taken me two and a half to do the trip rather than the ninety minutes I'd scheduled — I come round the mountainside to look down on a very curious sight. At first I think I am looking at an archaeological dig, the sort of thing that turns up on *Time Team*. There's no building here taller than a foot high, though their outlines are all visible among the piles of rubble. An enormous work of demolition has happened here. Forty houses have been flattened to no more than knee height.

This has to be an air strike, doesn't it? But it doesn't look like an air strike. That would leave a great hole. Here it's as if the houses have been individually knocked over and smashed, like someone's taken in a bulldozer. And, in fact, as my eyes start to be able to focus on the distance, there actually is a bulldozer

168

towards the back of the compound. It looks deserted. I wait for half an hour to confirm I can see no movement. Then I go down.

There's a smell here, a really bad smell. Bodies. That's weird because the Taliban always reclaim their dead, as do the local people. They wouldn't leave them rotting. Not unless they were terrified of something.

I walk up and approach the bulldozer. Clearly someone has landed a grenade pretty squarely in the cab. It's completely destroyed. It's an old Russian thing, grey under the cold moon. Could have been here a while but it still has tracks behind it.

I've looked at the bulldozer for long enough. I need to see what happened to the people here. I steel myself and approach one of the piles of rubble, the one that smells the most. This is not work anyone could relish but I start pulling back the rocks. I've removed four when I uncover what looks like a child's arm. I swallow and carry on. Next is a something else. A foot, clearly that of an adult. I keep digging and a piece of cloth is covering something. I pull the cloth away. It's clearly a burqa, or rather a chadri, the complete covering some women wear in the most traditional areas, basically a cloth with an area of net over the eyes. I look down and confirm what I thought. There's a hand with the remains of nail varnish on it. I've seen enough. Eighty Taliban fighters? I don't think so.

So what happened here?

I move around the village, trying to look for clues. There's the decomposing body of a donkey in what looks like a square. Plus there's an improvised football goal. The wood used to make it has been smashed down but markings of a penalty area still remain in the dust. This tells a story. Taliban are in the business of smashing anything Western — banning music, dancing and, yes, football. They've been known to kill whole villages. And yet this was spun as a Western victory. Why?

I check my watch: 4a.m. Time to head back to the ranch. I'm truly perplexed by what I've seen here. But then, momentarily, I freeze: there's movement on the hill from the direction I came. Shit. There's also, from behind me, the sound of engines. Double shit. Snick. There's a sound at my ear that I know too well — a lead wasp, a bullet. I hit the ground but I can't tell the way it was coming from. Snick. Another.

I've obviously picked the wrong side for cover. I scramble over the rubble of the smashed house and down the other side, two more bullets smacking into the rocks at my feet.

I clamber down the other side. The mountain drops away steeply and the cover is sparse. If whoever's shooting has an IR sight I'll be a sitting duck if I go down that way. The Taliban don't have them, but this guy's just put two bullets a bit too close to my head for comfort.

Vehicles are now streaming into the village. They stop and men get out and begin searching, lights on top of the vehicles scanning the darkness. One bloke has a powerful hand-held torch that scans the rubble where I am. This is not looking good. There are shouted voices, screaming in Pashto. If it's the Taliban, I'm dead.

Someone fires a burst into the rubble. This lot might be ANA so I'm not about to start shooting back until I know for sure.

I move around to the side of the building as quietly as I can, the AK47 in my hand. As I come around I'm faced directly by a guy in a turban. He's surprised to see me but not that surprised and he levels an AK at me. He's not ANA, he might be Taliban, he's definitely going to shoot me if I let him. I give him a burst from my AK and he hits the ground. No arsing about now, I run down the side of the house. As I go I can see he's wearing a black turban, as far as I can tell by the moonlight. Taliban. Has to be. I've got to take the fight to them. They don't know how many they're against and might just run for it. I go straight for the nearest vehicle — a pickup with a driver and a bloke standing on the back with an AK. I take the gunman first, dropping him off the back, and pop the remaining two rounds in my clip at the driver. I can't tell if I've hit him because I have to get around the pickup and into cover.

I've got to find some way out of here. If I take the truck I'll be a big target. I need to slip away somehow. A terrible hail of fire comes from all sides, rattling the truck, and I honestly can't believe I've not been hit. I crawl down the length of the vehicle, the bullets all around me. I get another clip into the AK as I go. I make the driver's door but it's a joke trying to get it open. As soon as I touch it the car lights up with bullets. No checking to see if their mate in the passenger seat is still alive, this lot clearly do not give a fuck. If that's how they treat their mate, what are they going to do to me?

I get my answer in short order as two of them come running around the truck, one from each direction. This is a bad idea as it quickly dawns on them they'll be shooting at each other. They hesitate and I put a round into the one in front of me, roll under the truck and shoot the other one in the nuts as I do so. Both go down but now I really have set up home in Fucksville. A storm of bullets comes in at the truck. I reply with the AK and give them a reason to keep their heads down with a sharp burst in the direction of fire.

I see the grenade at the last second. That's the image that's imprinted on my mind, the image that stays with me.

I guess it must have detonated because there'd be no other reason for the sudden blackness that engulfs me.

CHAPTER
SEVENTEEN

Movement, fast movement. I'm being dragged somewhere. I can still remember that thing rolling in front of me. Why aren't I dead? I should be dead. Stupid thoughts go through my mind. "They don't make grenades like they used to", snatches of songs I knew as a kid. I feel resentful in a stupid, stoned way. Jesus, I hope I'm not missing a piece of my head.

My ears are ringing like they're running the test card in my brain and great blotches of light are swimming about my eyes. What's wrong with my hands? They're tied behind my back. Why can't I walk? My feet are tied too. Lights out. A bag goes over my head and I'm on a floor. By the ridges it must be a pickup truck.

Slowly I'm piecing it together. The grenade, the one whose shape seems printed on my retina, was an American stun grenade — an M84. I remember the distinctive holes in its side — it looks a bit like a garden bird feeder but you won't be getting many sparrows in your garden using one of them. In the confined space under the pickup it must have knocked me cold.

Bang. There's a smack into my ribs that pushes all the wind out of me. The boys who have hold of me in the truck clearly want some payback for what happened to their mates. Smack. Another one. Harsh voices. I can't tell what they're saying but it isn't "One lump or two, vicar?" Or maybe it is. A third blow goes into the small of my back and I shout out in agony. I hear a barked command. Hopefully it's "He's had enough." Smack again. No, it's "Hit him properly." A terrible kick into the base of my spine and I feel my legs go numb.

Then there is another voice. One word. "Stop." Then it's repeated in Pashto. Someone just spoke English.

The pickup jerks into life and we're off over some bumpy surface. At least I've sent my coordinates to Mick, for what it's worth.

The truck rumbles on for a couple of hours. Underneath the hood I feel the gradually increasing warmth that tells me that the sun has come up. Then I'm being lifted from the truck again. I'm picked up bodily and slammed down, my knees forced up into my chin. My head is wrenched back and the hood is lifted. A rock is shoved into my mouth, big enough to be uncomfortable, and then tape is put across my lips. I try not to swallow; try not to panic. I can breathe through my nose and luckily my airway is clear. It's only pain. I can almost believe what I'm telling myself. Then there's a clunk and it goes very dark through the hood. There's the smell of petrol. I've been put into a car boot. For a second a wave of panic does hit me and I have visions of being burned alive in the car. No. If they were going to kill me I'd be dead by now.

The car pulls off and the journey seems never-ending. I pass out at certain points, the pain in my mouth excruciating. Cramps shoot through me and I desperately want to stretch my legs. It will end, it must end, I tell myself. I'm desperately thirsty but at least I don't want to piss. Eventually I lose all feeling in my legs, which is some sort of relief, though my head is battered and bruised from the constant pounding of the car.

I try my bonds but they're proper, full-on handcuffs.

The car stops and I think I'm going to be let out. But then it starts again and we're away. I can't tell how long. I begin to hallucinate, or to dream, I'm not sure which. The grenade, Ben, Chloe at home, Mick. So much for the coordinates I texted him, we must have been travelling a day now. My nose has filled up with hard desert bogeys from the dust of the roads and I have to keep snorting out to be able to breathe. All the time I'm on the edge of panic.

I hear noises that sound like we're driving through a town and then we're climbing on a long bumpy track. It starts to get cold. Very cold. My head hits the floor repeatedly and I eventually tire my neck by straining to keep my skull from being battered.

Then we stop. I'm desperate for release. But none comes. The fuckers leave me there. Are we off again tomorrow? I can't let negative thoughts into my head but a straight assessment of my situation tells me I'll be lucky to survive much more of this confinement.

After what seems like hours the car pulls off again and I begin to shake. What does you in more than the restraints, more than the lack of water and food, more than the incessant banging of your head against floor, is the uncertainty — not knowing how long you're going to have to undergo this ordeal is the real torture.

Suddenly the car brakes sharply. There are footsteps and the boot opens. I'm pulled out, manhandled. They were messing with me, trying to psychologically break me by fooling me into thinking I was in for another day in the boot. At least that's what I hope.

I force myself to think through the situation logically. If they're trying psychological tricks on me it means one thing — they're looking to question me. They can't do that with the stone in my mouth. All I can think is that they'll have to give me a drink.

I'm dragged for a little way and I can feel myself go down a set of stairs. Then I'm pushed into a chair. I'm shaking and trembling. It's not fear, though I'm not exactly relaxed. It's just my muscles are still recovering from the confinement and the cold. I feel myself lashed to the chair and my boots are pulled off me.

I can smell nothing from all the dust up my nose but, when my sense of smell does return after an hour or so, I wish it hadn't. Urine, shit, blood. The familiar stench of a torture chamber.

There's no chance of sleep in that position but I'm desperately tired. My throat is sore, every joint is screaming, my neck feels like someone has a knife in it and I can hardly breathe. Then, after who knows how long, I hear: "Would you like a drink?"

The tape is ripped off my mouth, I spit out the stone and I feel a bottle of water pressed to my lips. I glug it down as fast as I can, the water spilling over my neck and chest in my desperation to gulp it down. The bottle is withdrawn.

"Who are you?"

I'm trying to think straight. Is there anything to be gained by lying about who I am? No. What I'm up to — yes.

"My name is Nick Kane." I can hardly speak and he makes me repeat what I've said. I'm trying to place his accent. It's not Pashto or Dari, the other local language. His English seems very good. I'm guessing Pakistani, educated at a decent public school in England.

I can't see anything as the hood is still over my head. There's a light somewhere — a bare bulb — I can tell that much.

"What were you doing in Priand?"

I don't know what to say. This isn't Paddington Green nick and the penalty for keeping silent is likely to be a lot worse than a copper getting narky. I weigh up my options — I can see no point in lying.

"A friend of mine was killed in London. I think it might be related to whatever happened in that village."

There's no comment. Just the sound of him walking away. He's going upstairs, I can tell. Then the light goes out. It's pitch black. Do I try to escape now? No. This is the first part of my captivity. If they're not vigilant now, they never will be. Also, my legs are completely fucked from my time in the car. I couldn't run if I tried. Still, I try the chair, move about on it. It's solidly constructed but I might have a chance of smashing it if I fell over.

After a while — it's very difficult to tell how long — I hear two sets of footsteps coming back. Two people.

I'm tipped back on the chair, slammed into the floor. Then there's the sound of sparking and a smell of ozone. Electricity. My shirt's stripped off me and suddenly I'm in agony, a burning sensation all across my chest, my muscles spasming. My captors don't say a thing, nothing at all. All there is is the crackle of the electrodes and the smell of my burning skin.

They go away again, leaving me lying on the floor in complete darkness. Through my pain I try to gather my thoughts. This is the game; they want to break me. The stupid bastards don't realise that there's no need to. I really don't have anything to hide from the Taliban, nothing at all.

I have nothing to tell them, no details of troop movements, no secret agenda. I'm not even that useful as a hostage. How many times do you hear on the news "Contractor killed in Afghanistan"? Not often. I'm a freelancer, worth nothing to anyone. My only value is as a Westerner — being British. The government will have to act eventually but sympathy is scarce for mercenaries — which is how I'll be regarded.

I stamp down the negative thoughts inside me. How I feel about it, what I fear, doesn't help in this situation. I have to think of a way out of here.

For the first time I notice how cold it is in this place. I'm starting to shiver.

I have to wait another long interval before the footsteps return.

"Who are you?" The well-spoken man is back.

I hardly get a chance to answer before the electrodes are applied again. It's one of those pains you feel everywhere at the same time, in your head, in your teeth, right down to your bollocks through to your knees.

This isn't looking good. If they think I'm holding out on them, they also aren't going to expect me to tell them the truth straight away. I killed one of them, maybe more, and have at least wounded two others. If they clock me as Special Forces they'll expect me to resist for days. Which equals being tortured for days, whether I'm telling the truth or not.

There's nothing for it: I just have to put up with this for a while. They're not going to kill me or they would have killed me already. There comes a point where they have to realise there's a limited value in brutalising me. Let's just hope it dawns on them sooner rather than later.

The electrodes go on yet again and I black out with the pain. Then I can feel them reviving me. More water is shoved to my mouth and I gulp that down but then the electrodes are reapplied. This time the charge is weaker.

Finally it doesn't hurt at all. There's some conversation and shouting. It's almost funny. I think the car battery they've been using has gone flat.

The chair is pulled back upright.

"We don't have to do it like this."

The first voice again. I guess it might take them a while to locate another car battery. A few minutes, at least. I have that long to start a rapport with this man.

I know this guy's culture. It's very macho, full of front. If I look like a victim I'll end up as one. I also need to flatter him. He's a leader, he's feeling pleased with himself for having captured a Westerner. From his educated voice I guess that the praise of the country boys I encountered in the fire fight isn't going to be enough for him. I was only educated in a Southend comp but that's a damn sight better than most of the yokels here would have had. What to say?

"That would appear to be the intelligent view," I say.

He laughs. "But you haven't been very clever, have you?"

"I've had a good run, it had to end somewhere."

I hope that will increase my value to him, increase his pride in having caught me, if he thinks I've done this sort of operation before without being nabbed. As a matter of fact, I have.

He says nothing again, just paces about me.

"What were you doing in Priand?" he asks again.

"My clients are interested in what happened there."

"Which clients?"

"Global News."

"I don't think you're a reporter. It appears to me that you're trained in a little more than shorthand. You killed four men."

"Sorry." It sounds weak but I mean it. If they'd have come along and said, "Hello, chap, what's going on?" rather than trying to ventilate my hide with AKs then no lives would have been lost. In fact, they'd probably have been able to disarm me just by talking to me. I'm not going to open up on twenty blokes unless they open up on me, am I? So, if they hadn't been so aggressive I'd still be sitting here on the naughty chair and their mates would still be walking around.

"I'm an ex-soldier. The mission was seen as too dangerous for a reporter. I just had to gather information."

"And what information did you gather?"

"There are some dead families there. Civilians."

He seems to digest this information for a while. "I still think you are lying," he says finally.

"I'm sorry to hear that. I expect that means you'll be torturing me some more."

He seems to think for a moment. Here's a bloke who doesn't like being second-guessed. It's a slim chance but I'm trying to shove him down the route of peaceful interrogation. Some hope. He smacks me really hard in the face, breaking my nose.

I shout out, much more than I need to. This isn't the situation to be saying, "I felt nowt, is that all you've got?"

Blood fills up the back of my throat. I think he's dislodged a tooth. Great. Second one in a fortnight.

"Which interest do you represent?" he says.

I really don't know what to tell him. I just clam up at this point. He needs to feel he's worked for his information if he's going to believe it.

So the electrodes come back. I take a couple of beatings, during one of which he nearly manages to pull my ear off. I'm manacled to something. It feels like a pipe.

Then they go away. I'm drained, numb and beaten. I think they've broken some of my ribs. And they don't come back for a long time. I can't judge how long; it's almost impossible to say. A very long time. Like I've said before, uncertainty is as bad as the beatings. You don't know how long you've been left for, whether anyone's ever coming back. The only thing that gives me hope that they haven't left me for dead is the bottle of water they've placed by my side. I take little sips, try not to gulp it down, ration it as I don't know when they'll be coming back.

It's a matter of days, I can tell. I struggle against the pipe but it's no good. They've manacled me with my arms in front of me, which is a mistake but I can't get any leverage on the pipe. I can risk a peek out of the hood but nothing more. If I take it off then they'll realise their mistake and do something about it. The one time I try it makes a real noise and there are suddenly heavy footsteps on the stairs. I take another royal kicking.

When the well-spoken man returns he asks me if I'd like something to eat and drink. I say yes. He says I can have something as long as I just tell him what I was doing there.

I don't know why it's taken me so long to come up with this but finally a word comes into my head.

"Bulwark," I say. "I'm from Bulwark."

Bad move.

"No," he says, "I know you're not. Thank you. That confirms what I was suspecting. You are British Intelligence. Special Reconnaissance Regiment, by my reckoning. I've done my research on you, Mr Kane, and your name is about all you've told me that's the truth. Goodbye."

He says something to someone, I don't understand what. There's a click — understand that. It's from an automatic pistol, the sound of a round being drawn into the chamber.

I think of Chloe, back home. Nothing very sentimental, nothing insightful. I just see her face in my mind and think about how much I'll miss her and how she'll miss me.

An angry voice, the same one as was interrogating me. He's shouting at the others in a tone of superiority, like he's telling them not to be idiots. Suddenly I'm being unmanacled from the pipe and dragged forward. It's as I suspected — we're in a basement somewhere. Shooting someone in a place like that is a bit of a lottery — you never know where the bullet's going to end up once it's been through its target.

They need a better killing ground than this.

I'm pulled to the bottom of the stairs where my feet are kicked from under me. I'm left on the floor for a second. There's more shouting from right next to me and my interrogator's voice coming down the stairs. Then the man right next to me curses under his breath. That's an exchange I don't need a translator to help me with, a discussion between a boss and a junior employee happens in any sort of workplace.

"Can you give me a hand with this?"

"No, do the job I pay you for."

"Arsehole."

I lie still and limp and I hear the man next to me go up the stairs again. He's forgotten one fairly important fact. He's manacled my hands in front of me. Now I can just take off the hood. I do. I'm in a tiny basement lit by a single bulb. There is blood all over its grimy walls. I'm not the first guest to have been entertained here.

There's a sound that tells me my hosts are about to rejoin me. Quickly I pull the hood back down but only enough so I can still see out of the bottom of it.

Two sets of feet come down the stairs, one in boots, one in flip-flops. They pick me up and start to pull me upstairs, shouting at me to stand upright to make it easier for them. In English, again. Weird. No time to think about that. There are two of them. In my state I'd need a weapon to take them out. Luckily, they've brought one with them. Looking down I can see a gun in one of their belts. It's a Smith and Wesson model 29 — a .44 magnum in most people's vocabulary — Dirty Harry's gun. No wonder the well-spoken man said not to fire it in a room like this. You could eat a sandwich while the ricochets from that bounced about the place.

They're taking me up on my back, head first. There's one behind me on my legs. The other's above me, his hands underneath my arms. It's now or never. I go to stand up. As I do so, the one with the gun in his belt is slightly surprised and leans back. I trap the arms of the guy behind me under mine, smash my head back into his nose and mouth and then jump forward at his mate.

We go down the stairs with a terrible clatter and I pull the hood off as we fall. I know that it's pot luck if

I get hurt myself here. You can't legislate for every eventuality and all I know is falling down the stairs in a random heap where I could break a leg or worse is better than whatever this lot have in store for me once they get me where they want me.

We land on top of the guy with the gun, the one behind me desperately trying to free his arm. It's a miracle but no one is badly hurt, for now. Everything comes in a rush and I know my adrenalin is up. My vision has constricted to a tunnel and all I can see is the gun in matey's belt. My hand goes to it as the joker behind me gets his hands free.

The gun owner is understandably reluctant for me to take his weapon away and both hands come down on mine, trying to stop me pulling it out of his belt. Bit late for that, son. I click off the safety and fire. Half his upper thigh and most of his knee is blown away and he loses interest in fighting me, and just falls back. There's the sickening zinging sound of the bullet, which has gone through him, hit the floor and then done a quick pinball around the cellar. The gun's still caught in the remains of his belt and I try to jerk it free.

The bloke behind me has got his arm around my neck, he's trying to choke me out but hasn't got a fucking clue. I've got my chin well down and my shoulders up. He pulls me to my feet and the gun still won't come free from the belt. Time for a different approach. I let go, put one hand on the crook of his arm and drop down, throwing him over my head. Then I'm on him, legs around his neck.

I get him in a triangular leg strangle, which may seem a little arts and crafts for a mortal battle, but it's effective and allows my hands to be free. I finally pull the gun clear of the dying bloke's belt as two more goons appear at the top of the stairs. I give the first a double tap. I'm surprised by what it does to him. It doesn't so much wound him as crater him, punching a huge section of his chest away. He drops straight to the floor, the bullets going clean through him. I fire off another two shots. The second man stands at the top of the stairs for a moment, pausing like a skydiver just after he leaves the plane. That moment when gravity seems to be wondering what to do with him before sucking him earthward.

He too falls, forward, bizarrely, over his mate, to lie dead at the top of the stairs. I retain the stranglehold on the bloke underneath me and keep the gun levelled up the stairs. I've fired four of the six shots it holds. Another fucking poseur's gun, if this was a proper military automatic I could have seventeen in the magazine left.

I maintain the stranglehold for another thirty seconds. Matey is spark out and I'm not sure if I've killed him. I've been put in that hold in training myself and the little lights come on after about a second and a half of the guy getting the strangle on your neck. I've never known anyone stuck in it for thirty seconds. As if to answer my question he starts breathing heavily and turns to one side. I wish he hadn't done that. It means one thing — he's got to go. He could call for help there

186

could be weapons secreted here that I don't know about.

In the end, I just hoist him upright, out of the firing line of the top of the stairs, put my arms around his head and twist. There's a crack and that's him done. Not nice but necessary. He should have kept still.

I search the two guys around me. It's then that I realise something about them. This lot aren't Taliban. They're dressed in relatively western clothing. One has a fucking Madonna keyring. I take his keys, none of which fits the handcuffs. Bollocks, no time to waste. I get my boots on as quick as I can. Then it's up to the top of the stairs. My leg's in agony but there'll be time to think about that later on.

It's a cheap and dirty room, lino floor, bed rolls, a little camping stove. One of the blokes at the top of the stairs has a Makarov with a ten-round magazine. That's more like it. There's also a bottle of water next to him. I drink it in almost one gulp.

I check to see if there's a round in the spout of the gun. There is. He's also got a mobile and a decent wedge.

Whose number can I remember? No one's. Great. Actually, I can: John's in England. I hope this bloke had some credit left. There's no car outside the building, as I can see through the broken glass of a windowpane. My friend the torturer is nowhere to be seen either, which is a pity because I'd like to serve him a spoonful of his own medicine.

First I need to find out where I am. I step outside and nearly collapse. Stretching above me about 400 yards away is an enormous structure in raw concrete jutting strange projections into the sky. I recognise them. Diving platforms. I'm on Swimming Pool Hill, one of the most notorious places in Kabul. I wasn't in a house but some sort of disused plant structure — the purification part of it, I guess, but stripped of anything usable.

This is where the Taliban used to take anyone they didn't like — criminals, homosexuals, women who had offended them in some crazy way — and push them off the high board on to the concrete floor of the pool. Those who survived were deemed innocent and allowed to live — as best they could with horrific injuries.

However, the guys who were with me weren't Taliban, though the exact variety of torturer they were didn't really concern me while they were electrocuting me.

I look around over the bare hillside, a litter-strewn wasteland. Someone brought me here, back to Kabul. Why?

I can't think of that now. The adrenalin is starting to wear off and the pain is kicking in. My legs are seriously painful, with the beating and with inactivity. I'm handcuffed, my ribs feel broken, maybe my jaw too, I have burns on my chest and hands, my ear has a deep cut in it and my right eye is starting to close. Obviously I took a clump in the scrap on the stairs and didn't notice it at the time.

I need to get hold of Mick. I check the phone's number and text John with it, having to remember it as it disappears from the screen when I start to text.

"Call Mick Price, Corinthian. Need evac. Contact this number." It says "sent" but I have no idea whether it will get there, I just hope John gets the message. I can't stay here because who knows who might be coming back. I might even meet them on the road down the hill into town, though I'll minimise the chances by taking the back route. One thing's for certain: if I do meet them, there better be at least twenty of them again or it'll go very differently this time. I conceal both guns in my belt, and start walking down the hill.

CHAPTER
EIGHTEEN

Mick doesn't come but, just a street away on the main road, I can see taxis driving past. I hail one down, and the driver eyes me warily as he sees the cuffs. A London cabbie would rightly drive straight past you if he clocked those. In Kabul, though, they do things differently.

The taxi's a Toyota Corolla estate painted in yellow and white — meaning it is actually an official taxi, as much as official means anything here. I lean in to see him and I can see he has a stocky old Soviet Tokarev T33 pistol in his hand. He's smiling, though, and speaks to me in Pashto. Then he has a good squint at me and shakes his head. He's about to drive off when I say: "ISAF." I point to myself. "ISAF hospital." He looks surprised and gestures for me to get in.

He puts the Tokarev on his lap — sooner him than me, there's no safety catch on one of those. I hope he's remembered to leave the chamber empty of a bullet.

Then we're off. I'm in a state of paranoia by now and keep wondering if he's taking me the right way. Eventually I decide he is. We come to the ISAF hospital and pull up in the street 100 yards short. We don't want to get mistaken for suicide bombers. I get out to pay him and I gesture to my belt — the guns.

His eyes widen, particularly as he sees the cuffs, but I make another gesture, I point to the meter — does he want them in lieu of the fare? He shrugs and then nods. I pass him over the guns and put my finger to my lips. He smiles and laughs. That's the Afghan sense of humour for you — he clearly knows I'm getting rid of a couple of hot guns and he thinks of me as a bit of a naughty boy, rather than a probable murderer.

I get out and walk the last yards to the barriers at the front of the hospital. Suspicious guards cover me as I approach but I shout out that I'm English and I'm hurt, I need some help. They come running forward. After that, relief sweeps over me and I remember little else. The guards have English voices; I'm carried in. The doctors are German and are concerned. There's a bright, clean light to the place, a bed, a drink. I'm suddenly aware that I'm filthy. They're cutting the clothes off me. I hear the doctor draw in breath as he sees the burns on my chest. A hacksaw's brought in and the cuffs are cut down the middle, severing the chain. It feels good to be able to move my arms again, even though I get shooting cramps when I do.

After that someone cleans me up. There are dressings placed on my wounds. I have a cut in my leg I didn't know about — that's stitched up, as is my ear, and I finally get a drink of water and bite to eat. Tinned pasta never tasted so good.

More than the actual physical care I'm getting, it's good just to be back in an environment where someone's looking out for you. Isn't that what life should be about — people caring for each other, helping each other out? That was the major part of being in the army for me, to be part of a team of people who backed each other up and to feel you were actually doing some good in the world.

I sleep, clean sheets, a clean pillow. As I do, words that the faceless torturer said to me come back to me. I said I was from Bulwark and he seemed to regard that as a decisive piece of information. He absolutely knew I was lying, even if he couldn't recognise that I'd told him the truth the second we sat down for our little chat.

So why would that be? I'm still pondering that one when the Afghan National Police come to charge me with murder the next morning.

CHAPTER
NINETEEN

It's 7a.m. and everything is happening so quickly. There's a noise at the door and a tall Afghan with striking blue eyes is standing over me. He's wearing something approaching a uniform and he has three other blokes behind him. None of them are armed and I'm glad of that — the hospital has clearly made them leave their weapons outside.

Where are the embassy? Where are Corinthian? Where is anyone from my side?

"Nicholas Kane?" he says, pronouncing my name well.

"Yes."

"I'm arresting you for murder."

"What murder?"

"On Swimming Pool Hill. You fled the scene in a cab. Your gun has been recovered and will be compared to bullets found at the scene."

I feel the blood drain from me. The cab driver clearly decided he could make a few extra quid handing the guns to the police and telling them where I was — effectively selling me to them. I know from my limited experience of Afghan jails that you need clout of some sort to get someone dear to you out. Money is best but influence or favours will work too. I bet a pound to a penny that the taxi driver has just freed some cousin by sticking me away.

"I was never there."

"A gun has been recovered and we have good fingerprints from it." He adds nothing to this. Terrific — in my beaten-up state, I forgot to wipe those guns down. My prints could be all over the Smith & Wesson. I was trying to pull that out of the guy's belt for a long time. I had blood and dirt all over my hands. Yeah, that'd give a good print all right.

Rule one in this situation is clear: do not leave the hospital. This is a military hospital — ISAF ground, I am under ISAF jurisdiction. In fact, it's like an embassy. They can't shift me from here without the hospital director's say-so.

He'll give his say-so, though, once he understands I'm accused of murder.

The German doctor comes in.

"What's happening?" he says.

The policeman confirms that they want to take me away.

A thought occurs to me: "Check this lot are actually cops," I say. I'd do it myself but I'm on a drip.

They pass ID over to the doctor. He nods.

"It seems they are," he says.

"Then if you're satisfied we'll take him with us."

I can see that unless I do something smartish I'm heading down a long black hole. Once you're trapped in the Afghan legal system you are beyond the help of your own country.

194

But then luck turns my way, for once. The doctor shakes his head. "Out of the question."

"Why?"

"This man has life-threatening injuries. Move him now and he will die. He needs a course of intravenous antibiotics. He won't be able to leave hospital for at least another week."

I could kiss him, even though he's German and I can barely forgive him for his nation's record of scoring every penalty they ever take.

There's a lot of haggling between the two of them.

In the end the policeman reaches a compromise. He'll leave two guards in the room but I can stay there until I'm fit to be transferred to the Mir prison. I can already see a relapse coming on at about day six.

The English-speaking cop leaves; two guards remain. The German medic sits down on my bed. "Trouble?"

I rattle one of the cuffs at him. They still haven't taken them off and I'm wearing them like I've suddenly decided to resurrect the punk look.

"I was kidnapped and had to use some vigorous tactics to get out," I say.

"How vigorous?"

"Very vigorous."

I can see in his eyes that we've reached an understanding.

"Is there someone I can call?"

"How about the British embassy?"

"We called them. I called them myself three times."

"And?"

"They said they were looking into it."

"Looking into it." I've got no time to waste here and can't wait for the pen-pushers to get their act together. "Call Mick Price at the Swedish embassy. Get him over here."

"OK. Mick Price. I can keep you in here for a while but not indefinitely."

"I understand."

"Good."

I lean back on the bed and look up. As soon as I do, one of the guards comes and slaps me across the face, says something incomprehensible to me and pulls out the drip from my arm. The line comes free of the needle they've inserted into my arm.

I've no idea what he's trying to say to me but I don't think it's "Any little thing you need, just mention it and we'll be glad to oblige." He's giving me a taste of what's going to happen when I get out of there.

There's another quick burst of Pashto from the doorway. The guard looks round, his face like a little boy's who's been caught with his hand in the biscuit tin. Then his face hardens as he sees who has been speaking to him. It's a woman. Beccy. God, it's good to see her but it seems that I'm the only person who feels that way. There are plenty of Afghans who are capable of understanding that we do things differently in the West but this bloke's a country boy, clearly, and he isn't taking orders from a woman.

He starts shouting at her, becoming quite hysterical, waving his arms around. The other guard starts screaming at her too. Beccy takes it in her stride. I clearly hear the words "Fuck off" from her at one point — which are understandable in any language.

Then he starts shouting at me and pointing at her.

"What does he want?" I ask.

"He wants you to tell me to mind my place."

"Tell him where to get off," I say.

"I already have. This is an international hospital so we play by international rules. Outside that door it's Afghanistan and we play by his rules. Inside here it isn't, and we don't."

Beccy speaks again to the guards and they really go mental this time. This causes people to come running. The first is a tall Dutch doctor, a woman. Beccy tells her she wants a bit of privacy. If you're looking for a culture clash, Dutch women and Afghan men are about as far apart as world views get. The Dutch doctor points at both the guards and then at some chairs outside. She's polite about it and smiles but they simply do not want to leave if told to do so by a woman and that only serves to add more shouting and screaming.

Now the male German doctor comes in. He begs for a bit of calm and eventually it quietens down and he persuades the policemen to sit outside the room.

"What did you tell them?" I ask Beccy.

"I said they had to follow what the doctor said or she'd have them thrown out."

"Was that really necessary?" the German doctor says to her. "You know how things work here."

"Sorry," she says, "I've just had a bad day."

The doctors go and Beccy closes the door on the guards. Then Mick's big face pops round the door.

"All right, boss?" he says.

"How do I look?" I say.

"I've seen you better." He sits down on a chair. "Well, chin up, eh? I've bought you some sarnies."

"I've eaten."

"I'll have them then." He dives into the plastic bag he's brought with him. "Like old times, ain't it?" he says to Beccy, waving a flatbread sandwich at her.

She ignores him.

"What happened?" she asks me.

"I went up to Priand to have a look at a site that I thought might offer some clues to Ben's death. I got caught there."

"By who?"

"Don't know. Anyway, I was bundled into a car and taken to Kabul. There I was interrogated and, when I got the chance, I made my excuses and left."

"Best plan," says Mick, "how many did you kill?"

"About five in Priand."

"Good man."

"But it wasn't Taliban who interrogated me. These guys weren't fundamentalists, I could tell from the way they were dressed, the way they spoke."

"What did they want?" says Beccy.

"They seemed sure I was working for British Intelligence."

"But who are they?" says Beccy.

"I don't know. The bloke who interrogated me was Pakistani, I think."

Beccy's looking at me directly with a shrewd expression on her face. "If you're into any illegal stuff it would be a good time to mention it now."

"Other than being accused of murder?"

"What?" says Mick.

"There are four dead Afghans up on that hill," Beccy points out, "and the authorities are getting understandably annoyed with contractors bulldozing around the place, slotting whoever they like."

"News travels fast," I say.

"It's on the TV."

"Shit," says Mick.

"Any idea who they were?" I ask.

Beccy sighs. "Well, it's a bit embarrassing, actually."

"Why?"

"They worked for us. For Bulwark. Only as local guides but we'd employed them."

That explains how my interrogator knew I wasn't a Bulwark man.

"Looks to me like you've been compromised," I say, "they were definitely at it in some way."

"At what?"

"I don't know but you don't go kidnapping and torturing people for no reason."

"Might be bored," Mick jokes.

"Let me know when you're coming back to England," I say to Mick, "so I can alert the authorities."

He shrugs again and sinks his teeth into another flatbread sandwich.

"So these were the people you shot?" says Beccy.

"Yes."

Beccy puts her head into her hands. "I don't know what to make of this."

"Me neither."

"I need to go," she says.

"What for?"

"I need to ask some questions about all this."

"I think I have a week in here at the most. After that I'm nicked by the ANP."

"It was self-defence," says Mick.

Beccy shakes her head. "That's not going to make a lot of difference in the current political climate. The authorities are facing criticism that they're Western puppets. This is a chance to show they're not. You'd be the fall guy."

Despite the attention of the police, I've been feeling quite buoyant until then. I'd been so delighted to get off Swimming Pool Hill that I've been sort of living in a bubble, a mental fantasyland of hot meals and a nice bed. Beccy's words burst it.

We all look at each other in silence.

"Let me see what I can do," says Beccy.

She leaves and the Afghan guards immediately try to come back into the room. The way is barred, however, by the formidable presence of Mick. He says nothing to them, just stands looking at them in the doorway. I've noticed before how Mick not saying anything to you is more intimidating than a lot of people are when they're screaming in your face. They go and sit back down.

Mick asks for details of the trip and I tell him. Despite the pressure I'm under it's good to talk to him. He's a great soldier and he can understand the decisions I made and advise me what I might have done differently. It's like a debrief on the mission. Mick doesn't have much to say about it, other than it would have been ideal to put the site under surveillance for longer. Beyond that, if you're faced with twenty blokes on your own, then coming out alive has to be regarded as a result.

He asks me how I escaped and I tell him. I also mention the gun and the difficulty I had getting it free once I'd used it to kill its owner.

"Yeah, he had a .44 Magnum, ten-inch barrel. It was like drawing a broomhandle out of his trousers, Christ knows how he walked around with it," I say.

"Anderson used to have one of those," says Mick.

"What?"

"Yeah, before he got those Desert Eagles. That was his gun, he used to pose about with it. Bulwark get all the best equipment too, so it's not like he never had a choice."

"Have you ever seen one of those on anyone else?"

"Not round here. It's all ex-Russian stuff or the stuff the Yanks gave them to fight them. I've never seen another CP boy with one of those."

He's right: it doesn't work for CP. You can't have a gun with a barrel so long you need arms like a gibbon to draw it.

Something else strikes me about what he says.

"When you say the best equipment, what do you mean?"

"Everything: best armour, best comms, best cars."

"What have they got in the way of vehicles? Anderson was in a Hummer."

"They've got a few of those but he just grabbed hold of a load of Swiss Mowags. Latest model. Lovely if you can get your hands on one."

That was the profile of the truck I saw at Priand. Anderson's been out of town for days. This is one big heap of circumstantial evidence but it's enough for me to think I need to look into it further.

"Mick," I say, "do you know where Anderson's crew live?"

"Yeah, near the Afghan International. They've got a block for Bulwark staff about two hundred yards away. It's got a lot of security, though."

"I want to go there. Can you get me out of here?"

"I can get you out but it'd be better just to do one," he says, "I've got contacts and I can get you on a transporter out of the country. No fucking idea where but out, being the important thing."

"I've still got some things to clear up," I say. I need to talk to a few guys from Brad Anderson's team, see what they know. Like I said, I don't think Brad is the sort to keep stuff quiet in front of his mates. Again, I have a lot of circumstantial evidence. If I can shake down one of Brad's guys I might get more. If I'm lucky, I might even get the man himself.

Mick shrugs. "What are you going to need?"

"Is there much security on there?"

"Just guys on the door, I think. There's barriers at each end of the street, a guy on the car park at the back."

"Will you help me get out of here?"

"OK, but promise me that you get out of Afghan as soon as you can when you've done what you need to do."

"Definitely."

"Fair play. Can you walk?"

"Yeah."

"How are you going to manage for antibiotics?"

"I'm OK." The spiel about the antibiotics was for the benefit of the Afghans.

"Good, unhook yourself from that drip and we'll be off," he says. He flips out his mobile and sends what looks like a pre-prepared text. Then he opens a bag.

"Here." He throws some clothes at me — a tracksuit and some flip-flops.

"What about the guards?"

"Sorted, son." He taps the side of his nose.

I quickly put on the tracksuit and my boots. I'm stiff and aching but not too bad.

"Ready?"

"Yeah."

He takes something else out of his bag — short green cylinders about the size of a small canister of hairspray. Flashbangs! I don't believe what I'm seeing.

"Mick, are you nuts?"

He gives me a look that says, "Yeah, what do you think?"

"This is a hospital. There are people here that the shock might kill. On top of that the security is US marines. They have been known to shoot first and ask questions later."

"Can't make an omelette without breaking eggs," says Mick. "These have got CS gas too. And it's a repeater."

That means it will go off several times. I can't shake the suspicion from my mind that Mick just wants an excuse to let one of these off.

"There's people with breathing difficulties in here," I say. Actually, that's given me an idea.

"Have you got a packet of cigarettes?"

He fishes in his pocket and produces twenty Lambert & Butlers.

"Go and offer one to the guards," I say, "and make sure they light them."

Most of the time we try to avoid culture clashes and spend a good deal of time and effort fostering understanding and compromise. But in this situation, bollocks to that. I'm going to use some creative friction between East and West to get what I want.

Mick is a top bloke and a real soldier. He trusts me, knows I have a plan, so doesn't even bother to ask me why I want him to do this. He goes out into the corridor and says, "Here, boys, no hard feelings."

The guards are momentarily nonplussed. Mick is a big unit and if he offers you a cigarette you naturally feel inclined to take it whether you smoke or not. They look pleased and he lights up their fags for them. Of course, this sparks up the smoke detector in short order and out comes the Dutch doctor.

"Put those out," she says, pointing at the fags.

From the end of the corridor a couple of brick shithouse marines come down. Excellent, one of them is the sort of parade-ground, crew-cutted badass you see screaming into the face of new recruits in films about Vietnam.

The guards have had half an hour to ruminate on what they should have said and done faced by a bossy woman and this time aren't letting it go easily. They want to regain some respect.

One of them actually blows smoke into her face. Ohhhhh, shit. She goes utterly mental, which makes them start laughing which makes her even more angry and she tries to bash the cigarette from his hand.

Now he jumps on her and starts slapping her, as does his mate. The marines, having been bored shitless doing guard duty for weeks, perk up at the first sign of action and wade in to rescue the doctor. Both cops are bundled out, one receiving a fair dig in the ribs from a truncheon as he does so.

That's our cue to leave. Outside the door, I'm really relieved to say, is Arnan, this time in a car I've never seen before — a knackered Toyota Camry. And then we're off into the Kabul traffic.

"Arnan," I say, "get round to the Bulwark building."

"You can drop me off at the embassy first," says Mick, "and here, dopey bollocks, you might be needing this." He takes off his ankle holster and passes it to me, along with his P99. "There's a full clip in there," he says, when we pull up at the embassy. He also hands me fifty dollars. And from inside his bag he produces a Fairbairn-Sykes fighting knife — a commando knife to you or me. I take it gratefully. Close up, there's no deadlier weapon. It's intimidating to be faced by a gun but there's something absolutely hard-wired into the human DNA that says "beware" when a knife is produced and none more than this particular knife. It's designed for one thing — killing people — and you can tell that by just looking at it. This too has an ankle strap, but, in this case, it's far from ideal because I have to conceal it so it can be got out quickly. I can't be rolling up my trouser leg if someone's bearing down on me. In the end I stick it up my sleeve and the elastic of the strap holds well enough on my arm. I'm not going to get a super-speedy draw out of there but I can't walk around with it in plain view.

"Might not want to have to cause too much of a row if things get fun," says Mick, "or there again, you might." He hands me the bag with the flashbangs in it.

"Thanks, Mick," I say, as he gets out of the car.

"Nick," he says, "try to remain in one piece, won't you?"

"That's the plan," I say.

And then we're off, through the Kabul traffic and towards the Bulwark building, where I intend to get some answers.

CHAPTER
TWENTY

The building itself is no great shakes — just a functional, Soviet-style block, big expanses of concrete and cheap metal-framed windows — but it's in a side road that's closed to traffic. I don't know how they've got the right to do that because there are a number of small shops opposite, but there are big concrete barriers at both ends of the street to stop suicide bombers. They're unmanned but they'd certainly be effective against car and truck bombs.

I really need to do a recon — keep an eye on the front and see which of Anderson's guys I recognise comes back.

We wait in the car for a while just shy of the barriers but their security get sniffy and come out of the building to check on us. The guys on the door are Pashtuns — smart uniforms with holstered pistols. There are two of them. Arnan gives them a bit of chat and they seem satisfied.

Arnan drives us around the back and we park up in sight of the block's car park compound. There's a barrier on that too, with a guard who's sitting on a stool at the side of the road with an AK across his knee. He's listening to the radio and appears to be smiling to himself. Hey, he gets paid for sitting on his arse all day listening to music. It's a big improvement on some other life options that face blokes from his background, so he has reason to be happy.

Arnan takes us round the front to a long row of shops, each of which seems to sell everything — camping gas, clothes, cloth, bread and, as it turns out, tea by the glass. We sit at the front playing backgammon and I have a good view of the building.

One of my problems is that my beard is now well developed, I look a bit fucked up, I'm wearing cheap clothing and could quite easily be an Afghan. My feet are still a giveaway but I've done what I can, making them dirty to disguise my white skin. However, it might have been an advantage to come dressed as a Brit here. Given a shave, a business suit and a briefcase I might even be able to walk straight through as a Westerner. This, however, is going to be trickier.

First, though, we have to get our mark. I was hoping for one of the guys who was working security for the businessman I met in the Afghan International. It's 9 a.m. when we start watching; by the time it gets dark no one I've recognised has left or entered the building.

I'm feeling incredibly exposed just sitting playing fucking backgammon for nine hours but Arnan tells me not to worry about it. Guys do, he points out. "What else are we going to do if there's no work?" he says wryly.

The Afghani guards don't come out. It's midnight before one of the grunts I saw in the bar comes home. He's still tooled up — big pistol on his hip, carbine across his front and he's wearing a ballistic jacket. Again, he may as well have a sign pinned to his chest saying "Suicide bombers, take note: Westerners live here". Immediately Arnan walks around to the back of the Bulwark building while I stay at the front. Our mark goes in and I wait.

On my side, no light comes on.

Arnan comes back. "Third floor, fourth light along," he says.

Good, we know where he is. I know what to do now. There's no massive anti-suicide bomb security so I guess that the bottom flats might be deserted. It's quite difficult to defend these buildings so they just have to hope that the suicide bombers are predictable — that is, they go for convoys or higher-profile targets like hotels and restaurants. By not filling the lower rooms they at least get some protection and I've noticed that none of the lights are on on the first two floors.

That won't stop a suicide bomb killing people but it will mitigate its effects and, putting it brutally, make the bomber go where he'll get more return for his investment.

The empty lower rooms provide a point of access and therefore a potential burglary weakness but there's no real way of getting in with the guards there and on a busy street. Then I have an idea.

"Go to the International and tell the Global News correspondent that the head of security at the Swedish embassy wants to talk to him now. He has a big story for him. Phone Mick to get him to confirm the story.

He must go to the embassy. Mick won't talk to him any other way."

He nods and runs across the lanes of traffic to the International. Global News'll need security if he's going to travel and he'll have to call his guard. They might have one guy with him if he's tucked up for the night but Bulwark are lords of the overkill. If he's going to move, they'll want a team.

I move round to the back of the building and past the guard. It's a different guy but he's still listening to the radio. He's not exactly dozing on the job but he doesn't look that vigilant either. The compound has a high wall and it's topped with barbed wire. However, whoever put the wire up hasn't done it very well. There's quite a dark space at the side of the building where an alley runs alongside it. That alley is barred by a metal gate but the gate has no barbed wire on top and is effectively a ladder up on to the compound wall. There, the wire is lower than on the rest of the building and it's supported by a couple of wooden stakes that rise out of the wall. They'll provide good support to balance on when nipping over the wall. Add this to the fact that the guy on the main car park entrance can't see the gate from where he is and you've got a weakness.

I walk down the side of the building. It is poorly lit here and there aren't many people in the street. No point hanging around.

I skin up the gate on to the wall. Unfortunately there's only so much pain the excitement of this sort of thing can mask and I'm still in a bad way. My leg gets a sharp stabbing pain as I scale up, my ribs are agony and my neck feels like someone's set it in concrete. Never mind, get on with it. I'm on top of the wall quickly, propelled by adrenalin. I have a hand on the stake, one leg across the wire, two and then I have a drop of ten feet to the car park floor. There's no way of hanging off the wall and dropping like that because I'd get caught in the wire. So I just jump.

I don't cry out as my battered legs hit the ground but there is the noise of me landing. The ground is a sort of herringbone brick affair. The guard doesn't move.

I squint through the darkness. There, on the same wall I'm on, is the unmistakable shape of a Mowag. I quickly make my way along the wall, crouching low behind the line of cars. Then I'm at the Mowag and I roll underneath it.

I have a good view of the third floor and, as I look up, I see the fourth light along from the right turn off. Result.

I wait, flat to the ground. After twenty minutes, footsteps approach — big boots, a crisp step. Most Afghan shoes are flip-flops or knackered ex-military boots. This guy sounds like he's treading the square at Sandhurst on passing out day. I can feel my heart beating. This guy's a meathead, so he might not be rational. If he fights I'll have to kill him, which will have meant I've spent a day losing at backgammon for nothing.

Bleep. That's a relief, it's central locking. This is going to be easier than I thought. I slide out from under the car at the passenger side, open the door and get in at the back. I don't believe it, the idiot has got his MP3 player headphones in. I can hear what he's listening to — "Killing in the Name" by Rage Against the Machine at top volume. He's fiddling with the comms system on the car, trying to confirm he's on the move. He's clearly unfamiliar with the way it works.

I place a hand over his mouth and put the knife to his neck with a gentle jab. That wakes him up. I take my hand off his mouth and tug his headphones out of his ears.

"Always reminds me of Christmas, that song," I say. He swallows heavily. A drop of blood is making its way down the blade of my knife.

"What's your name?"

"Richard."

"Richard what?"

"Goddard." His accent is Midwestern, but his voice is trembling.

"Well, Richard Goddard, I've got some great news for you. You have every chance of living to see tomorrow if you play your cards right. If you don't, I will kill you without thinking about it and be downloading some proper fucking music on to that fancy Walkman of yours before the night is out. Do I make myself clear?"

"Pretty much."

"Good. Now, I want a couple of answers out of you, that's all. After that, you can drive me out of here and we'll work out a way for you to stay alive without dropping me in the brown stuff."

He swallows again, hard.

"Put your hands on the steering wheel."

He does.

"Now, your training doesn't seem to have been up to much so I'm going to explain some basics of close-quarter battle, which should be self-evident, but just in case. Even if you have your hand on your gun with your finger on the trigger, even if you didn't have the safety catch on, which you do, in the time it takes you to turn your hand and shoot me, I will have pushed this knife through your carotid artery and probably, because I'm something of a bastard, through the soft palate of your lower jaw, up into your eyeball."

That last bit's made up for effect. Not the bit about me being a bastard, obviously, the bit about the eyeball. Just cutting the main artery supplying blood to the head will do, there's no need to tie a bow on it.

"In the plainest possible language, you will be dead and the shock will make you drop your gun. Now take that fucking cock replacement off your hip and drop it into the footwell to your right."

He unholsters the Desert Eagle and throws it into the footwell.

"Shoulder holster."

A Glock comes out.

"Ankle. Lift your leg up, do not bend forwards."

Some snub-nosed affair I can't quite see is tossed into the footwell.

"Any others?"

"There's a shotgun, a couple of SMGs and a carbine in the safe behind you."

"OK. I've now drawn my gun with my left hand. I'm going to sit back. If you attempt to move, I won't shoot you unless I have to. I'll use the knife and you will feel it. Do you understand?"

"Yes."

I sit back.

"Put your hands back on the steering wheel. Do not put your hand to your neck."

He does what I tell him.

"Tell me about yourself, Richard."

"What about me?"

"Who are you, where do you come from?"

"I'm out of Jefferson, Missouri. I joined the army two years ago, an infantry unit."

"Which one?"

"It don't matter."

"Why not?"

"I never finished the training."

"Why not?"

"Mindless bullshit."

"What do you mean?"

"Getting your balls busted over nothing at all. Learning useless shit. I didn't join the army to learn to iron creases into my pants. I wanted to shoot some fucking guns."

I can't say I find my heart bleeding over this but I try to sound sympathetic. It sounds odd but there are areas of similarity between what counsellors do and the skills an interrogator needs. You're looking for a rapport. That can be established even in a weird situation with a knife at the guy's back.

214

"So you came here?"

"I bullshitted the resumé and they took me."

"And you got to shoot some guns?"

"Yeah, I did."

"At Priand?"

"Yeah."

So he was there. This is better than I expected. I was prepared to find out I was wrong — despite my captors walking around with Brad's gun, despite the Mowags, despite my gut feeling. I was also prepared for this bloke not to know what I was talking about. As it is, I've come up lucky. I don't say anything for a short while, in order to increase his stress.

"Look, Richard, I can see you're a decent guy and you're trying to help me. Now I've got one very straightforward question. And I already know the answer to it. So do not lie to me. What happened at Priand?"

He bends his head and makes a strange noise. He's actually started crying. I didn't expect that.

"Take your time, mate," I say. I've got him where I want him psychologically so there's no point in any further aggression. I went for the aggressive approach in the first place because I had no chance to isolate him, work on him and develop a relationship. This, though, this is a bonus. He clearly wants to open up to someone.

"It wasn't meant to happen like that," he says.

"How was it meant to happen?"

"We were leaning on some guys. We make a little money in opium, just providing a bit of protection for the guys going to Pakistan. The guy who lived there had a lot of clout down in the valleys, in the poppy-growing areas. He looked like he was going to buy into this 'legitimate future'-type deal — no more opium, just legal crops. We went to talk to him, that's all. Brad said we were just talking to him. And then . . ."

"And then?"

"Someone started shooting. And then we started shooting and then it didn't stop. Brad had a fifty-cal and was just going mad. By the end . . ."

"Yes?"

"We had to finish it. There couldn't be any witnesses or we were all looking at life in an Afghan jail."

I have the strong impulse to stick him with the knife at this point. I control myself and make myself speak with an even voice.

"And yet there were witnesses."

"There was a Brit taking some engineers up that way. He came by while we were demolishing the village."

"You mean burying the dead children."

"Yeah, that." He's crying properly now. Guess he just found out that killing people isn't like it is on *Call of Duty: Black Ops*. Particularly if they're four-year-olds.

"You've got brothers and sisters?"

"Yeah."

"How many?"

"Two brothers, fourteen and sixteen."

"There must have been kids that age there."

He doesn't reply to that, just keeps sobbing.

So Ben wasn't even there when the shooting took place. And yet he's meant to have killed himself in a fit of guilt. Not likely.

"And what did the Brit say?"

"We told him it had been a fire fight."

"And he didn't believe you?"

"I don't know what he believed."

"Did he say anything?"

"He said it was convenient that we had a bulldozer standing by. I thought that too, man. Brad got it driven down by morning. Bulwark were using it up the valley. Lucky, I guess."

It does seem that Richard managed to miss the fact Ben was being a tad sarcastic at that point. I look at the back of his shaved head. I know his type. Richard has no deep culture of his own, no imaginative life beyond the lurid video games he plays and the half-understood lyrics of the heavy metal songs he listens to: no spine and no curiosity about other cultures. That's OK, there are plenty of squaddies like that — it's the army, not the diplomatic corps after all. He ain't going to be munching Ferrero Rocher at the ambassador's receptions. But if you take someone like that, give him no guidance, no framework, no discipline and a bad commander, what do you end up with? Dead women and kids and a bulldozed village in the Afghan mountains. It sounds like it was a terrible overreaction to a perceived threat. But perhaps I'm being generous.

I make him tell me the story again, and again. Then I make him go over it in detail, only backwards, starting with the massacre and running me all the way back to his brief spell in the infantry. Then forwards again. He omits nothing. I can tell he's telling the truth. One fact emerges during my interrogation, though.

"Brad said he thought the British guy was going to rat us out."

"You didn't think you had to kill him too?"

"Brad made a call."

"What sort of call?"

"I don't know. Bulwark have contacts, man, you know that."

"No, I don't, what sort of contacts?"

"The sort that can get to a guy and shut him up."

"Well, they shut him up good and proper. They shot him, Richard."

"I'm sorry."

"Yeah, I don't suppose that means a lot to his wife and kids."

Suddenly vehicles are coming into the compound, at least two of them with headlights on full beam. Shit, they must have wondered what happened to Richard and now they've sent for back-up to find him.

"They missed you at long last."

"Yeah."

I say nothing.

"Where does it go from here?" His voice is shaky.

"It makes it harder to get out without me killing you."

Ain't that the truth? But this is a fucked-up country and the raw fact is that killing a Westerner will make it ten times more difficult for me to get out of the country than killing an Afghan. Even if I'm convicted of killing the Afghans, there's a chance I'll be bargained or bribed out. It's happened before. Kill a US citizen and things get very hairy indeed.

I don't want to kill this kid, either. I've never really wanted to kill anyone at all, it's just that in my line of work it's fairly unavoidable if you don't want to be killed yourself. He's just a dumb, sheltered piece of shit from shitsville who found himself up shit creek in want of a paddle. He'd have been fine spending his life lurching between the mall, the bowling alley and the burger joint. Out here in the real world, though, he's going to get eaten alive. The lights have turned towards our car. I need to get out of there.

In the end, I just say, "catch." I throw one of the flashbangs into his lap and get out of the side of the vehicle away from where I came in. There's the familiar ear-splitting noise, the enormous flash and a burst of CS gas. I'm through the door, holding my breath with my fingers in my ears, rolling down the line of cars.

There's a taste of CS gas in my mouth and my eyes are watering but I can see where I'm going. There are footsteps running towards the car. I quickly make it down the cars and make my way towards the gate. All attention has gone to where the explosion happened. There's another huge bang and I can hear shouting, coughing and retching. A gun goes off. Great. I think Richard's actually found his Desert Eagle despite the flashbang. He's out of the car, I can see in the lights of the other vehicles. He can't see though, and he's staggering about firing madly. It's a good fucking job the Health and Safety Executive aren't here. The sound of it alone would have them insisting on ear defenders for the lot of us.

The noise has caused the guard on the gate to come running forwards with his AK levelled. The Mowag is there with its engine running and it does occur to me for a second to just take the piss and steal it. As it is, I just walk past it, using it as a shield between me and the fun and games on the other side.

"Get your hands above your head."

I look round. Jesus, I've got done with my own trick. Emerging from underneath the Mowag is the unmistakably huge figure of the other guy who I had the run-in with on the plane, all inflatable arms, over-white teeth and, more tellingly, MP5 submachine gun.

There really doesn't seem to be anything else to do but obey him.

He comes up and gives me a good dig with the business end of the gun — straight in my already-damaged ribs. I go down like a sack of wet sand. He puts the boot in and I feel like I'm going to vomit. I consider going for one of my guns but there's no chance of that — his weapon's right in my face. I can hear sirens blaring from across the city but the Bulwark boys are sealing the compound, shoving curious people back inside. Lights are coming on in the building, everyone who has woken up is looking down at me. This is not going well.

Now he's screaming and shouting for the others to come. They do, three of them.

"Get this motherfucker inside," says the guy who's hit me, "get him inside!"

The other three descend on me and now is the time to go for it. Only a maniac would start shooting into a scrum of his mates. I get the P99 free and smash the first in the head with the butt as he bends to pick me up. Then I sweep the legs from the second, bouncing his head off the ground and covering the other two guys with the P99.

This is clearly a tester for them as they start barking commands at me, which don't really gel.

"Throw down the gun and stand up slowly."

"Drop the weapon and lie on the floor."

Well, make up your minds, ladies. It's time I pointed out a very simple fact.

"I can shoot you, you can't shoot me," I say. "You lay down your weapons."

"We are not about to do that."

"Suit yourselves." I click off the safety on the P99.

"Nick!"

It's Beccy's voice. Where did she come from?

"You know this guy?"

"The bastard tried to kill me." It's Richard. He's reappeared with the old Desert Eagle, about the size of a field piece, waving around in his hand.

"Actually, Richard, I did my level best not to kill you."

"Nick!"

"Yes, Beccy?"

"We need to talk about this."

"I'm not talking to anyone who's got an MP5 stuck in my face."

"Put the guns down. Todd, that's an order."

"You're not in our division, lady, I don't take orders from back room staff."

"You do if you want a job in the fucking morning, now put the gun down."

He lowers the weapon.

"Anyone raises a weapon and I will kill *him*," I say, nodding towards the MP5 man, "no matter who is shooting."

This is true. He's directly in front of me and I can just level and fire without turning. Facing three heavily armed men I'm dead anyway, so it would just be an indulgence to try to shoot the one who fires at me. I'll take the nearest target of convenience.

Oh shit, Richard raises his Desert Eagle. Still feeling sore from our time in the truck, I guess.

"Richard!" Beccy again. She walks in front of his gun, which is something I'd hesitate to do with him in his condition. "Put it down."

Weirdly, this seems to get through to him and he lowers the gun. He seems almost touched by her gentle manner. I know what's happened to this kid. He has been playing with the demon of violence all his life. At Priand it bit him in the arse. Now he wants reassurance, kindness, the idea that there might be a future where he doesn't see those dead children's faces in his dreams every night. In short, he wants his mummy. It's OK. We all do eventually.

The people are still looking at us from the upper floors, sirens and flashing lights are at the compound gates, which have been locked. It won't be long before the police get involved, though, which is bad news for me.

"Come on," says Beccy.

"Where?"

"Follow me."

Doesn't seem I've got much choice. It all goes in a rush then as we jog towards the accommodation block. We go in through the building. Beccy speaks to the guards. There's a short period of arguing and then they let us in. They lock the building's doors behind us. At least it'll hold up the cops once they've come through the gate.

We go down the ground floor of the building. It's bare lino on the floors, strip lights above and has the stale feel of a place that is rarely used.

She opens one of the doors and we all troop in — me, her, Todd, Richard and another meathead they have with them.

It's a bare office stocked with the sort of furniture MFI rejected in the 1970s — plastic wood-effect desk, knackered metal chairs with foam poking through the fabric of their seats. I don't bother to sit, although I feel like it. I have a feeling I may be wanting to leave in a minute. Beccy tells us all to put the safety catches on our weapons and put them down.

"What's been going on?" she says.

The situation would be funny if wasn't so serious. It's almost like she's a headmistress who's called us into her room to account for our actions.

"Ask this guy," says Richard. His face is swollen with tears.

"Nick?"

"I came to get some answers about what happened at Priand."

"Did you get them?" says Beccy.

"Yeah," I say, "you should know: it was your company that was responsible for the massacre."

"What?"

"Your guys here have been doing a little deal with the local opium barons. Someone wants to quit. The boys don't like it. They go to sort it out and, owing to a combination of indiscipline, stupidity and nerves, end up killing a whole village."

"What have you told them?" says Todd to Richard.

"The guy had a fucking knife at my throat." He points to the mark where I used the old "steel reminder" to jog his memory.

Beccy nods. "You've been dealing opium?" she says to Todd.

"Yes. Not dealing, providing security."

"Using Bulwark resources?"

"It's all cleared, man, check it out if you don't believe me. Part of the strategy," says Todd.

"What strategy?"

"This ain't *Murder, She Wrote*. You want an explanation, ask your bosses. Which leaves us the problem of what we're going to do with this motherfucker, since he's such a fucking brilliant detective."

"Killing an entire village is part of our strategy?" Beccy says, an incredulous note to her voice.

"Just a perk on the side," says Todd with a wink.

"It wasn't meant to happen," says Richard.

"We need to kill this motherfucker now," says Todd, pointing at me. He opens the flap on his revolver holster. I'm not arsing around, I take the commando knife from my sleeve. I wasn't bull-shitting about the relative speeds of knives and guns. I'll have kebabed him before he gets the pistol halfway out.

"No, Todd, that's an order," says Beccy.

"I'm a little deaf from the fire fight," says Todd, "I'm afraid I didn't hear what you said."

He takes a Glock from his shoulder holster. Oh shit. The other guard gets in on the act and produces a pistol. It's decision time.

I look at Beccy. She looks at me. Then she gives two taps on her chest. That's an old 14 Company signal. It means "yes". In other words, kill them. She hasn't got a weapon but it's an unmistakable sign to me. It's not one she would make accidentally, it's too distinctive.

I kill Todd. It all happens in slow motion. Todd takes one straight into the unarmoured part by his neck just above his vest as I knock his gun aside with my free hand. This knife was designed to be able to kill through the three-inch-deep clothing of a Soviet soldier's winter uniform, so it easily punches down into his chest cavity. I wasn't messing about when I hit him and the force of the blow sends him crashing back into the chairs but I've kept hold of the knife. I turn to the others but, as I do, there are a couple of muted thumps and two louder thumps. Both Bulwark boys are dead on the floor, slick pools of blood seeping from their heads. Beccy has a Walther P99 in her hand, fitted with a silencer.

For a second I'm open-mouthed.

"Why have you got that?" I say, nodding towards the silencer.

"I was intending," she says, "to kill you. And quietly."

CHAPTER
TWENTY-ONE

There are three dead Bulwark employees in the room, a smell of gun smoke hovers in the atmosphere.

I look at Beccy. "You were going to kill *me*?"

"Yes."

"Why?"

"I think you know."

"I don't, or I wouldn't have asked why, would I?"

"Think about it, Nick, I'm sure you can work it out."

I look at the bodies.

"I'm not sure I can. You killed two of the Bulwark boys. That's your Christmas bonus fucked, love."

She gives me a look. Then the penny drops.

"You're not Bulwark, are you?"

She says nothing. And I realise. She's never left, has she? SRR must be all over Kabul, along with every sort of military intelligence. Is she part of that?

"Smack?"

I see a flicker of a "yes" in her eyes.

"And, hang on, you thought I was involved in that?"

She hasn't put the Walther down. OK, it's hot, so she doesn't want to put it back inside her jacket or wherever she got it from. If she was going to holster it she'd need to take off the silencer. But why doesn't she put it on the desk? Doesn't she trust me? Well, since she said she was going to kill me then obviously not. Hang on a minute: is that off the agenda?

I glare at her. "I've got nothing to do with it. The nearest I get to drugs is fucking Boots."

"That's not my information."

"Well, your information is wrong."

"Ben was working for a firm that was smuggling heroin out through Pakistan."

"No, he wasn't."

"Yes, he was. I've seen the file, Nick, it's as thick as a phone book. Sentinel Securities were involved in it — Ben's lot. Then something went down at Priand. We know it was a war for control of the opium trade."

"I don't know what it was but my mate Ben, *your* mate, wasn't involved in it. Look, we should have this discussion somewhere else."

"No, we should have it here."

"You're thinking of killing me, aren't you?"

"No, I'm thinking of letting you go. If you answer my questions satisfactorily, you've nothing to worry about." Her gun is levelled at me.

"Right."

Thinking about letting me go. Implying there's a possibility she won't actually do that. Part of my mind is already doing calculations. I'm nine feet away from her. She has the gun pointed at me, the safety disengaged, and she is expecting me to attack. Also she looks calm. Todd and the Bulwark guys were excited, almost raving. Adrenalin can take you two ways. It can make you react faster or it can slow you down. Anyone who's been in a violent confrontation will know the experience of it all happening in slow motion. If you have the training — or if you're a natural at fighting — you can use that to your great advantage. Most people, though, find it's as they're watching themselves from outside their bodies. They can't connect, can't make the limbs respond and do what they want. Beccy's not in that zone. My only option is a forceful, aggressive attack which frightens her so much that she forgets to pull the trigger. But Beccy's a trained soldier, not a shop girl. It's a hundred-to-one shot I kill her. If I got odds like that on a horse, I wouldn't back it.

"So why am I alive now?"

"We were interested in what you'd do out here, who you would contact. We were surprised when you went to the men in the jail and we thought you might rattle a few cages, frighten some of the smack dealers. We knew you'd want revenge for Ben and we were interested to see who you'd come for. Then the people you were leaning on would start reacting to you and we'd have a chance to find out how far the corruption went."

"So why haven't you got the boys out of jail?"

"They're clearly heroin dealers. That's my briefing."

"From who?"

"Reliable sources."

I'm still looking at the gun. Do I go for it? Hang on a minute, this is Beccy. Is it going to end like this?

"So what do you want to know?" I say.

"Who were you sent here to kill?"

"No one."

"I've seen the file, Nick."

"Well, the file is wrong. I've been ferrying wankers around the Isle of Wight for the last six months, I've been nowhere near a drugs deal. Where did you get this information from?"

"The sources are good ones."

"No, they're not. Look: if I find out who killed Ben I'm going to present the evidence to the police. I'm not here to kill anyone. My friend was killed, that's what I believe. I have found out why, and that might lead me to who. Ben and me were soldiers and we fought to uphold decent values — democracy, the rule of law. Yes, nothing would please me more than to find the bastard who killed him and take him out, but that's not how it's going to happen. I'm doing this by the book."

"And the book has left how many dead so far?"

I shrug. "I've been defending myself. I haven't fired unless I've been fired upon. Christ, I'm lucky to be alive."

"There's a dirty war going on here, Nick, a war behind the war. I believe you are part of that."

"No, your Bulwark boys are part of that, as you've just seen."

She nods. "So you're not working for the Chinese?"

I can see she's thrown that into the questions to try to shock me, see what response it gets. But it gets none.

"No. Although I'm interested to hear that they're involved. A bit disappointed, actually, I was hoping to narrow down the field of suspects for Ben's murder. It just went up by 1.3 billion, which is a bit of a pisser."

She pulls in a laugh and then thinks for a bit.

230

I say, "So are you going to kill me? It would seem ungrateful after all we've been through. I would remind you that you saved my life in Iraq. What were you doing, just saving me for later?"

She did as well. We were undercover in a car and she overheard a street vendor calling in some hit men. We'd been compromised and, because she spoke the lingo, we got out of there.

She remains silent. I try another tack. "Do you honestly believe that me and Ben were involved in this? Really? Beccy, I have a kid. If you think I'd get involved in heroin, think again. I've spent years fighting people who get their arms from drug money. I'm not going to get involved in a business that puts British soldiers, a fair few of whom may be mates of mine, in the firing line. Ain't gonna happen."

She looks at the floor. "What were you doing up in Priand, then?"

"Trying to find out what went on. Ben ended up at a fucking counsellor, for God's sake. He wasn't exactly a navel-gazer, was he? And look, old Richard down here told me the two lads currently sitting in the Mir prison were just passers-by on the massacre, as was Ben. Go and confirm the story with them, if you like."

"Richard might have lied. They might lie."

"Richard was as thick as a post. He wasn't capable of lying. He was barely capable of shutting up. I'm surprised he was allowed to live." Suddenly, I get a flash of temper. "If you want to kill me, why don't you get on with it?"

"You have no idea," she says, "how much you have to thank me for. There are elements here that would have arranged a convenient accident for you the moment you hit Afghan soil."

"Why's that?"

"Because you came here to kill. Believe me, I've had to fight very hard to keep you alive."

I look her in the eye. "I came here to find out why Ben died. That's all."

"He crossed the wrong people. If he was involved in the massacre at Priand, then some people wanted revenge. It's why the Afghans came for the guys in prison."

"How did they come to be blamed? Who pointed the Afghans in their direction? Richard said they had nothing to do with it," I say.

"Did it occur to you Richard might have been spinning a line? We now know there is a Bulwark faction that has been dealing smack. Maybe they were part of that."

"No. Richard's story was too consistent, too well remembered. I interrogated him for an hour."

"Right." She stares hard at me.

"I'm not a heroin dealer. All I know is something very odd has gone on with whatever file you've seen. Also something very messed up happened up in those hills."

Beccy looks as if she's weighing up her options. Finally she says, "I want you to come in with me."

"Where?"

"Somewhere we can check out your story."

"Interrogation? That's not going to happen."

I see her fingers move on the handle of the gun.

The mobile buzzes in my pocket.

"Do you mind if I get that?"

She waits a beat or two, before saying, "Go ahead. Put it on speaker, though."

I answer it. "Nick, it's John." His voice buzzes out into the room.

"How you doing?"

"I've been talking to our guys on the ground in Afghan. That whole sector's not being handled by SOCA — it's a military intelligence job, classified. I could hardly get any information on it at all."

"Is that normal?"

"Very abnormal. SOCA's in everything out there."

"Did you get anything at all?"

"Yes. There was a question of investment there — until about ten months ago. There was a mining company, it's an offshoot of the Venezuelan government. It was trying to set up something."

"Mining what?"

"Lithium. The stuff in your mobile phone. Apparently they found some. But they withdrew."

"Why?"

"There was a sudden-flare up of violence in the area. The local guys aren't Taliban at all and it came as a surprise. Incursion from Pakistan. Also Bulwark's spending in Kabul increased hugely at that time. The western military don't have a big presence in that area. It's just Bulwark and the ANA. The increase in spending is timed almost exactly with the increase in violence."

Beccy's listening intently — I can almost see the cogs whirring in her brain. It seems that this information is as new to her as it is to me.

"Could have been them fighting it," I observe.

"Yeah, or funding it."

"Are you serious?"

"There are huge payments going to Bulwark Kabul for a month before the upsurge in violence. Proves nothing but it raises a doubt."

I think of those Mowags up in Priand. What were they doing there? Not keeping the peace for sure. And the Bulwark operatives who took me to Swimming Pool Hill? Were they bringing me back so someone in Kabul could get a good look at me?

"Thanks, John. Beccy's here, she says hello."

"Hello, Becs!"

"Hi, John."

"All well?"

"Can't complain."

I turn off the phone.

"Did that sound like it checks out with your story or my story?" I say.

"Your story."

"Right. Think about it, Becs, you're being asked to believe that me, Ben and John all suddenly decided to have a complete character transformation and start dealing drugs. And massacring kids."

She swallows. "The report was clear."

234

"Well, someone has been spinning SRR or MI — whoever it is you're working for — a line, haven't they?"

"And why would they do that?"

There are footsteps outside. A voice speaks in Pashto.

"Shit," says Beccy.

"What?"

"Afghan National Police. The guards must have got suspicious and called them."

"Are you disappointed that I'm going to do life in prison before you can shoot me?"

She pulls out her mobile phone. "I'm going to call my boss," she says. She presses quick dial.

"Cadwell? A spot of bother at the Bulwark main accommodation block. I have Nick Kane here and we've had a gun battle with the heroin runners from Bulwark. Yeah, Bulwark. Unfortunately the ANP are at the door and it looks as though this one might be difficult to explain away."

She listens for a second.

"Very good." She turns to me.

"Put on Todd's vest and lie on the floor."

I don't question, just do it. The vest has a conspicuous puncture wound on the front where the knife went in and is heavily stained with blood. He has four clips of ammunition for the Desert Eagle in his trousers. What was he planning to do? Demolish a house? This could all get interesting; I take them.

I tuck the Glock into my shoulder holster and quickly unbuckle his Desert Eagle thigh holster and tie that on, along with the gun.

"You're wounded," she says to me, "and you have to get to hospital." She squints through the venetian blinds, using the little holes that take the cords to see through. "The street is filling up with cops," she tells me. "They're swarming all over it."

She unlocks the door and then she calls out in Pashto. I don't know what she's saying but I guess it's along the lines of "Help". Boots come running. Beccy calls again. She knows better than to open the door. Training standards in the ANP vary wildly — largely because there's no guarantee a trainee won't send his brother along on days he can't make it. So the boys can be trigger-happy.

The door opens and a big Afghani copper, his pistol in his hand, steps quickly into the room. He has a radio.

Beccy is weeping now, gesturing to the bodies. She points to me and says something then points to Todd and, in the middle of her sentence, two words stand out clearly: "Nick Kane."

The guy gets on to his radio and barks into it. There's a crackle and then a reply. He points to the body and shouts at his men. Two cops lift Todd and drag him out of the room. As they come out, a press of cops comes in, all eager to see what's gone on, flip-flops all over the lovely pristine crime scene. So much for *CSI Kabul*. These guys are a defence lawyer's dream.

Beccy speaks to them, much more deferential than she was in the argument in the hospital. This goes down a lot better with the cops. I hear the words "ISAF hospital". Two youngish cops lift me up to my feet.

236

Then I'm dragged along out of the back of the building and into the car park.

We arrive at the Mowag and she unlocks it. More cop vehicles are coming into the car park, coppers spilling from cars. Everyone seems to want to help load me into the Mowag. I get in the back and Beccy jumps into the front and has locked the doors and started the engine before anyone can object.

There's no clear senior officer here and everyone just watches as she backs it out of the compound gates. Then we're on the streets of Kabul.

"Your boss is a bright bunny," I say.

"Not really," she says, "he told me to blame you for the killings."

"Military Intelligence's caring, sharing side in evidence again?" I say.

"Exactly."

"So where now?"

"Priand," she says.

"You haven't been there before?"

"It's classified."

"Even to you?"

"Yeah."

"So why go there now?"

"Because we need to find out what's going on up there and that's not going to happen if we stay here. We need a proper recce and that could take weeks. Call your mate, Arnan. We can't travel in this thing, lovely as it would be."

"I haven't got his number."

She tosses me her mobile. "Under A," she says.

"How have you got his number?"

Puh-lease, she says with her eyes.

I dial Arnan and we agree to meet just out of town where we can use his car.

I am harsh on the Afghans sometimes but most of them are beautiful people. Try saying this to a London cabbie: "I'd like you to drive in your own car for three days through a mine-infested, bandit-ridden country over roads that resemble a ploughed field to the middle of a drugs war where you know your fare has already been kidnapped by the Taliban and passed over to torturing maniacs with Madonna keyrings. It is very likely you will be shot. I will give you fifty pounds for it, though there is no guarantee you will be paid."

"I'll be on my way in ten minutes, boss," says Arnan. "Do you mind if I bring my cousin?"

CHAPTER
TWENTY-TWO

It's difficult to leave the Mowag for Arnan's beaten-up Toyota. Satnav, air-con, MP3 player with — admittedly — Richard's iffy taste in music for a cramped back seat with the foam sticking through.

As it is, Arnan's arrival is nearer to an hour. We keep off the roads, inside a big garage owned by some mate of Arnan's. Beccy makes Arnan promise that, should we need it, the truck will be in one piece when we get back. Afghan mechanics would strip a Mowag in about twenty seconds if they got the chance and use its components to fix everything from cars to washing machines.

He smiles at us, waves his hand and says, "This isn't the Mowag you're looking for," in a way that I think is meant to sound like Alec Guinness in *Star Wars*. His point's clear. He doesn't have the power of mind control, so this vehicle's too hot for him to handle. Still, Beccy suggests that he sell it. She can't talk to him directly as that's not the custom so she writes what she has to say down and I give it to him, as if it was my idea. He calls someone in who reads it and nods. He can say he found it and get a reward back off Bulwark.

On my request, Arnan has brought some clothes for us: a tribesman's get-up for me and some of his wife's dresses and a full chadri — the so-called "shuttlecock" burqa with only a grille for the eyes — for Beccy. She won't need to wear this on the Highway 1, but as we get nearer to Marjul it's a case of "better safe than sorry". Local warlords do enforce the dress code down there and, if we meet a Taliban roadblock, it's going to be easier for everyone if she blends in.

Arnan's also been and raided Mick's kit, so we have a couple of military sleeping bags, a basha for some sort of shelter, a survival kit full of goodies and thermals for us both — a bit big for Beccy, but better than none. There's also a decent pair of binoculars. Beccy takes the first-aid kit out of the Mowag and quite a lot of weapons out of the safe in the back.

There is some serious kit there — an M27, for a start. This is a gun I've never seen before, brand new. It's a squad automatic weapon — designed to give infantry teams suppressing firepower. I'm struck that it's incredibly light and magazine fed. Frankly, I wonder if it's up to the job. There's another similar weapon with it — an M249 light machine gun. I'd have preferred the original Belgian Minimi, which is what I trained with, but this is a near exact copy. This fires about a thousand 5.56 rounds a minute and, if it opens up, the advice is keep your head down. It's light enough to carry, has a bipod and a belt feed firing two hundred rounds a belt from its distinctive plastic box. It's heavy but worth carrying. However, that has to go in the boot of the Toyota. There's an HK417 — a good underslung grenade launcher with ten 40mm rounds. That's always worth having.

There's also, unbelievably, two Claymore antipersonnel mines. Again, worth having because you can pretty easily discourage people from following you with a couple of those.

Arnan's mechanic helps us stow the stuff under the back seat of the Camry and even, in the case of the M249, ingeniously under the bonnet. These guys are marvels. We'll only have Arnan's AK in the case of an ambush but we've plenty of stuff to take with us if we need to go cross-country.

So, if anything, we're overequipped in the weapons and ammo department, slightly light in the comfort stuff and in fairly unsuitable clothing. Good for disguise, not for endurance. We have a decent packed lunch that Arnan's missus has made us, along with a few water bottles, and we can pick some stuff up on the way. Apart from that it's going to be a hungry little trip. Never mind. We'll make do.

Pamir's eyes light up at the sight of the guns. I give him the Desert Eagle. He looks immensely pleased, as well he might. I show him how to hold it to stop the whip on it but he seems to need no introduction. He's an old hand. Kids today, eh?

The car pulls out of Kabul under a big white moon that hangs above Television Hill. Beccy takes a call. It's from Cadwell, her boss, her real boss in whatever aspect of MI she's in now.

"Yeah, it's sorted," she says.

Then, "No, he got away."

And after a pause, "Yeah, I'm going after him. Hello, hello, I'm losing the signal."

I glance at her — she's on the back seat next to me. Ideally I'd have gone in the front to check for any problems but culturally it just isn't going to work putting Arnan's in the back with Beccy. There's no way she can go in the front seat while there are blokes in the car, either. No point moaning about it, it's just the way it is.

"It's going to be a tough one explaining why you're missing for such a long time."

"Not really, I have autonomy. Cadwell's the overall boss, but I'm not reporting to him every second. He's got his own work to concentrate on."

"Which is?"

She smiles enigmatically. "Messing people up."

"Same as all of us, really."

"I thought you were here to save the world, Nick."

I return the smile. "I am. It's just that sometimes requires messing people up. You'll look good with that M27, by the way. It goes with your eyes."

"I bet you say that to all the girls," she says.

I pop an antibiotic.

"Believe it or not, Beccy, I haven't had much opportunity for chat-up lines around here. 'If I ask for a bucket to wee in are you going to beat me some more?' "

"Now I bet you do say that to all the girls."

"Only if they ask nicely."

She smiles again and up ahead, past Arnan's head, I see a roadblock.

CHAPTER
TWENTY-THREE

It's the police and they're on high alert. No doubt they're a little bit upset by now and would love to have a long chat to talk it all through with me — the hard way. Luckily they're looking for two foreigners in a state-of-the-art battlewagon, not four Afghans in a broken-down Toyota. I don't bother touching the Glock under my thigh. If we get pulled by the police, the tactic is to come quietly. They're not the enemy and we've no rationale for shooting them. The fact that they're going to lock me up for the rest of my life is not justification enough to start slotting them.

They don't even search the car, just have a few words with Arnan and wave him through. As dawn comes up we've made good progress and pass the place that sells the fuel where we saw the Taliban guy last time. Here Beccy puts on the burqa and we receive few looks as we blow the filters and refuel.

No Taliban about, which is a good sign. There are a good few army convoys rolling along this morning — big bulky Mastiffs, Jackals on their flanks. We follow behind them, leaving a respectful distance between us. No Taliban are going to be shooting at us while they're there. They do fear the Mastiffs because they know their mines normally can't hurt them and all they do by exploding an IED is give away their position. That is unless they're expecting them, in which case they'll double or triple the size of the bomb.

Then it comes time to get off the highway and hit the dirt. Immediately, in a small mud-brick village, we clock Taliban. They're everywhere, black turbans out in force. We're only five kilometres from the main drag but these boys don't seem to care.

Arnan bravely keeps going but there is going to come a point soon where things will get hairy. We're getting looks here, not up close, not hostile, but looks nonetheless. We're strangers and someone is sooner or later going to ask us what we're doing here.

The car carries on and after about a couple of hours the road is blocked just before yet another small village. Ten Taliban are sitting around on their haunches carrying a really unpleasant array of RPGs, AKs and, crucially, some whacko-looking heavy machine gun on a wheeled mount. It looks like an old Soviet NSV. It's got a belt of ammo fed into it and I know that it will make short work of our car. Thirteen rounds a second and it'll put holes in your truck from three-quarters of a mile away. It's a tasty bit of kit. The road is straight and I know there's no way we can just accelerate through there.

Arnan has been busy, putting a Koran on to the dashboard tray.

We pull up at the stop and Arnan gives his normal cheery "hello". These guys, though, are serious and approach the car, looking all around.

They glance at the Koran and he yaks on with them but even I can see they don't look impressed by his story, whatever it is. They ask him and Pamir to get out of the car. Pamir does, with difficulty. He's stuffed the Desert Eagle down the back of his trousers. It's not a gun that stuffs anywhere easily.

I remain in the back of the car. The conversation is becoming heated. At least we're too close for them to use that NSV, though the guy operating it looks stoned enough to start shooting at whatever hallucination wanders into his field of vision.

I have my hand on the P99 I've stuffed down the side of the seat.

"This is going badly," says Beccy under her breath.

"What are they on about?"

"They want all sorts of detail off him and I think they're going to call to check his story out."

"Well, it was nice knowing you," I say wryly.

The interesting thing is that, throughout this encounter, the Taliban haven't looked into the car at all. Maybe it's because there's a woman in there.

Suddenly, I can't believe my eyes. Pamir has drawn the Desert Eagle, and points it at the centre of a young Taliban's chest. The man starts backing away.

Everyone else levels their weapons. There is really nothing we can do here, just sit tight.

"*Butch Cassidy and the Sundance Kid*?" I say.

"Yeah, didn't enjoy the end, did you?"

"*Bonnie and Clyde?*"

"A man and a woman, in a car, machine-gunned to death. Now why couldn't you think of *The Sound of Music?*"

"If you can get this lot singing 'Doe a Deer', the drinks are on me," I say.

Something's weird about the way the Taliban are gesturing. There's a lot of waving of hands, as well as guns, expressions of "No! No!", real vehement disagreement.

Pamir is screaming at the kid in his sights, Arnan has produced a Tokarev, everyone is waving a gun. All of a sudden, a big bloke with a long bright red hennaed beard comes striding through the crowd. He kicks the boy who Pamir is targeting across the back of the legs, sending him sprawling to the floor. He points an AK at him and the boy lies wriggling and pleading.

"What's happening?"

"Pamir has accused him of looking at me."

"And they're going to shoot him for that?"

"The big guy saw the look. It's his father."

The man speaks to Pamir. He shakes his head. The man turns the gun away and waves us through. Arnan jumps back in the car, as does Pamir, and we're off.

"Good idea, tell him good idea," I say to Arnan, "a good trick."

Arnan translates and the kid says something back.

"It was not an idea," says Arnan, "he was looking at her."

"She's in a burqa," I say.

246

Arnan shrugs. "Pamir defended her honour. They understood that and knew their man was in the wrong. That's why they let us through easily."

"Crazy," I say.

"Just think of it as if he'd spilled his pint," says Beccy.

"Oh, right, yeah. Oh well, that puts it in a light I can understand."

We keep on down the narrow dirt track. There is a river here and we wind alongside it for a while. The road is becoming impassable. Since we last came down here it has rained and it seems there's been a lot of heavy trucks through the area.

"A strange combination," says Beccy.

"Yeah," I say.

"What do you mean?" says Arnan.

"Big trucks. Clearly a convoy," I explain. "No sign of IED activity, nothing burned out, not even any signs that a bomb went off and didn't work."

"Maybe lucky?" says Beccy.

"There is no such thing as luck in Afghanistan," says Arnan.

She nods.

A boy with a donkey is coming the other way and Arnan stops to talk to him. I can't speak Pashto but I can understand what he says.

"Taliban, Taliban, Taliban." He waves his arm down the road.

This has become too difficult. By the satnav on Beccy's phone we're about fifty kilometres from our target. In the middle of a big Taliban build-up, we're bound to run into uncomfortable questions soon. I think Arnan has been brave enough. It's time he went back to Kabul.

"Can we take the fields here?" I ask Beccy.

"I think most of the Russian mines have been cleared by now and there's no big reason to think the Taliban will have put anything new down here."

"Shall we do it then?" I ask.

"Yeah. But I'm not spending the next three weeks in this get-up."

She speaks to Arnan. Pamir starts laughing but Arnan seems to take her seriously. We get out of the car and she goes to the boot and fetches my discarded tracksuit.

She offers it to Pamir. He looks at it and nods. Then Beccy walks off down the track. He changes into my tracksuit and puts his Afghan clothing on the bonnet of the car. She returns, takes it and goes off again. Five minutes later she comes back. Pamir bursts into laughter, as does Arnan.

There is no way that Beccy can pass as a boy. Her face is too feminine. Luckily she hasn't got big tits, so that's not a problem, but she's still obviously a woman, despite the baggy pants and top.

"You look like a girl," I say.

"Don't worry, I've done this before."

"When?"

"In Kabul. My intelligence-gathering capabilities are compromised as a woman. Sometimes this is the only way."

"But you don't look like a male."

"No, not to you. But remember, this isn't a cross-dressing culture. Here, if I'm dressed as a man, I'm a man. People might think I look a bit girly but they won't think I'm a girl, it's just not an available thought over here."

I look at Arnan and Pamir. Arnan is well educated, speaks great English and has lived in England. But still, he finds it hilarious that Beccy is done up in male clothes. He keeps shaking his head.

"Are you sure?"

"Yeah, let me tell you a joke. A man walks up to a policeman. He says, 'Do you fancy a bit?' The policeman says, 'Your place or mine?' "

"That's not funny."

"Why?"

"Don't know, just isn't. It's not really a joke, is it?"

"In the early seventies in Britain it was. It's a Monty Python sketch. It was funny because the idea of a policeman being homosexual was something the culture couldn't even picture. When someone suggested it, it made people laugh because it seemed such an odd idea. So that's why these two are killing themselves here. The idea of a woman dressing as a man is literally unthinkable to them. They've never even thought it might be possible. The other way, yes. Men can disguise themselves as women — the Taliban have done it — but it would never occur to them a woman might do the same."

"I have no idea what you're talking about," I say.

"The disguise will work, believe me."

We take the big rucksack and the weapons. We've a good quantity of ammunition from the Mowag. I wrap the M27 and the HK417 in a bit of cardboard from the back of the car, tying them loosely with twine. It won't fool anyone up close, but from a distance it'll make it difficult to pick them as such modern guns. The Taliban do have a bit of modern kit but we're not Taliban and it would raise questions if we were caught with them.

I'd love to take the light machine gun but that's not going to happen now. It's too heavy for a long mission and the grenades can provide covering fire as easily — at least if we're close enough.

"Good luck," says Arnan.

For a second Pamir goes to touch Beccy on the shoulder and then his face falls. He starts talking quickly. "Tell him not to worry," says Beccy to Arnan in English.

She turns to me. "I told you the disguise would work."

We arrange an RV here in two weeks, agreeing that if we're not here by then Arnan shouldn't hang about. We take what provisions we can and head down off the track. We're sparing Beccy's satnav batteries so we boot it up, get a bearing and then turn it off and use the torch compass Mick's provided us with to keep going.

It's crop fields here and we take minor paths. We have a disguise, we have a story we've concocted — car broken down, heading on to relatives up the valley, afraid of bandits on the road. Beccy can handle that. I'm just going to keep it zipped and hope they don't challenge my silence.

250

If the area hadn't been cleared of mines there's no way I'd be on these little tracks. However, it has. Still, I'm cautious. We've decided to trust our disguises so we're not going to move patrol-style with supreme caution. Instead, we're trying to walk casually, blend in with the background. Our first contact with hostiles will be through talking, we hope. Nonetheless, Beccy's up front with her eyes peeled and I'm bringing up the rear in a sort of sneaky tail-end Charlie way.

It's slow to move like this, though, and it's very hot. We go ten kilometres and check our position. The track has taken us back towards the road. To be safe, we should really try to make it to the opposite side of the valley, particularly as night is falling.

We cut across, going through fields and past grazing goats. When we reach the river we're lucky there's a ford one kilometre downstream. We cross and continue down that side of the valley.

As darkness falls we eat the first of our provisions, taking it easy because we know these have to last a long time. Then we make the decision — continue on by night. The moon's a good 'un — bright and yellow — and it'll be safer to move through the dark and hole up during the day. It'll be warmer like that, too. We fill up our water bottles at the river, adding the drops of iodine from the first-aid kit. It tastes shit but it means the water's sterile.

Then we press on, making good progress — a couple of clicks an hour, which is phenomenal under the circumstances. At dawn the calls to prayer from unseen villages echo around the hills and the sky is pink and lovely. For a short time you can even find yourself forgetting what's going on in this country when it's capable of producing such unique and beautiful moments. We climb the hillside a little and bivvy up in the shadow of a big boulder. I collect a few other rocks from around the mountain to break up our outline if we're seen from above and we sleep in shifts. She has two hours, I have two hours, then the same again until dusk. I'm already starving. There's a point at which you get used to reduced rations. You're still hungry but you're not fit to keel over all the time. I'm not yet at that point.

We kick on under the big moon. We're beginning to see little compounds on this side of the river now, which worries me. We don't want to have to explain ourselves.

We make good progress again, not resting at all. At one point, across the valley we see the lights of a convoy. I wonder who they are — it's not usual to travel at night.

"Do we need to look at that?" says Beccy.

"Tempting, isn't it? What do you think?"

Beccy sighs, puts her hands on her hips and shakes her head. "I don't know. Part of me is really curious, but the other part is cautious. I just don't know."

I stand at Beccy's shoulder and stare across at the convoy. What would we gain by doing a recon? It could be nothing, meaning we've lost valuable time. We're travelling by night, after all, and I want to get to Priand as soon as I can. And if it's something, we could get caught up in a bit of a clash. We could get injured, or killed, and Ben would remain in the eyes of the world a suicide.

"Let's leave it," I say eventually. "It's best that we get to Priand as soon as we can — we need to understand what's been happening there."

Beccy nods her assent and we move off again. As dawn approaches we make camp, this time in better terrain — a scrubby wood. This area of the country is becoming mountainous but it doesn't seem to know whether it's Greece or Switzerland. There are a lot of small pines like you might see on the hills on a Greek holiday but further up there's a covering of pines. That's quite unusual. A lot gets stripped for firewood.

We wait out the day but the night is suddenly cloudy. We can't see properly to move so we wait it out until morning, shivering together in one sleeping bag.

We're huddling together for warmth, that's it. The threat of imminent Taliban contact tends to take your mind off romance. Also, I can tell Beccy isn't up for it, more to the point. All that's on either of our minds is keeping warm. On a night as cold as this, if big Mick was here I'd be in the bag with him.

We can hear more convoys in the other valley. What's going on here? We understood there were Taliban in the area. If convoys are coming through with their lights on there either aren't any Taliban about — which means they're coalition convoys — or it's under their total domination and the trucks belong to the Taliban. From what I've seen I'd guess it was the latter.

The next day is still cloudy and we decide to move. It's good to get going again after such a cold night and we're closing in on the objective. Today we pass some goatherds but we just give them a wave from the distance and they wave back.

Now we're on the plateau. We've actually come up a bit higher and look down on it. It's an incredible sight, stretched out in front of us for miles, the flat khaki of the plain broken up by the little outlines of animal enclosures, a deeper green around the river in the distance, villages and compounds dotted across it.

From up here it looks like a giant Zen garden. Rachel, my ex, was into that sort of thing and I bought her one from Tesco one year when Chloe was little. It had a little rake with it, I remember, and Chloe swallowed the tip and had to go to casualty.

I try to put these thoughts out of my mind. I can't think of my family while I'm doing this.

If we can move across closer to Priand then we'll have some great OPs to choose from in the mountains.

The valley curves around into the distance. It would be good to be in a landscape like this with Beccy for some other reason. Imagine if we were tourists, hiking in these hills in a time of peace. All day alone in the splendours of nature and then back for a meal at a village followed by a night of . . . did I say it was off my mind? Well, the sun up here is stronger and it seems to have warmed me up.

We drop down and begin to skirt around the mountainside. There are no tracks as such but the way forward is fairly obvious. I do worry that we might be seen, so we keep below any ridges and keep descending. We can see less from the valley floor but we can be seen less too.

Our first contact comes at around eleven in the morning. We're walking down a long slope of tiny stones, when we hear voices from below us. There's a compound, just a single unit, among the green scrubland. Sitting outside it talking are three black-turbaned Taliban. They're just sitting around on the floor chatting.

I motion for Beccy to stop. We freeze to the mountainside. We're in a terribly exposed position if they look up. The mountain becomes steeper in front of us, almost a cliff. We'll have to drop to the track by the Taliban if we want to go on. We can go back and over the top of it or we can bluff our way through this lot.

Zip! A stone at my feet leaps up. We're being fired on. More shots rattle around us above our heads. Too high. There's a shout from below. All three Taliban get up and point their weapons at the hill, scanning for us.

The shout's come from the roof of the compound. There's a bloke on top of it. He's got an AK and he's done the whole clip in the first burst. He's reloading.

I don't even bother to take the cardboard off the bottom of the HK. I just line him up and squeeze the trigger — on the gun, not the grenade launcher. He goes down. Beccy aims the M27 at the three below and fires. That does the trick, the ground writhes with dust as the bullets smash down. One bloke goes straight down, the other two roll for cover.

Shit, we need to do this quickly. It's imperative we get out of here as quick as possible. Gunfire's common in these valleys but someone will come and check it out. The enemy have retreated to the doorway of the compound. What's that saying? In for a penny, in for a pound. I scramble as far as I can around the hillside while Beccy puts suppressing fire down.

As the slope begins to become too steep to walk on, I can just get an angle on the doorway. One grenade in the pipe, I squeeze the trigger and it flies forward. There's a loud explosion and Beccy's already running, half sliding down the slope. There's another burst of fire and she gives the signal to me to advance. I come down the hill.

The boys in the compound are all dead. We quickly check the bodies. Nothing. In the compound, though, are some water bottles, flatbread and cheese. And a motorbike — a little Honda 100 with the keys still in.

"Yes?"

"Yes. Actually . . ."

She recovers a couple of turbans from the men. Beccy jumps on the back of the motorbike. We go five hundred yards off and put the turbans on. Black turbans. We're now Taliban. This bike is a find. It's almost the Taliban's signature mode of transport. They use them for reconnaissance. Well, we can use it for the same thing. It lets us get around without attracting suspicion.

We ride down the track and on through several other compounds. We see some dust coming at one point so stow the bike behind a wall while a pickup truck full of Taliban zooms past.

We travel on around the mountains. I guess we must be passing the ANA post where I stayed the night. It'll be north of us, fifteen or so clicks. Beccy's a bit concerned about the range of the bike but there's half a tank in there and these things sip fuel. We'll be OK for a while.

The mountains are like a stadium around the massive flat expanse of the plateau. Here, though, there is a line that extends into the plateau, almost cutting it in two, rising like a dragon's back from a lake. The hills rise steeply and sharply from the plain but, as I know, they are climbable. This is an excellent vantage point from which to survey the town.

There's the question of where to dump the bike. Nowhere immediately presents itself. However, as we pull onto a more substantial track, there's a culvert going over a little ravine. I stow it in there.

As the sun falls we make our way as best we can up the hill overlooking Priand. I can see it clearly. It actually sits on a slight hill, I realise now, and the plateau falls away sharply at the rear of the compound to where I was trapped on my last visit. That's why I couldn't drop down the back of the village — it's just too steep.

Unlike my last visit, the place is banged out with trucks. These aren't Afghan jobs, they're western — no decorations for a start. Afghan trucks are known as jingle trucks because they're all done up with chains, bells and tassels. They're incredibly colourful, like something you'd see in a carnival. These trucks are nothing like that — they're really modern. Army?

257

Maybe. I'll see in the morning. The mountain is rocky enough that we don't need to dig in, just settle in behind some boulders.

I take a scout higher up the mountainside for a stream because water's running low but there's nothing so we'll have to manage our supply carefully. I look back to where we came from. I can't see as far back as the compound where we engaged the Taliban. I guess they'll have found the bodies and be looking for us by now but we've put a good distance between us and them. Then I come back down the mountain to Beccy.

"No problems?" I say. It's only a whisper, we need to keep noise to a minimum in case there are any enemy nearby.

"No."

"Could be a tricky one, this."

"Yeah."

"Miles from home with no back-up."

"If this is the 'let's have a shag in case we die tomorrow' conversation then forget it. Bad soldiering, it would make too much noise. I stink anyway."

"Excellent," I say.

"Why?"

"Well, if we get back to Kabul then you can have a shower. Then you won't stink, and . . ."

"Dream on."

"I will."

We do the shift thing again and I see lorries coming and going all night. At first light I get the binos on the situation. It could be the army. They are in a uniform of combat trousers and black bomber jackets. But there's

Taliban amongst them. It's unmistakable. The trucks set out across the valley with the black turbans in attendance. There are Mowags there. Are the Taliban providing security for Bulwark trucks? It's certainly not the US or ISAF with Taliban in tow.

"Do you believe what you're seeing?" I say to Beccy.

"That looks like something more than helping out a few drug lords," says Beccy. She looks puzzled. She clearly can't work out why MI haven't noticed this themselves.

"How much are they exporting? There's enough trucks to export tons of it there."

"It's the right way for Pakistan," she points out.

"We should watch this a bit longer."

"Yeah. Food situation's not good."

"Water neither, but one more day and we'll make our way to the river."

"Right."

We wait throughout the day. It's boring and uncomfortable but we can't afford to move around. At one point a load of heavily armed Taliban come past us in a pickup but they just speed past our position. Interesting. Looking for us after finding the bodies at the compound? Probably. Ah well, it's a fact of life now, no point worrying about it. They've gone but if they come back, they come back.

After the dawn convoy leaves there's not a lot happens. And then, at sundown, we see a Hummer streaking across the plain. It stops about two kilometres outside the town and four blokes get out. I look through the binos. One of them is the unmistakable figure of Brad Anderson — dyed blond hair, chemically enhanced muscles. He looks big even in the distance. Brad leans smoking and chatting against the vehicle. Eventually, with the sun casting the long shadows of the hills towards him, he opens the back of the truck.

Something is removed. It looks like a giant cocoon at this distance. Then it seems to split at the back and I realise I'm looking at someone's legs.

One of the other boys takes out a spade and, as night falls and my vision fades, they start digging.

"There's something here," I say to Beccy, "that we need to take a look at. They're burying somebody out there."

Immediately she takes out the compass and we get a bearing. In this land of corpses a secret disposal like that is something to notice.

CHAPTER
TWENTY-FOUR

Tonight the moon is back, the stars are thick and deep and the plateau is in front of us like a still and silver lake.

We descend the back of the mountain. I estimate the burial site at six clicks but it might be more than that. From the high level there's very little need to bother with navigation. We can pick our way clearly. Not that there's anyone to RV with, at least we hope not.

We hide the backpack and travel light — though I still have ammunition stuffed in the webbing under my Afghan gear.

When we get to the plain things are more difficult to see but we make our way around to a place directly below our original position and set off on our bearing.

There is no cover, we're horribly exposed and if you're going to lay a mine anywhere, this is where you'd lay it. The technical term for this land is alpine meadow but another might be "mine layer's paradise". There are dogs barking everywhere in the distance, so at least if we disturb one it's not going to create any notice — as long as it's tied up.

We move forward cautiously, checking to see if we've been observed and keeping low to the walls of animal pens, ducking behind rises in the ground and, as we come around the town, even crawling at certain points. I'm nervous, here. The going is very slow indeed and come dawn it's possible we'll be caught out in the open. We can rely on blending in to an extent but it's a risk, particularly after our little knees-up at the compound.

Finally we make the river. We've clearly missed the burial site. We pull back to where we crossed the truck track. It's not a road, just the path the trucks have made as they head south.

There's a bend of the river we used as a landmark, though, and about two hundred metres away from it we begin looking for disturbed earth. After an hour, Beccy finds it.

It had occurred to me before this point that I had nothing to dig with but the ground has only just been put back down, there's no frost and it's easy to move it with my hands. Beccy helps out and, as we do so, there's a familiar buzzing sound up in the sky. It's a drone. I tell myself that there are no ISAF forces in the immediate area. What's it up here for, then?

Clearly someone's seen the truck movement and wants to check it out. With its IR cameras we're going to stand out like a long skirt in an Essex nightclub. Digging at the side of the road. If this was an area where ISAF were running convoys I'd give us about twenty seconds to live.

Beccy looks at me, I look at her, but we keep digging. Time is short and it's either going to drop something

262

large and unpleasant on us or it's not. It passes over, just as I uncover a hand.

This is a shit awful job but it has to be done. We pull the body free and, to my surprise, I find another behind it. Both are male, quite recently dead and, from the look of them, Gurkhas or something similar from what I can tell in the moonlight. They bear signs of torture on their bodies — they're heavily bruised and both have been subjected to the same electro treatment that was used on me.

We peel back their clothes, looking for any identifying signs. No documents at all.

Without speaking, we start to strip them. On the lower leg of one of them is a hammer and sickle inside a red star. Not Gurkhas, then. These guys are in their mid-to-late thirties and, at the time they were recruited into the regiment, Nepal was in the middle of a Maoist insurgency. The communists didn't like the regiment recruiting and would stage raids on recruitment days. The Gurkhas don't have a lot of time for the reds, on the whole. I look as close as I can. Just at the bottom there are some small Chinese characters. I think it's actually the Chinese flag with something written underneath. No time to think about it right now.

We rebury the bodies and check the time: 3a.m. Too risky to go back across the plateau. The slope up contains the shrubby trees before it becomes impossibly steep. There's not as much rock cover here, though there is some, so this is going to be hard routine until nightfall, once we've dug in as best we can.

We go up as high as possible and hide behind the biggest rock we can find, which isn't big. At least we filled our water bottles from the river.

We put on some camouflage, using the bushes, and we wait the day there, which isn't exactly comfortable. One benefit of our water situation is that at least neither of us wants a piss. At one point some locals come past but they don't like the look of the disturbed earth and quickly hurry on by.

I whisper to Beccy. "Do you think they're a problem?"

She nods.

And she's right. After about an hour we hear the rumble of tyres. I carefully roll out from behind the rock and put the bins to my eyes. There's a Mowag, complete with grenade launcher turret, and a pretty full-on Hummer adapted to take an open turret on top. There's the unmistakable outline of a .50 cal. Terrific. If that opens up on us we'll be reduced to something you can inhale. Also, the gunner's very well protected, surrounded on all sides by armour and thick bulletproof glass. You'd need to be good, lucky and probably both to get him with a gunshot, even from quite close up.

The trucks stop and the front door of the Mowag opens. Anderson gets out. He comes over and inspects the grave. He prods it. We've put a good hundred vertical metres between ourselves and him. I'd guess we are half a mile away. We should be OK.

He has five or six men with him and, oh dear, we are not going to be OK. He goes to the Mowag and gets a bloody great German Shepherd out of the back. I would put money on "Mr Logistics" Anderson not being able to find us. He's clearly a good organiser and he's a big Mary so he'd be a handful in a scrap but I'd take my skills on escape and evasion against his any day. Introduce Scooby Doo into the equation and the maths is this: heavily armed men + trained creature with hypersensitive nose = game over.

The plan becomes one of last resort. We have to attack them. How many troops can they spare once they discover the contact? Quite a few, I should guess. I don't know these mountains, either, so getting off in one piece is going to be very hard.

Beccy and I exchange glances. She has her hand on the M27. The dog's barking madly, straining at its lead.

"Go get 'em!" shouts Brad, and lets it off. At which point it shoots forward and starts digging up the grave. Never work with animals or children, eh? If it wasn't so serious I'd start laughing. I catch myself making an error here. I've come to regard Brad as a clown. Not so. He's clearly trusted by Bulwark to handle some fairly major stuff. He's dangerous, having massacred a village, and he's offed at least two more in the grave down there. The fact he's never going to get on *One Man and His Dog* is neither here nor there. He's my enemy and I need to respect him.

It is hilarious, though. Brad's straining at the dog, pulling it back but it simply is not having it and is burrowing into the mound of earth. Brad's men are clearly pissing themselves too, I can hear them laughing through the thin mountain air. And then he shoots it. I swear to God, he pulls out his Desert Eagle and puts a slug the size of a comet through the dog's head. The mountains ring with the sound of the shot and the dog slumps on the grave. That stops the laughter pretty quickly.

I go back behind the rock and shrug. Beccy shakes her head slowly. If I catch Brad I'll be handing him over to the police if I can make anything stick on him. If Beccy gets hold of him I don't fancy his chances. She loves dogs. Let's face it, most people do.

When I look out again, the men are bundling around the camp looking for footprints. Shit, they find some. I was pretty careful pulling out but it was dark and sometimes you just miss something.

One of them gestures up the hill. Brad's in a temper, and shouts for them to make their way up the hill and then jumps back into the Mowag and speeds off down the valley. The men do precisely nothing. That is, they scout around on the hill for a bit but then return to the Hummer after an hour or so and sit smoking after they bury the dog. The night air is crisp and, even at this distance, we can hear what they're saying quite easily. Just the normal soldier bollocks, really. Taking the piss. They're English, it sounds like.

There are four of them and clearly this is not a unit that runs on much respect. As soon as the officer leaves they're taking it easy, feet up. As the sun begins to dip, Brad returns in the Mowag and starts screaming at them. We can hear virtually every word. He tells them to do what they're paid for and get up and look for

266

whoever's sneaking around the mountains poking their nose into his business.

They say it's dark and they haven't got night sights and he says they should have thought about that when they were sitting on their asses doing jack shit earlier on. They can stay out there until they find the guys they're meant to. He stands and watches as they go in a four-man patrol up on to the hill. Actually, these guys obviously have some experience, as they move forwards in good order, point man looking out at the front, everyone else attentive and covering the ground well. I can't help thinking this would be a decent unit if it respected its leadership.

As soon as Brad's on his way again, though, they come right back down the mountain and sit down again. One of them turns on the lights of the car and they use those to see by. One of the guys is nervous but I distinctly hear the words "Sniper" and "Bollocks, he'll have been out of here yesterday if he's got any sense."

He's right as well. To fire a shot now would be to compromise ourselves terribly.

The best thing to do would be to wait until they go to sleep, or most of them do, launch a quick, ferocious attack and nick their Hummer. Then we can get up the valley, see what there is to see and hide in the hills when Brad and Co come looking — or just drive out as best we can using Google Earth and the satnav. That idea makes me uncomfortable, though. From hearing them talk I can tell these guys are Brits. Now they've got a pack of cards out. Not sure this mission is all that engaging when they include them in the basic kit.

These guys may just be honest Joes trying to earn a crust. They may have had nothing to do with the massacre so I can't just stick a grenade in among them.

A different idea enters my head. These guys are British Army; I'm British Army. That means something. Yes, there are people who would slot their grandma for two bob but the army tends to weed most of them out. They're psychologically weak.

Most soldiers have a good sense of loyalty to the army, their regiment and the immediate guys around them in ascending order of importance. So maybe, just maybe, I can talk to them — especially given the fact they obviously don't have a heap of respect for Brad. And why should they, as by now he's probably drinking tequila shots, smoking a big cigar and acting like he's in a shit film back at Priand instead of being out here with them?

So maybe I can reason them into letting us go. No. Stupid plan. I'm allowing my desperation to get the better of me. Best idea is to wait until it's as dark as it's going to get and they either get bored and go or at least some of them fall asleep. Then we sneak out of there. And then I hear a voice as clear as a bell.

"Fifteen two, fifteen, four and the rest won't score."

I recognise the voice, I'm sure. In fact, I'm sure I've played poker with the geezer. I leave it another hand and I'm certain. I hear the distinct Manc tones.

"And one for his kn-ob!" He pronounces the K and splits the word in two. I can't believe this. It's Dave Henshaw — a special forces bloke I worked with for a

268

while in Serbia. He's one hell of a soldier and a very clever guy but not someone who ponders too much on the wider questions of life. If you ask him about anything outside of soldiering then his response is usually the same: "Don't know. Don't care."

"Henshaw, you mug!" I hiss off the mountain.

Suddenly it's all scrambling for weapons and looking out into the dark. The lights on the truck go off.

"Who said that?"

"It's me, Nick Kane, you muppet."

"Nick!" He gestures for the other guys to lower their weapons.

"Look, I've got Beccy with me, if I come down this mountain are you going to kill me?"

He thinks for a minute and then says, very slowly and deliberately, "No, I'm going to ask you for the tenner you owe me."

We come scrambling down the hill to a bit of "Who in the name of . . ." and general sounds of amazement.

"Give us a couple of them ration packs and a drink," I say.

Dave does so. Me and Beccy get some water down us and then hit the beefburger and beans. After so long without any proper food it tastes great.

"Well, Nick," says Dave, "you disappoint me. I always knew you were a weirdo but now you've gone and joined the Taliban. And as for you, Beccy, I didn't know they let women in."

"It's not me who's joined the Taliban. What are you doing rubbing shoulders with them?"

"Don't ask me. I come up here a week ago. I was meant to be in the north of the country but they wanted me to find someone."

Dave would be your man for the job on that one. He's an exceptional tracker. Which begs the question of why I haven't been caught before by him.

"To find me?"

"No."

"So who?"

He points at the grave. "I caught 'em but what happened afterwards was nothing to do with me."

"Who are they?"

"I was brought in from Kabul, made to sign the Official Secrets Act and told to come up here. I was tasked to find communist agitators in the area, I had to find them."

"Communist agitators?"

"That's what those guys were doing. This is all part of a secret deal. We're buying the towelheads off over here and, for some reason, the Chinese don't like it."

"So what are they doing here?"

"Spreading worldwide revolution." He says it like a thick kid who has crammed for a test and is reading out what he's remembered in front of the teacher, barely able to contain his delight that he'll then be able to forget it.

"Bollocks. There was never even evidence they helped out in Nepal and that was a full-on communist insurgency."

He looks mildly puzzled.

"They're communists," he says. "He's Chinese and he's got a hammer and sickle tattoo. What more proof do you want?"

"Well, quite a lot, actually. Every secretary in England's got a tattoo in Chinese characters."

"These two weren't secretaries. They put up a good scrap."

"I'd put up a good scrap if I thought I was going to fall into your hands."

"Yeah, you'd lose."

I laugh. "It's good to see you, Dave."

"Yeah, you too. So what are you doing here?" he says. "Was it you who took out those Taliban."

"Why would that matter to you?"

"It doesn't. They've bought off the Taliban around here. That's the deal. They've agreed a truce of some sort. Or at least they think they have. The usual shit."

He's right here. There are all sorts of secret wars going on all over the planet and some involve quite strange bedfellows. It's not inconceivable that there might be a secret deal with the Taliban. Politicians have been arguing for it for a long time and I know some tribesmen were given cash to lay down their weapons. And the threat of communism does strange things to the heads of the top boys in the UK and US armies. At the end of the Second World War we disarmed the Greek communists who had been fighting the Nazis for the whole war and gave the weapons to the fascists who'd been supporting them. Our ruling class just trusted the stiff-right-arm brigade more than they did the reds. Can that have been happening here? And what about the Venezuelan mining company the boys in prison said they were working for? That country's pink-ish, isn't it? Have there been commies up here?

"There's one problem. If this is a truce, why aren't there any army here?"

"Taliban won't let them in. Has to be contractors."

Does that sound reasonable? Does it even sound plausible? Yes, I suppose. If Bulwark can deliver quiet in this region I guess a lot of people at the top won't mind how they do it. I can't see the Brits sanctioning a massacre, though, or agreeing to cover one up. But maybe I'm being naive.

I have one question. "What was in the trucks?"

"They didn't tell me and I didn't ask. Maybe they're building a control base."

This is what I mean about Dave being a great soldier. He does what he's told and literally doesn't think about anything outside his orders. Those weren't building trucks. Definitely not. Why carry bricks sealed in a brand-new lorry? A load of bricks might protect you from bandits if they're carried in the open. They're less likely to want to steal them — unless they're thinking of building a house. A closed truck lets a thief's imagination run riot.

"I need to get down the valley," I say, "any chance of a lift?"

"Why not?" says Dave.

Dave now takes a big risk. He has a chat with the other lads. He tells them to tell Brad that he's gone up the valley to try and cut off the escapees. It takes a bit of explaining but not much. The lads know we've done a few Taliban in the past few days and their attitude is "good luck" to us. Everyone here isn't comfortable with what's going on but they're soldiers, or at least they were. They know that war is odd and dirty and that the clear battle lines the politicians like to present to the press don't always reflect the reality on the ground. Still, they don't like the Taliban and are pleased to help anyone who seems to be killing them. Also, Brad isn't well liked. I get the idea they enjoy jerking him around.

"We'll plot up here for the night," says one of them, a hard-looking little Welsh bloke, "you run 'em up the valley and be back before Action Man gets back in the Mowag."

"If he does get back?" asks Beccy.

"We'll bullshit him," he says with a shrug.

"Gleaming," I say.

We drive on up the valley and it's good to be in the comfort of the Hummer. I fill Dave in on why I'm here. The Hummer's got a mobile phone adapter in and it fits Beccy's. She plugs it in and turns it on. She texts a code to Cadwell to say she's OK. There's a message from John. She passes the phone to me and I play it.

"It's about the Venezuelans. I've been in touch with them and they're majorly pissed off. There's a haul of lithium up there, a lot of it, and they'd struck a deal with the locals to extract it — they were forming a cooperative with them. Then the Taliban come pouring in all of a sudden and the deal's off. No mine, no cooperative. They've tried to get back to the area but they've lost three blokes trying to do it. More when I get the info."

"So you think Ben discovered someone shifting a bit of smack down here?" says Dave.

"Seems most likely," I say.

"Still don't quite see why they'd slot him for that," Dave muses. "It's not news, is it, that drug dealers do bad things, particularly in remote areas? And it's not like we're not trying to stop them shipping it out to Pakistan anyway. A lot of people die around opium dealing. Are ISAF going to drop everything and come pouring up here just because a few innocent civilians get killed? Locals are getting killed all over this country."

What did I say about Dave not being a deep thinker? He sees the world in a very straightforward way but, sometimes, that's worth a stack of degrees. If not the heroin, then what? I think about Bulwark. It's a global group — security, arms manufacture, heavy industries and . . .

"Yeah, they do have a mining division," says Beccy, reading my mind.

We make good progress down the valley, though Dave's careful as he goes. It's a long way and I'm glad we didn't have to tab this in the dark.

"Help yourself to the chocolate, by the way," says Dave, noting that we've eaten it all.

"Thanks," I say, cracking open a bottle of mineral water.

At the top of the valley, a road has been cut into the side of the mountain, a proper big thing in tarmac laid down on a steel mesh support. Beccy and I glance at each other.

"You've not been up here?" I say to Dave.

"We've been looking up in the north," he says.

"Drive up?"

"The car's got Bulwark passes on," says Dave, "let's see if they work." Not a bad idea.

We pull around the mountain and become aware of a light source on the top of the hill. The curve of the plateau and the intervening mountains has shielded it from us so far but, as we round a bend, it appears. It's like something from a fantasy film, the mountain's faintly lit up from behind like it's opened to a hoard of treasure.

"If there's a flying saucer in there, you're on your own," says Dave. "I don't do aliens."

"How about that girl from the stores?" says Beccy.

"The exception that proves the rule."

We drive on and there is very little to indicate that anything is really happening here, other than the road.

"What's meant to be here on the map?" I say.

Beccy studies her phone. "A big flat bit," she says.

"I thought we'd just come off a big flat bit."

"This is a bigger flat bit. It's salt flats, I think."

"Gate," says Dave.

And there, across the track, is a chain-link fence with a hut next to it. Two guards get out. They're big guys with crew cuts, M1 assault rifles and combat trousers.

"Bulwark?" he says.

"Yeah, Bulwark," says Dave.

"Problem?"

"Serbs," he says.

"That's not necessarily a problem."

"It is with these guys. Arkan's old boys," Dave says. Arkan. I remember him. Serbian football hooligan turned military leader and war criminal. Assassinated back in 2000, if I recall correctly.

"Who's employing them?" says Beccy.

"I thought you were the insider," Dave asks.

"I never found out about this."

"They have certain talents that could be useful out here, I bet," says Dave.

One of them comes alongside the car.

"Are you OK to be up here?" he asks. He speaks English well. He doesn't seem like a murdering paramilitary bastard, which he almost certainly is. He peers at our windscreen stickers — there's a pass ID on it that I hope will do the trick.

"Brad sent us up," says Dave.

"I haven't heard of it."

"He's coming up in a minute."

The Serb stares into Dave's eyes.

"Radio's down," he says, "so I'll believe you. Go on."

He opens the gate and we go in, over the brow of a hill. Dave brings the Hummer around and positions it facing the gate. Good idea in case we need to make a sharp exit.

"Wow," says Beccy.

"Yeah," I say, looking out from the hill. "Never seen something like that."

CHAPTER
TWENTY-FIVE

In front of us, stretching away into the distance, are miles of flat white salt. At the limit of the horizon I can make out another dark line. Impossible to tell but it could be some sort of other barrier fencing off the flats at a distance before anyone can see what's going on here. The view is eerily beautiful under the moonlight and subdued lights of a fairly big camp.

"What is this?" I ask.

"It's a dry lake bed," says Beccy. "I've just googled it. It's the biggest one in Afghanistan."

A series of huge pools has been dug near to us. Under the eerie light they vary in colour from clear and silvery to an almost luminous green. People — Afghan and Western — are taking samples from them. Is this what lithium mining looks like? I'd imagined a pit head of some sort.

The place is a hive, even at this time of night. Some people are down at the pool, a couple actually in it. There's a canteen in a prefab hut, and scoff is ready, going by the smell. Then there's a lorry park and several accommodation blocks. We get out of the Hummer. Dave puts his helmet on. He's clearly expecting a bit of trouble here. He doesn't particularly stand out — the guards have helmets on too. It's cold up here and a helmet is one extra layer on top of a forage cap. On a slope looking down at the pond are four or five Taliban, AKs at their feet. He could be right about the trouble.

"That's Mullah Kabir," says Beccy.

"Who?"

"He was the governor around here before the Taliban got kicked out. He's back. He's been a royal pain in the arse for years."

I can't tell you how this bugs me. To have a straight line of fire on one of the Taliban's top boys and able to do nothing about it. Mind you, if we've found some sort of peaceful solution, all to the good. People have had to swallow worse compromises. Killers go free but, if it means they don't do any more killing, perhaps it's worth it. On the other hand, it still doesn't describe why my mate was killed, why there are two dead Chinese blokes down in the valley or why such secrecy attends this whole thing.

We walk around the site. At the back of the cabins is something we really didn't expect to see. There's a whole mule train: eight mules all in a line. They seem incongruous in this area. There are baskets lying on the floor beside them. They're stuffed with bottles of what looks like a thick brown liquid — opium.

"Mining smack," says Dave, "that's a new one. I think I've just resigned."

I can't put this together at all. Is this mine a front for opium trafficking? It looks like it but surely Bulwark wouldn't allow this to happen so openly. Or is it just that the same boys running the mine are running the mules?

We can't stand looking at the smack for ever but as we go to move, we look up to see one of the Taliban staring at us.

And then it starts going wrong. Mullah Kabir sees us and gestures for us to come forward. He says something to Dave that, clearly, he is never going to understand.

Beccy replies for me but the Mullah isn't a fool — far from it. I can see he's immediately suspicious of us. He starts speaking in a very slow and thoughtful way. Beccy is talking twenty to the dozen.

He's seen her speaking to Dave, clearly, that's what his gestures say. He says something directly to me too. I don't reply and I point to my throat. We're ten feet from them. The mullah shakes his head. He's clearly seen me speaking too.

And then we hear a voice from the gate. "Get your hands up. Get your hands up!"

Clearly some sort of communication has been established with Brad and our cover's blown. The Serb guy is running towards us, assault rifle pointed at us. The Taliban are between him and us at the moment but that won't last long.

Things seem to happen in slow motion, the Taliban are peeling away, going for their AKs, the guards are screaming, levelling their weapons.

There is a golden moment of confusion in which we can act. As soon as anyone gets a clear shot at us, we're dead or compromised. We have a choice. Normally I would surrender but these guys have had one pop at me, they're not going to give me a second chance. Plus we have no back-up, no chance of anyone coming to help us out or even noticing we're captured. We haven't let Mick know our coordinates and, even if we had, this is beyond his help. If we're taken we'll be keeping the Chinese fellas company in no time. I think all that after the fact. There and then, I just squeeze the trigger, putting a burst into the crowd in front of me. It's funny how people react under fire. The Serb is looking for a target but it's all confusion and he can't tell friend from enemy. As the Taliban guy in front of me falls, I get a clear shot at him. The last of the magazine goes into him.

Dave fires a burst from his SCAR — a US-issue 7.62 assault rifle — the M27 bangs into life and people are flying everywhere, shot, jumping to evade, scrambling down the slope.

The Afghans are incredible, though. Mullah Kabir has balls of brass, I'll give him that. He just stands directly in front of us and starts firing his AK as he brings it level but Dave is so close he could almost kiss him if he wanted to. He doesn't kiss him, though, he just double-taps the mullah's face.

"Withdraw. Hummer!" I shout.

Beccy reloads as Dave stabs a Taliban in the throat with the muzzle end of his now empty gun, sending him sprawling backwards. As he hits the ground Beccy double-taps him with her pistol. Our fire is withering and there are no more left.

280

Immediately we go into evasion mode. I bang off a couple of grenades, which keeps the guys down the slope honest, and then run back while Beccy and Dave cover me. Once I'm at the Hummer, I'm on the .50 cal. There's a 100-round belt in it, there's a good line of sight down the hill but still I won't fire indiscriminately. I'm shooting only at people who shoot at us. Either that or I fire into the ground. I'm just trying to make sure no one comes up that hill after us. The gun booms into life, sending carrotsized chunks of steel screaming down the hill at supersonic speeds. It's a major encouragement to keep your head down. There's not been the body armour or helmet invented that will save you if you cop one of those. It'll chew through the armour on a Hummer no problem as well.

Dave makes the Hummer with Beccy close behind and I strap myself into the seat. It's fashionable to sit on the strap to fire, and it is useful if you're a shortarse, but Dave doesn't hang about in these situations and it's clunk click every trip when he's at the wheel.

He smacks it into gear and we're off, smashing straight through the chain-link gates and hammering down the track. Already it's all going a bit freefall in the turret and I'm glad I'm strapped in. Coming up the track are a line of Mowags. In the dark and with the dust I can't see how many.

I can't open fire on them because I don't know who they are. The turret seems to explode around me and I'm in a world of shit.

The Hummer takes a mad dive off the side of the track and for a second I think we've lost it but Dave's just gone around the oncoming trucks. I press the pedals, swivel and see I'm facing the side of an Eagle IV, dropping away from it like I'm on a mad roller-coaster. It's got a grenade launcher, fully automated weapons system on the front. Hence the explosions. These guys appear to know what they're doing.

The world is oddly quiet, I can't hear a thing, it's like I'm watching the battle underwater. The gunfire and explosions have done for my ears. I press the thumb trigger on the .50 cal and bang as many rounds as I can into the Eagle. I've got no idea if its armour is up to a .50-cal round or not but there's only one way to find out.

Dave can't carve back up on to the track, the gradient's too steep, so we're going along on the slant while he looks for somewhere to either drop down or get back up. Another volley of grenades comes towards us, I just see the movement in time and drop into the turret, shoving myself down as far as I can go. More explosions and the ting ting ting of fragments against the armour.

Dave dives again and I feel a sickening drop followed by the vehicle levelling. Then another and another. Finally there's a bang and he's hit the plateau floor. Then he hits a hard left, screaming down the plateau. Oh, well, I don't suppose things can get much worse.

Wrong. The boys on top have got their trucks turned around and are following Dave's path down the mountain. I stick another burst into them and I can't tell if it hits them with all the dust that's being kicked up. More grenades come raining down in front of us and for a second I can't see anything at all. It's thick with smoke. They've clearly run out of explosives and are just chucking what they have at us — in this case, smoke.

Advice on the motorway when faced with fog is slow down. Dave seems to have skipped that bit of the Highway Code, although I don't realise it for about five seconds. For that time I don't know where I am. I can't hear, I can't see, only the shaking of the truck tells me we're moving at all. Then the smoke clears and for a second we're flying. Suddenly, I'm thrown back in my seat and Dave has emergency stopped. Shit, I know what he's planning.

I have about thirty rounds left in the .50 cal. There are three trucks. There's very little short of a light tank that will offer protection against a .50 cal fired close up.

The first vehicle breaks through the smoke about a hundred yards away, gleaming under the big moon. It's flying, slightly to my right, about sixty yards off. I do not mess about, hitting it with full automatic fire straight at the windscreen. I see the bullets sparking off it everywhere, lighting it up in metal flashes. The windscreen goes in at about fifty yards but the truck doesn't stop, it just careers on past us, as do the other two. They've been going too quick, failed to react as they've seen us, and gone streaking by. Dave hits reverse and we go screeching back into the smoke. There's a big bang. Sounds like the Eagle I hit has crashed.

A pair of hands from below have an ammo box. Beccy shoves, I pull and it comes up — it's very heavy and difficult to pull. I jettison the old one and fit a new belt in. I'm doing it almost by feel, the smoke is that dense here.

Again, it's like being under the sea, there's a sudden stillness, a calm. We hear the two trucks turn around. This time they're moving really slowly. It's run silent, run deep, but this smoke isn't going to last for ever. Dave doesn't move the truck at all; just keeps it idling. They'll have difficulty hearing us after the noise of the battle and above the sound of their own engines.

Two incredibly bright lights are quickly joined by two more. They're moving slowly, trying to use their headlights to pick us out.

That isn't going to do them any good at all. It won't help them see us because the light just reflects back off the smoke but it picks them out nicely. It's difficult to judge distance in this murk but I aim the .50 cal at just above the lights and give it a second burst. I really have done in my hearing because I can't even hear the gun going off, I just have a high-pitched ringing in my ears. Instead I just see one of the lights go out, sparks through the fog, and I follow it with another quick squeeze.

The other truck's lights abruptly go out as they realise they've made targets of themselves but I still shoot off a couple of rounds in the general direction of where they were.

There's one remaining headlight on the other Eagle and Dave drives towards it slowly. We edge forwards and draw level. In the eerie glow of the light I can see it's a right old mess in the cabin. The faces loom from the fog like drowned men from the wreck of a ship.

The Hummer shakes slightly, and a figure crosses the headlights. I think it's Beccy, I don't know why but I have that sense. There are flashes in the dark. I really can hardly hear a thing but it looks like a small arms exchange. Then the smoke clears slightly for a second. Beccy is in the driver's seat of the Eagle, leaning across what's left of the driver. The grenade launcher moves and fires, fires and fires again, grenades pumping out into the air. Then Beccy jumps back into our truck, the smoke grenades land and visibility is zero.

Dave drives forward carefully. We're going slowly, I think. Bang! A big collision. Flashes wildly going off everywhere. No time to think, I just level the .50 cal in their direction and give them the full belt. The flashes stop. Dave reverses. There's the sound of tearing metal. He's run into the other truck. I can see nothing at all but I hit them with the .50 cal point blank. This is a gun that was developed to go on Second World War bombers, to bring down fighters.

There are a peculiar series of bright flashes as the bullets chomp into the armour of the truck. We go forward again and suddenly we're out of the smoke. Rule one of evasion is put as many miles between you and the enemy as quickly as possible.

The Hummer will make us visible but, with this barrier of smoke in place, we have a chance that we are invisible for at least a few minutes. There are some hills going across the plateau about five clicks away. If we can get behind them, we can lose our pursuers and think about dumping the truck, though we'll be loath to do that unless we really have to. It's armour, it's shelter. It's very visible but I've seen no choppers in the area. Still, we have to assume they're in radio communication and can mobilise Taliban roadblocks all around the valley. So the answer is clear: get off the plateau, ditch the truck and scarper cross-country on foot. From there we pick up a road and try to make contact with Beccy's handler or Mick.

Dave takes it up to the top of the clock — around 50 mph over this terrain — and I scan for enemies. Nothing so far. In no time we're at the hills, growing up from the earth like islands from a lake. They're incredible things, tall and severe, like something from a fairy tale. There are rolling hills to the west, going up into mountains, folds of earth wrapped around each other. You could get lost here, which is what we intend to do.

Dave takes a hard right and we've ducked behind the huge buttress of a hill in a stony ravine. If they want to ambush us here we are royally shafted but we can't think about that, we just keep going, up and around, winding through the hills.

We can't see the plateau from here, so they can't see us, though I think it's only a matter of time before we're contacted again.

I seem to have lost my turban somewhere along the way. Still, the Taliban disguise is going to be worth nothing as soon as word goes out over the radio.

We'll be OK as long as we don't come across a compound or a village. But as the ravine broadens, we come across a compound. What's more, it comes across us.

There's a roadblock across the road, and a tripod-mounted Barrett M82 pointing straight at us. This is what used to be called an anti-tank weapon but now is known as an anti-material weapon. It won't go through a tank's armour but at fifty yards it'll penetrate the Hummer's windscreen and come out the back.

I look up. There are ten men up to our right-hand side, strategically spaced so there's no way I can get them with the .50 cal at one sweep. Four have RPGs and the rest are equipped with small arms. Most tellingly, one has a command wire in his hands. I look down. There's freshly dug earth at the side of the vehicle. We're sitting right next to an IED.

Someone pulls at my foot. I look down. It's Beccy. She makes a sign, crossing her hands over each other face down. The signal is clear: "over". Very slowly, I put my hands into the air and look up at the hills around me.

There are some situations where you just have to say, "You got me".

CHAPTER
TWENTY-SIX

I get straight out of the turret through the top. This could go seriously wrong if they discover Beccy is a woman. But there really is no other way around this. Four of them come bundling down the hill. At least they're unlikely to explode the IED now with their mates next to us. That said, it's still a no-win situation. By the time I get the Glock out I'll be shot by one of the guys on the hill. If they haven't got a clear line on me, they have a clear line on Dave and Beccy.

I'm fleeced of weapons, as are Dave and Beccy — though they somehow don't manage to notice she's a woman while they're doing it.

One of them, a little guy with a shrewd, foxish face, starts barking at us. Beccy replies, gesturing back down the valley. As she moves her hand every gun comes up to the firing position.

The little guy waves them down. He looks at the front of the Hummer, which clearly has a bit of a scrape on it. Then he walks up to me and shakes my clothes. Little bits of stone fall out of them, pattering on the ground. I'm bleeding, I realise. I honestly haven't notice until that point. No wonder with so many grenades going off, and cars flying around, my clothes have filled up with half the plateau floor. My hearing's coming back slightly but it's undercut with a test card bleep.

Mr Fox looks at Dave. He points at him and says one word very clearly. "Bulwark." From the reaction of the tribesmen I can see this isn't a good thing.

Beccy shakes her head and talks rapidly.

The man holds up his hand.

"Let him speak for himself," he says in very clear and surprisingly posh English.

"Have a look down the plateau," says Dave, "there's three Bulwark trucks burned out thanks to us. You can consider those my resignation letter."

Mr Fox still isn't convinced. "Hmm, you're not in a convoy," he says, cogs clearly whirring.

He turns to a couple of his men and speaks to them. Then he waves his hand and invites us into the compound. As I walk forwards I hear the Hummer being started up. It drives past us in through some wide gates.

We're taken into a comfortable room with cushions on the floor. Tea is brought to us in little glasses, along with dishes of pistachios. Everyone crams into the little room and sits looking while we chat to the chief.

"So," he says with little preamble. "Just what are the three of you doing here?"

I see no point in bullshitting here. "I'm going to level with you, sir. A friend of mine — a good man with a wife and a son — was killed because of something he saw here. I'm looking to find out what because I want to bring the men who did it to justice. I suspect it was to do with what went on at Priand."

His eyes widen.

"It's very simple what went on there," he says, "there are great mineral resources here. We had negotiated a deal with the Venezuelans to develop them. Everyone in the valley was to benefit and the villages were united. However, this country needs strong men. We had one in my son. He kept the Taliban out and imposed peace on the land. But he was tricked, lured to a meeting in Priand. He was killed and the village massacred, as a lesson to others around here."

"A lesson from who?"

"Bulwark. We had rejected their proposal to develop the lithium mine. So they got rid of our leadership, put the people in fear and brought the Taliban back in."

"They struck a deal with the Taliban?"

"Everything is possible. The Taliban are not fools. While my son was alive he had the people behind him. They could not come here. Then they are gifted this area. Bulwark's presence means the coalition won't trouble them if they keep quiet, they reap the money from the mine and use it to fund the war elsewhere."

"And the coalition doesn't know about this?"

"Things are not clear here. Deals are struck. The Taliban today is tomorrow's ordinary farmer, maybe businessman if things go well for them. The hard core will always fight but around them . . ." he put his hands into the air, ". . . things float. In the end, most people have their price. The Taliban, Bulwark, ISAF, you, even me. Pay enough money and the Taliban will go.

Unfortunately, Bulwark has given them an incentive to stay."

I can see how this all works. This region remains secure, Bulwark get their mine and the contract for security around here and the Taliban get back-handers. I can't see why the coalition would stand for that. But if the Taliban don't call themselves Taliban, don't declare jihad, then they're just another bunch of farmers who used to fight the Russians and who now fight ISAF. They lay down their arms here; that's a victory. Still, though, I can't believe the Western forces would be so shortsighted. There's something more going on, I just know there is.

Something occurs to me. "You haven't been taken over by the Taliban. Very few villages near here still stand against them. How can you?"

"We are well armed and this side of the plateau doesn't want them. If they come here, they know they will bleed for every rock they take. So they leave us alone, for now."

"And the opium?"

"It's Afghanistan," he says with a shrug, "people deal opium."

I was pinning this whole thing on Brad. He was the one who squeezed the trigger at Priand, he's the one running the show here. But if Mr Fox is right, this goes much deeper. To where?

"The Taliban will be coming here soon, or Bulwark."

"They won't follow you this way," says Mr Fox, "not to this village. We've been clear they are not to come here."

We sit for a few more hours. And then a boy comes back and speaks to Mr Fox. He nods slowly.

"He confirms your story," he says, "you have had a great victory, it seems. Ask us how we can honour you."

"Your hospitality has been enough for us," says Beccy, who is trained in local customs.

"Get us to Kabul," says Dave, who hasn't.

Foxy nods. "That is impossible," he says.

"We'll give you the Hummer and all the weapons in it," I say.

"That's ours anyway," he says.

"I'll personally swear to you that, if I get a chance, I will kill the man who murdered your son," I say. "His name is Brad Anderson and I will kill him."

He looks into my eyes. "Yes, I think you will. Then we'll see what we can do," he says.

"That's how things work in Afghanistan!" says Dave under his breath.

Foxy hears him and smiles. "It's how things work the world over, if only you had the eyes to see it."

CHAPTER
TWENTY-SEVEN

We're taken out along mountain passes, following a group of ten villagers sporting a variety of weapons, including many of our own. I've been given back the Glock and Dave and Beccy have been allowed a side arm each but all the longs have been taken. Fair play, they're getting us out of here so they name their price.

It takes us four days to reach the road and it's fascinating to see just how well these guys know the country. There are routes here that I would never think to use — invisible until you're right on top of them, seemingly disappearing into walls of rock but turning at the last instant to reveal a way through.

There are people searching for us but we can see them from a distance, Hummers and Mowags prowling the land. But they're looking for three people, not a party of twenty tribesmen. Dave's been given Afghan clothing in return for his ballistic vest, helmet and all but his shreddies. And the Bulwark boys know that if you want to pick a fight with these guys you better be sure it's worth it. The .50 cal rifle alone can put a serious cramp in your day from nearly two clicks away and you can be sure that these fellas know how to shoot them. It can be used as a sniper rifle and the Afghan mountain guys are famous for their ability in that department.

We make the Highway 1 and an aged Corolla comes to pick us up. The guy in it speaks not a word of English but he looks scary tough. He's built like a horse and has two big scars running down over his face from his forehead, over his eye to his chin and he doesn't look like he was too pretty to begin with. He's not someone you'd want to see at your window at midnight. Still, after so long out in the wilderness and minging for a shower, the prospect of being back in a Kabul hotel means it's all I can do to stop myself from kissing him.

We thank our escort and then we're off down the road at Afghan speeds and it does occur to me that it would be ironic if I end up dying in a road accident after having a small army trying to put holes in me for the last four weeks. If I get back I'm going for a Sunday drive with my mum just for the novel experience of being driven slowly and carefully.

Beccy uses our driver's phone to get hold of her controller and I can hear him bollocking her down the phone, despite the fact she hasn't got the speakerphone on. She tells him she has big news, that there's evidence of a major collusion between Bulwark and the Taliban up in Marjul province, that she has been on the ground, interviewed locals and seen what's going on at first hand. He goes a bit quieter after that.

"He wants to meet you," she says, "and Dave."

"He can find me in the bar," says Dave.

"You'll have to keep your head down, Bulwark are all over the place and they have contacts," I say.

"So do I," says Dave, "I've called in a few of mine, I'm out of there on a Danish Frogman flight tonight. When I said he could meet me in the bar, I meant the one in Dubai airport."

Danish Frogmen are their equivalent of the SBS. They work on land as well as at sea, which is a good job or they'd have not a lot to do in Afghanistan.

"You going to go to the press with this?"

"I signed the Official secrets act."

"Do you think that was for real?"

Dave shrugs. "One way to find out, I suppose."

He gets an Internet connection on his mobile phone and finds the number for the BBC. Then he gets through to the news desk. A couple of hours later, there's a call back. The journalist is very interested in what he has to say and tells him to meet up with their man in Kabul as soon as he gets in. He's given a number and told to call it.

I'm pleased about this. Bulwark's criminality needs to come out one way or another.

There are roadblocks on the way in, but only ANP. The events of the last few weeks have disordered my head. I'm demob happy, my guard down. It's not until we encounter the third roadblock — on the outskirts of Kabul — that I remember what the action of the past few days has made me forget: I'm wanted for murder.

CHAPTER
TWENTY-EIGHT

We reach the outskirts of Kabul at about five in the afternoon. The car slows into a line of traffic. There are about ten cars and a couple of trucks between me and the police. There's a coned-off area where selected cars are being pulled to one side. They're coming down the line of cars, looking inside. I'm relaxed because I can't believe they're actually looking for me. The ANP have rather a lot of work in the murder department and I'm sure they think I've skipped town weeks ago.

However, there's a different attitude on display here. The normal ANP copper seems like a slightly bored extortionist, which is what he generally is. This lot have a bit more snap to their step.

They come level with us and look inside the car. We're all all right, except for Dave. He's wearing Afghan clothing but he has a big, sunburned rugby player's face with a splat of nose that looks as though it was applied by the same people who make Wallace and Gromit. He couldn't look more Anglo-Saxon if he had a sword up a Norman's backside.

The copper sees him and a hullaballoo goes up. Nine or ten come running over and the car's surrounded by ANP, AKs and pistols pointed at it.

They're screaming at us.

"They want us out," says Beccy.

We get out very slowly. They're not very interested in the driver, Beccy or me but they're screaming at Dave. One of them does speak to Pirate Jake the driver and we're covered by AKs but Dave is the centre of interest.

He's disarmed and cuffed and our driver is talking to the policemen. The driver is smiling and being reasonable, Beccy's doing the same.

The guys are on the radio and this looks grim. I do notice, though, that they're all junior officers — quite young. The senior guy's obviously decided roadblock duty isn't for him. Dave is put into a van. He goes quietly, giving me a wink before he's bundled inside. The roadblock has now been forgotten and traffic is streaming around us, bashing the odd cone out of the way as it goes.

We have fifteen minutes of haggling before the driver puts his hand on one of the young boys' shoulders and they embrace. Have we been sold down the line here?

The driver gestures for us to get back into the car. I do, as does Beccy.

"What?" I say to Beccy as we pull off.

"The driver has a brother in the ANP. He told them they picked the white guy up and were bringing him in. He was haggling for a reward."

"Why didn't he sell us, then?"

"He didn't sell Dave, you muppet, it's his way of getting us out of here."

She says something to him.

He shrugs and replies.

"He says he doesn't get a go in the Hummer unless he delivers us," says Beccy.

"His time in it just got reduced by a third," I say.

Beccy gets on the phone and tries to raise Cadwell but he's not there, as Sod's Law would have it. She leaves a message.

I can now only think of Dave. He can't get charged for what we did up in Marjul but he's in a hugely vulnerable position. One thing's certain: I'm not leaving Kabul without him. He put himself on the line for me and it's pure good manners that I do the same for him.

I make my own call — to Mattias, the Dutch commando guy who was observing at the Mir prison, using the number I memorised. There are systems for memorising stuff — you attach pictures to the numbers and turn it into a story, preferably quite a dirty one because they stick in the mind. His involves a girl with big breasts leaning over a gate while a fat woman does something unmentionable to Valentino Rossi.

I need to have him looking out for Dave if he gets into prison and I also now know those engineer guys have stumbled on a world of trouble. We need to think about getting them out any way we can.

I'm surprised when he remembers me straight away.

"Look," he says, "I've got some bad news. Your friends in prison, the engineers. They are dead."

"How?"

"Some of the other prisoners got to them. The radicals did for them."

298

I take this in for a minute. "Someone's got some explaining to do, then."

"Yeah, I should say so."

"They were segregated."

"Yeah."

"What do you think?"

"I think someone didn't like them very much and arranged for them to go. Annoyed the wrong guard, maybe," the commando guy tells me.

"You'd have to be pretty annoying to make someone turn you over to the Taliban in there."

"Yeah."

I explain as little as I need to about Dave. There was some trouble upcountry and now he's in the frame. It's a case of mistaken identity, I believe. I think they're looking for someone else.

This guy isn't stupid and he immediately understands that by "someone else" I mean me.

"OK, I'll look out for him. If you ever need anything, we're based by the airport. Big tower block, fourth floor. Dutch territory."

"What might I need?"

"I don't know. A safe haven. Our offices are Dutch. If you get in trouble, come there."

"Thanks, but look out for my mate if you can. It's him I'm worried about now. We should be able to get him out but a lot can happen while he's in there."

We come into Kabul under the huge hill of the TV station and into the city proper. Beccy turns her phone back on and calls Arnan. We need somewhere to stay, not a hotel, low key and safe. He says he'll get back to us. Ten minutes later there's a call and he has an address for us in the Murad Khane area down by the river.

It's a weird place — full of some of the oldest buildings in the capital, meant to be a cultural gem but to my untrained eye they look like any other part of this beat-up city. It's a busy, bustling place with a shedload of reconstruction going on. There's lots of street life, people selling food, building materials and other stuff from little shops. The buildings look as if they were built to resist a siege, which is just as well. They have thick walls and small windows. The driver asks his way and we're directed to a big mud-bricked place in sight of a mosque. It looks a something from the Bible, particularly as someone has decided to build a shack on top, which reminds me of Noah's Ark.

We knock on a knackered wooden door and it's answered by a young man. He leads us into a long corridor. Inside the place is amazing. The corridor is panelled in a light wood, all carved with little birds and the floor is tiled with a deep blue pattern. It was clearly once luxurious. It's as though the outside and the inside belong to different worlds. We go through and into a back room. The man opens a door and there is a small, clean room with two low beds with towels set out. There's even a washbasin. The boy leads us past it to show us, just off the corridor, a wonderful shower.

Beccy calls Cadwell again and thank God he picks up this time. He says he'll sort Dave out. Guarantees he won't spend an hour in custody. Least he can do for the help he's offered Beccy. Excellent.

I thank the driver while she talks to Cadwell. Then the boy disappears and leaves us alone. Beccy finishes the call and slips her mobile back into her pocket.

"What time is it?" I ask.

"Seven," says Beccy.

Beccy's arranged to meet Cadwell at ten. I desperately want to get clean but I feel guilty taking a shower while Dave is somewhere very likely taking a five-star kicking.

This is the plan: get in, contact Beccy's handler, debrief, try to sort Dave out and then get home. I know why Ben died now — to stop news of Bulwark's atrocity at Priand coming out. I had thought it was smack dealers. Wrong. This was sanctioned by the top levels of the company. Ben couldn't go to the police because he thought it might drop the Royal Engineer boys in it further. They were in prison. If it came out that Westerners had been responsible for a massacre it'd be the easiest thing in the world to stick the blame on them. I'm not in a dissimilar position. While Dave's inside I have to play it carefully. All I can hope is that Cadwell does what he promised Beccy he'd do.

Beccy goes into the shower while I check the corridor to stop anyone coming down it. No one does but the phone rings again. It's the BBC. They want to speak to Dave. I tell them what's happened.

The guy on the other end of the phone sounds stunned. "Look," he says, "I shouldn't even be making this call but I thought I owe it to you to tell you. There's a DA notice five on it."

"What's that?"

"It's a request not to report from the government. If the government wants something hushed up it puts a DA notice on it. There are five sorts."

"And what's number five?"

"Security and Intelligence Special Services."

"So you can't report on it?"

"We could, it's only a voluntary agreement but no one ever goes against them. I'm sorry, the story's dead."

Beccy gets back from the shower and I tell her what's happened. She looks surprised.

"I'll take it up with Cadwell," she says.

"Can he get the notice removed?"

"He can do anything," she says, "but first he better get Dave out. He's pretty sure he can."

When I get back from the shower, Beccy's already lying in her bed with her eyes closed.

I go and lie on mine and look up at the ceiling.

I look over at her and I'm surprised to see her looking over at me. We look into each other's eyes for a long moment. She says nothing, just slips out of the sheets and into my bed. A million and one things are going through my head. I feel bad because of Dave, I feel tired, sore, confused, relieved to be alive. But I also, it can't be denied, want her. I put my arms around her, feel her soft body next to mine and we kiss. We've been through a lot together and she's come through for me, backed me up, cared for me in the most meaningful way of all — by putting her life on the line. I've fancied her for years but there's more than just a physical thing going on here: there's a bond between us.

Three hours is over in no time and when it is, I look at her gathering her filthy Afghan clothes from the floor ready to go out into those dangerous streets again, ready to stand by me as I try to do the right thing and I realise, if this isn't love, I don't know what is.

At nine, she calls Cadwell. It's sorted and he gives us an RV — out of town. It's not ideal to travel by night but we can cut across the desert. How are we going to get there?

"He told me to use my initiative," says Beccy.

"Is that code for 'nick a car'?"

I go up on to the roof to have a recce, see if there's any car in a back street somewhere away from notice. I spend a good ten minutes watching the back of the building. Nothing doing. Plus big clouds are rolling in off the mountains. Great, it's about to throw it down. I come around to the front. Hmmm, hello, there's a Toyota 4×4 at the front. I haven't seen that before. It's a bit too exposed to easily nick it but that's not what I'm thinking about. It doesn't look quite right. Call it instinct.

When I come down I can hear voices from our room. Now I don't like this.

They're talking in Pashto. One of them is Beccy's but there are definitely at least three men in there. One of them's really screaming. I hear a smack and a shout from Beccy. Someone's hit her. I leave the Glock in my shoulder holster — no point introducing firearms to the situation until we know what's going on. I walk back up the corridor and watch what's happening.

It's three Afghan guys in official-looking uniforms, though I don't think they're police. Soldiers? Security guards, even? I can immediately guess what's happened. There's a reward for us and our driver has sold us. He gets his money for delivering us and then gets a second payment for grassing us up. But to who? Who are this lot? They could be anyone. Only three guys have turned up. That means it's not official business — yet. Maybe we've been sold to them so they in turn can sell us on to the police without our driver having to implicate himself. In one way, that simplifies things.

Beccy is still shouting at them. She has blood coming from her mouth. I don't know what to do. I've no way of immobilising these goons and I can't let them go.

"Hello, boys," I say. I'm peering around the door, gun in one hand. It's a less stable grip than two hands but it exposes a lot less of me and I'm hardly likely to miss at this range.

Bang! One's just turned and shot at me. I get a mouthful of plaster and am blinded for a second. I let go two shots and drop him. The other two have their attention taken by me and loose off a load of shots as I duck back round the corner. Thank God I'm against a supporting wall because the bullets don't come through it.

Bang and the sound of someone else hitting the deck. It could be Beccy. I jump through the doorway to see one remaining standing cop. He's half looking at Beccy, half at me. As he sees my movement he levels his

gun but I loose off a shot of my own. He goes down as
there's another bang — Beccy has shot him as well.

I look at Beccy.

"Cadwell?"

"Cadwell," she says.

We both know that we need to get out of here as
quick as we can. We don't want to have to explain this
to the police.

I rifle through the fallen men's pockets. One of the
corpses has a VW car key and, sure enough, it's for the
old Passat out the front. Well, there's one problem
solved. He also has an AK and a hunting knife. I'll have
those.

We pull out in the car. My ears are still ringing with
the gunshots but I can't hear any sirens coming to the
scene. Gunshots are not unusual in Kabul. Beccy
phones Arnan to tell him what's happened. He's not
very happy about it but says he'll try to sort it out. How
you sort out three dead bodies in your guesthouse, I
don't know.

My mind's tired with all the violence and I gaze out
into the dusk. Kabul's a wonderful-looking place in the
evening — almost medieval, a darkness you don't get in
the West. It's pitch black tonight, heavy cloud and now
there's a light rain in the air. Still there are amazing
smells of cooking meat and fires. Not that I've got time
to stop and take in the ambience.

Then it's out, out, out, in the dark.

We travel for two or three hours up into the hills, into
a thick fog. Only the GPS on Beccy's phone means
we're sure where we're going. When we get to the RV

there's a big old compound. To my surprise, we're flagged down by an Afghan guy in local dress. He's not armed so I get out to speak to him.

"Cadwell will be here shortly," he says. "You can park up inside the compound."

He has an accent like Prince Charles's. Probably not an Afghan, then. The disguise fooled me.

We drive into the compound and the gate's shut behind us. There are three other blokes, all similarly dressed, standing around a big blue Nissan estate.

"You can wait here," says the bloke who stopped us, "your transport's on its way."

The gates are opened again and the blokes drive off, leaving us on our own.

"So is Cadwell undercover too?"

"Well, he's meant to run a building project but it's only a cover story — there are no offices or anything," says Beccy. "He oversees the whole intelligence side of things, so he's not caught up in any one operation."

We spend the time checking our weapons and reloading. We've no way of knowing if we've been followed or if our position has been compromised and there's only one way out now. If we got bogged down in this compound on a mountain road there wouldn't even be one way out. Still, I'm not spending the rest of my life in an Afghan nick, so that's that.

Eventually there is the sound of a couple of cars coming up the road, the heavier sound of a truck behind. They stop outside the compound and someone approaches the gates.

Beccy goes to hide inside one of the mud-brick buildings to our left while I listen at the gate. If it's hostiles then at least Beccy will be in a position to surprise them.

"Nick, Beccy?" The voice sounds vaguely familiar.

Beccy opens the door and I cover her. Then someone steps round the gate, smiling. As the torch he's using splits the darkness I see he's wearing casual western clothing — a North Face jacket and walking trousers, hiking boots so he looks like he could be out for a day on the Pennine Way. The only thing that marks him as being something other than a civilian is the wireless earpiece of a phone headset at his ear.

But it's his face that takes my attention, his big, cheesy grinning, smiling face. I know him all right. He's the bloke who knocked my tooth out in Paddington Green.

CHAPTER
TWENTY-NINE

Cadwell opens the gate and the cars drive in, like prehistoric creatures emerging from the misty night. They're not Land Cruisers, as I thought, but big four-seat pickups adapted with covers at the back, like you see some builders use. Effectively, it turns the back half of the truck into a giant boot.

Beccy has come out of hiding and watches as Cadwell directs the trucks into the compound.

"This is your handler?"

"He's everyone's handler. He's the Alpha."

"Well, he took time out of his busy schedule to punch my face in while I was in Paddington Green."

She looks at me strangely. "Why would he do that?"

"I don't know but I'm about to ask him."

Part of me, of course, just wants to get on with this and get home but I'm the kind of guy who, when smacked in the mouth by a senior member of the security services, likes to know why. I'm old-fashioned like that.

The pickups line up in the compound. I'm pleased to see that each one just has a local driver and that there are no immediate signs of weapons. Call me paranoid but I haven't lived this long because of a sweet and trusting nature.

Cadwell comes up to Beccy and looks her up and down. He doesn't bother with niceties, just piles straight in.

"You have evidence that Bulwark have been conspiring with the Taliban?"

"My own observations and testimony of witnesses, sir."

"Well done."

He turns to me. "We're here to take you out of here. Your methods have been unconventional but you've turned up some important evidence that could be crucial to the future of Afghanistan. We're going to get you out of here on a military flight via Dubai this evening. Forgive the delay but I had some paperwork to sort out to make that happen. Enjoy this thanks because it's all you're going to get. What's happening at Marjul is highly sensitive and don't expect to read about it in the news. You will, of course, say nothing about it."

"Half-time, sunshine," I say.

"Yes, Mr Kane?"

"Where's Dave?"

"In the pickup."

I walk over and, sure enough, there he is, travelling in the back.

"All right, mate?" I ask.

"Sound." He has a broken nose. Ah well, it's not like it's going to ruin his looks.

"Why in the back of the pickup?"

"Cadwell thinks it's best I keep a low profile — he thinks Brad might come looking for me when he finds out I'm gone. Or send someone."

"Right." If Brad has bad luck he'll find Dave. He's not the sort of bloke you want to put in a corner.

I come back to Cadwell.

"You look troubled, Nick."

"I'd just like an explanation as to why you're being so helpful when the last time I saw you, you were beating the shit out of me."

"I was trying to help you and to help myself. I saw that, after the death of your friend, you would try to investigate. It's a sensitive situation here and I didn't want you messing things up, as you so very nearly have. So when I heard you were in Paddington Green, I decided to come down and try to persuade you to go back to your life on the yacht. You were identified as a risk and so you turned out to be."

"A risk to what?"

He comes up to me and stands very close to my face. "This is serious stuff, Kane. You've been out of the SRR for a while now and, to be honest, it's not much in the way of military intelligence anyway, is it? You were forever getting under our feet in Ireland and it was the same in Serbia and Iraq. We'll take your best operators," he gestures to Beccy, "but let's be honest, you're a lot better blowing things up and killing people than you are at anything that resembles real intelligence, aren't you?"

I do think of chinning him but decide not to. He's our way home. So I say nothing, just look him in the eye.

310

"You will be going out of here through the cargo gate of the airbase. You'll be going straight through and firearms are absolutely not allowed in the airport perimeter so you will leave your guns here for my men to dispose of. Any questions?"

We lay down our guns and I'm about to ditch the hunting knife when I think twice. He said no firearms on the airport perimeter. I'll stick this in the sharps bin, should there be such a thing, before we get on the plane. We're not in the airport yet and you never know.

We climb into the trucks. There's me and Beccy in one, Dave in the other. The trucks are cramped, low, noisy, uncomfortable and pitch dark. Never mind, I've had worse.

The trucks pull out and I feel them turn left and up the mountain. This doesn't worry me. It makes sense not to go back the way we came. Before long I feel the trucks begin to descend. Beccy and I hug each other and it's good to feel that this ordeal is over.

A text message buzzes into Beccy's phone.

"It's from John," she says.

The phone lights up the darkness of the van and I can see her face tighten as she reads it. She passes the phone to me.

It reads: "Checked Cadwell. Has false bank account under name Henry Green. Regular payment of £100,000 a month from hidden source. Account has been used to pay Cadwell's credit card bill. Money trail leads back to personal account of Sir John Carlyle — chairman Bulwark industries. Do you have a way out?"

"Tell him the Dutch have offered us a way out," I say.

"We should alert the ISAF!"

"We can't — the ANP are still looking for me. Just tell him about the Dutch."

She texts back while I get thinking.

"Is there any chance he was infiltrating Bulwark?" I say.

"That's a level below him," says Beccy, "and what are they paying him a hundred grand a month for? He should be running it for that, not infiltrating it."

"So he's been bought."

This explains everything — the DA notices, the information clampdown, how they covered up the massacre, even how someone had the nous and ability to slot Ben. And the police investigation was slight — the case passed over to military intelligence. Bulwark have used their dirty money to corrupt British intelligence at a very high level. I thought I was fighting a bunch of smack dealers when I first came here, then a corrupt multinational. It turns out I'm up against one of the pillars of British security.

There's a pickup directly behind us. No way of jumping out and going for it. One of us might get away, if we were lucky and didn't encounter a big drop when we jumped off the track the trucks are on. The other one would be done for.

The truck stops and in the stark light of the headlights behind us I see Beccy reach down to take the Walther from her ankle holster.

"You kept your gun?"

"Of course. Didn't you keep yours?"

"No," I say, "but I kept this." I take the knife from the sheath on my wrist and hide it under my arm.

"Cadwell's mine" I say.

"Sure."

It sounds naff but I ask her for a kiss. As we break she squeezes my hand. She says nothing but we both know that the likelihood is we're not getting off this hill.

The door at the back opens and I hear a voice. "Change of plan."

The voice is deep and American. I see a pistol move across the headlights of the truck behind. It's only a glimpse but I'd recognise its outline anywhere. It's a Desert Eagle.

CHAPTER
THIRTY

There are powerful headlights on me and I take a blow in the guts as I step from the truck. Beccy gets the same treatment and there's a shot as her pistol is taken from her.

"Bitch!" says another voice.

I can hear shouting from the other truck. This is the position of our maximum advantage. It all goes downhill from here. With the strong lights on me I can't even see who it is that's punched me.

I'm going to find out. I stand up and, as I anticipated, a kick comes in to put me down again. I've still got the ballistic jacket on, so it absorbs some of the force and I manage to grab the leg, and drive a reasonable sidekick into his knee.

Normally it's a very risky move to go to ground. It might be all right in your mixed martial arts but not where someone can come in from the side and practise his conversion kicking on your head.

However, here there are firearms involved and we're looking at a "least worst" situation. The closer I stay to their man, the harder it is for them to shoot me.

I turn on the leg I have in the crook of my elbow and stick the hunting knife into the inside of the thigh, going for the femoral artery, which will put him out of the game, or any game. My kick has wrecked his knee and he goes down, taking the knife with him. He screams as he writhes on the floor but I have no idea if I've dealt him a fatal blow. To be honest, I don't know what happens next. Someone twats me old-school style and all the little lights come on for a minute. Someone puts two shots into the guy who's hit me and he goes down. Beccy. Bang, bang, bang! I hear the Desert Eagle booming but something's wrong. I had the impression that Anderson was right next to me but that shot sounded as if it was further away. Everyone around me suddenly disappears, diving for cover.

I roll around the side of the truck. I'm now behind the lights and can see Beccy's got her gun back. She levels it at someone but his gun is on her. A man is sidestepping away from the truck to my left, trying to get a clear shot at me with his UMP — a machine pistol. Bang! A flash and the Desert Eagle booms. The man with the UMP falls and staggers. There are people running everywhere. I roll out to the corpse and I've got my hands on the gun. Did Anderson shoot his own man?

It's certainly possible, there's no order to this at all, people leaping around everywhere. Where's Beccy, though? She was there one minute, gone the next. There are any number of these goons here — I can see they've brought a Mowag and a couple of Hummers with them. It's not going to help Beccy if I get myself shot. I crawl back around the truck.

It's chaos, headlights starring the mist, shapes running everywhere. You can't tell who is who. Boom! Another crack from a Desert Eagle. Someone else is shooting one. I roll around the truck and collide with someone coming the other way.

I'm about to take him out when I see it's Dave.

He's got a knife with him, so I'm clearly not the only one who thought it was worth hanging on to a bit of back-up.

"How many enemy?"

"Eight brought me up here."

That's how many I counted. Brad's men on top of that.

Two blokes running towards us from around the truck behind us. Assault rifle rounds smash into the car above our heads. I give them two bursts of two shots. One goes down and the other decides life was sweeter behind some cover and goes back the way he came, arms windmilling like he's in a slapstick comedy. Dave doesn't need a second invitation. He goes round the other side of the truck in a flash and, from the fact a gun doesn't fire, I guess he's done for the bloke with his knife.

Men are running past us in the fog, unable to see anything out of the glare of the lights. I realise I don't even know where we are. Are we on a ridge, a plateau, in a valley? We could be in an aircraft hangar, for all I can tell.

I can't tell why we haven't been surrounded here. There's fire coming in from the right of the truck, out of the pitch dark. God knows who that is.

Suddenly there's an enormous thumping noise, like when you ring the bell with the hammer at the fair but massively bigger. Big slugs are tearing into the pickup. We've been flanked.

I roll underneath the truck again and, to my surprise, come out straight under one of the Bulwark boys who's standing on the running board of the truck, using the roof to support his gun. Two shots drop him. He falls straight off the step on top of me and I have to shove him aside. I have to move as best I can because my shooting will have given away my position. But I'm surrounded by open ground. I come out from behind this truck and I'm dead.

Then something weird happens. Everything goes quiet. It's a bizarre thing. We have two pickups about fifty yards from me. There's the pickup I'm hiding behind and three big military trucks down the road. Someone is groaning and whimpering but apart from that no noise at all. Everyone's hunkered down and waiting for the next move.

"Brad!" An American voice.

"Roger."

"You OK?" The voice is behind us, from down the line of military trucks.

"What we got?

There's a couple of shots but no reply. Someone — Beccy or Dave — has said "Thank you very much for shouting out your position" and taken him out.

All of a sudden I see someone come across the line of trucks, towards where Anderson has been shouting. I can hardly believe my eyes. It's Arnan's kid cousin Pamir. What the hell is he doing here?

He's got a Desert Eagle and he's making for where Anderson's voice came from, firing as he does so. It's insanely brave but he's not really holding the gun right. He's allowing it to whip up too much as he fires it. On round three there's a click and the gun doesn't fire. That much whip can unbalance the magazine on a gun like that. A hail of shots comes the other way, the gun flashing from beneath the far pickup. I count four and he hits the ground.

In the flash, though, I've seen that Brad's under the pickup.

I'm looking around for more of their guys. There's a fair few of them on the ground. I count six from where I am.

No one else fired at Pamir when he came forward. I think they're all dead or injured. I should approach the truck. It's a big gamble, though. Suddenly something makes it worth it. Three big shots from the far pickup and a round blasts the opposite side of the truck to where I'm hiding. Seven shots. If that's a .50 Desert Eagle, which I think it is, then that's all it's got. Good reason not to have a flashy gun.

Two targets in front of me — Afghan guys launching a brave frontal assault. I have no choice, two shots drop the first and only one shot drops the second. Out of ammo. I look down for the gun of the guy at my feet but suddenly I'm smashed to the ground.

Brad's used the distraction of the Afghan guys' attack to creep up on me and he's hit me with a serious tackle.

318

I see him at the last second and smash my gun into his knife arm. He drops the weapon but he's on me, trying to get me in a stranglehold, get his fingers into my eyes, taking any target of opportunity.

He's enormously strong and fighting for his life and for a second all the breath goes out of me and he's got a strangle on me. I've still got the UMP around my neck on its strap and I drive it backwards into his ribs but he's as strong as anyone I've ever fought and now he's got behind me and locked my left arm down with his leg, has enveloped my right with his right and with his free arm he's using the lapel of my jacket to strangle me. This is a strangle I've been taught and it's known as "the hell strangle" for the severe difficulty people have in getting out of it. Technically speaking, this is a choke, not a strangle. It cuts off the windpipe, not the veins to the head, so I have a little time longer than I'd have if he'd cut off my blood. Still, there is no time to hang about nor call for half measures.

And then I think of all those kids in that village, Ben, the counsellor, even those poor Chinese bastards buried and forgotten miles from home. Training can take you a certain way, do so much for you. But in a fight like this — tight confines, a bloke as strong as a bear against you — you're looking at something deeper: the will to survive. From somewhere there's more shooting but I can't think about that.

It's only that desperation that gives me the strength to turn into him, popping out my left shoulder as I do. It's agony but I get my teeth into his nose and take a good bit of that off, which causes him to let me go and put his hands up to his face. For just a second horror has kicked in and he's forgotten that the fact that he's just lost half his nose is of less importance than me finding his knife — which I do.

I drive it through his ribs and his hands come down to grab me again. He's punching me, biting at me but then he stops moving. Brad's dead.

My arm is out of commission and all I have is a knife. I get the gun off the dead guy at my feet. He's an Afghan and it's an AK. Not easy to shoot one-handed but better than nothing.

"Nick?"

It's Dave.

"Yeah?"

"All dead?"

"Yeah."

"Beccy?"

"Don't know."

There's a groan from underneath the Mowag. It's her. She starts to cough and to shout. Good, that means I can ignore her. I run to Pamir. He's lying on the floor with a big wound in his side.

"Dave, get a field dressing out of that Mowag!"

Dave runs over and comes back with the first-aid kit. He applies a field dressing to the wound while I get a drip into the kid, putting the bag underneath him to provide the pressure to get the fluid in. There's no morphine left. The skanky bastards have nicked it.

"You're OK, Pamir, you're going to be OK. How did you find us here?"

He doesn't understand me. In the heat of things I've forgotten he doesn't speak English. Beccy comes up, holding her side. I repeat the question and she translates.

"Anderson killed Arnan when he wouldn't tell where you were. Cadwell told him we were here so he came to protect us."

I can't find words for this. He kept them from surrounding us. I owe him my life. I squeeze his hand in thanks and we get him into the back of the Hummer.

Then I go to Beccy.

"You OK?"

"I got hit by something. The body armour took the impact but I think it's broken my ribs. What about your arm?"

"Dislocated." As I say the word the pain comes back to me.

"Milch technique," says Dave, coming back from the truck.

I remember that one from training. You lie on your back and reach behind your head to the other shoulder. It's painful but it avoids jolting and it does pop the shoulder back in. I lie down and perform the technique and with a snap feel it go in. It's going to be painful for a while but it'll do.

"What's the plan now?" asks Dave. Beccy's next to Pamir now, speaking to him comfortingly in Pashto.

I think for a moment. We've got to get some help for Pamir. And Beccy and Dave have got to get out of Afghanistan. It's not safe for them here. It's not safe for me, either, but I've got things to do.

"Get to the Dutch, by the airport perimeter. I'll call to tell them you're coming. They can get some care for the kid and stick you on a flight."

"What about you?" says Dave.

"I'm going to have a word with Cadwell," I say.

CHAPTER
THIRTY-ONE

There's a whole bunch of kit in the cache but apart from recovering my shoulder holster, Glock and some ammo, I'm only really interested in the Claymores. There are two. I want only one.

Dawn comes up no brighter but there's satnav on the Mowag and I get a bearing. We're on a mountain somewhere south of Kabul, inside a ravine. A perfect killing ground because the walls of the creek mean the gun flashes won't be visible from Kabul and any sound gets channelled straight up. They picked the right night too — intentionally or not — a good fog with no chance of being spotted from the air.

All I take from the Mowag is a pen and a clipboard that's on one of the seats. I'm going to need those. I also take a mobile off one of the bodies. On impulse I flick it to Bluetooth. St John. Seems it was Anderson following me all along. Odd, you'd have thought I'd have noticed someone that big. I call the Dutch guy and tell him to expect the team. He's good as gold about it.

"If you get there by eleven he goes out to a coffee shop round the corner to read for an hour. He's back twelve sharp," Beccy informs me.

"Bit lax, isn't it?"

"It's not always the same coffee shop. But he's like clockwork in his habits."

He should know that's dodgy. Mind you, I've heard of worse. One soldier back in the day in Northern Ireland used to get a chip supper from the same chip shop every Friday, 6p.m. sharp. He only lived because 14 Company got a tip-off he was being lined up by the IRA and intervened to stop it happening.

"Is there a password I'll need to get into the compound?"

"It should be on the phone's text. Cadwell's code name's Red Three."

I scan down. Sure enough, there it is. Firefly.

"You didn't get the text?"

"No. Should have been a warning, shouldn't it?"

"Yeah, right," she says. "Are you going to do Cadwell?"

"Yeah."

"Well. Stay safe."

She starts giggling and I can't help but crack a smile too.

"Can you see another way?"

"No."

Cadwell needs to be eliminated. This isn't just a matter of emotion — though there's some of that in there. It's useless to try to bring him to justice, he has hooks in everywhere, the legal right to suppress information and the resources to take me out.

It's all falling into place in my mind while I prepare to go down the mountainside. The whole lithium thing was so sensitive that he wasn't even using proper spooks to do his dirty work for him. He was subcontracting. Did Anderson think he was working for British Military Intelligence? Was it some sort of deal? His position in Bulwark remained protected, his opium smuggling undisturbed as long as he did a little freelance work for Cadwell.

How had they got the better of Ben? There could be hundreds of ways. Drug his pint? Simple but effective. Empty half a bottle of Rohypnol in there and he just looks pissed. Cart him back to the B&B and slot him. It's how I'd do it. Ben was a handful and you wouldn't want to try killing him when he was on his game.

So Cadwell must have been reasonably isolated in whatever branch of MI he was in. He couldn't employ proper spooks. So why move Beccy to Bulwark? That doesn't make sense. Unless he'd identified her as a good operator and hoped to turn her eventually. Or did he want to bring in Brad's bunch for heroin dealing, discredit them and put them in jail after he'd used them? She was the one to build the case, she certainly has the talent to do something like that.

For the most part it seems that Cadwell was outsourcing his skulduggery. That would account for the off-the-shelf bugging device. Clever, really. The last people I suspected were Military Intelligence. Cadwell knew how to cover his tracks — if the device I'd found at Ben's was state of the art I'd have suspected MI straight away. But if Ben's place had been bugged with a state-of-the-art device I'd never have found it. As I think this through, a cold wave washes over me. What's the implication of that? They wanted me to find it? Or was it just there to signal to Ben that they could hit him at home when they chose?

Brad was a useful operator but he was a bit of a loose cannon. Had I been set up to kill him? Why not just get an Afghan to pop him here? Because that doesn't seal off the risk. And besides, I'd presented myself to them. They knew they could get me to kill Brad by manipulating me, giving me the chance. If they'd used an Afghan there was always a chance, no matter how remote, that something would come out. He planned it like it was hermetically sealed. Everyone dead — the potential whistleblower in Ben, the bloke he knew would come looking for answers, the slightly unreliable operative, the engineers. He cleans up all the mess with witnesses, even everyone who took part in the massacre. Brad was the last one left. I killed all the rest. I've been doing his dirty work. Now he'll want me. Well, he's going to get me.

So why set me up to be killed on the mountain? Cadwell knew I'd found out too much, knew Beccy had. He wanted Brad dead. He sticks us all in the same arena and at least some of us die. Less to worry about.

I get changed into the uniform — if that's what you can call it — of a Bulwark man: combat trousers, camouflage bomber jacket with the Bulwark insignia on the side, body armour. I cobble it together off the bodies — not a pleasant task. Some of the stuff is too bloodstained to pass muster and I end up in a pair of slightly too big trousers, decent boots, a sweaty T-shirt and good body armour.

I take an ID that most resembles me. Section Leader Michael Neumann. The only problem I have is that he's clean-shaven in his picture. Apart from that he looks enough like me. Never mind: people do go a bit native over here. I put on his shades and his bandana. I take a sports bag for the Claymore, some ammo for the Glock and that's it.

While I've been getting ready, Beccy has bound up her ribs and has helped Dave get Pamir into the back of the Mowag and make him as comfortable as they can. I've managed to get hold of the Dutch, and now all Dave and Beccy have to do is get to their embassy. Sounds easy, but I know that there's many a slip between cup and lip.

Dave leans out of the window of the Mowag, Beccy's seated in the passenger side.

"You look like Lord Twat of Twat Hall," he says. No change there, then.

I shake his hand.

I go round to Beccy's window. "Let's hope the Dutch have got a plane. If they have, you be on it whether I'm there or not."

She nods. I kiss her goodbye, which isn't all that pleasant with a split lip. As the adrenalin is wearing off I realise I'm covered in bruises. With a wave of his hand, Dave pulls the Mowag away. This is it — I'm all by myself now.

I get into a pickup and head back down the mountain.

As I drop down the mist clears and Kabul is laid out in front of me in the morning sun, the light catching windows and windscreens in flashes. I can see the airport road from here.

I travel down the mountain and around the outskirts of the city. It's midday by the time I get to Cadwell's gaff. I park the car just off the highway, put the Claymore into a plastic bag and stuff that inside my body armour. Then I walk the two hundred yards to the roadblock at the top of Cadwell's street.

There are two young American guys there, clean cut and bored.

"Good morning," I say to the guards. We're right on the airport road and it's a bit like trying to conduct a conversation by the pit wall at Monaco. Possible but not easy.

"How can we help?"

I flash my ID.

"I've got a meeting with Red Three here," I say.

"Where's your car, man?"

I stiffen, suddenly doing the drill sergeant impression. I am supposed to be a section leader, after all.

"I understood you were here to ask me for a password, not poke your ugly misshapen nose into business that doesn't concern you."

"Sorry, guy, chill out."

"No, I am not going to chill out. You heat up. We stick you here for one reason. To ask for a password. Now ask me for the password!"

"What's the password?"

"Firefly."

He nods.

"Good for you. Now when Red Three comes through here do you think you could try to act like a professional soldier and just ask him for the password without burdening him with speculation, conversation or masturbation?"

The kid goes bright red and I can see I've made my point. Nothing like driving it home though.

"Aren't you forgetting something?"

"What?"

"You haven't asked me to sign."

"Oh yeah, sorry."

He produces a clipboard, I sign Michael Neumann and then I march on to Cadwell's house at my best parade ground clip. Cadwell's place is actually one of the more interesting buildings — a restored 1930s job in a light blue colour, all arches. It's a sort of mock gothic, mock Arabian, mock God knows what thing with plenty of decorative plasterwork laid on in swirls and points.

The front door is rather exposed to the road and in clear view of the checkpoint. Still, the guards have been shamed into not wanting to meet my eye and are paying studied attention to the road in front of them. There are two flats. I hadn't counted on that. Never mind, get on with it. I ring the bell on the ground floor. Nothing. Then the top. Nothing.

I'd hoped Cadwell might be late going for his coffee so I could just force my way in and silence him with the pistol. Clearly, that's not going to happen and this place has a good bit of security on it — alarms on all windows, the basement sealed with a heavy metal door of the sort they put over drug dens when they've shut them down. Mind you, one piece of good news is that — as I can see from looking at them — the alarms are basic shock sensors. There's no sign of a movement detector in the flat. The one thing you must always assume about an alarm is that it's turned on. However, in my experience, most people go through a month of enthusiasm, when they religiously arm it every time they go out, before the whole thing becomes a pain in the arse. Still, I'm not going to be tripping any shock sensors so the alarm shouldn't be a problem.

The guards are still looking up the street. I have to look like I've gone in so I nip around to the side of the building, out of their sight. At the back is quite a pleasant garden, green and well stocked with flowers. Looks like our boy might be a bit of a gardener, when he's not in the mass-murder business. There's no way in. Now, I could just lay low here and just wait for him to come back and then nip round and force him in. A bit risky, though. Hello, the top flat doesn't look like it's got any alarms on the window.

There's a shed at the back. This is a secure compound, so there's no lock on it. I open it up and, hey presto, there's an old wooden ladder. The garden's well hidden by trees so, though I'm about to take a risk, it's a calculated one. I pocket a big screwdriver and find some cord. Then I take the ladder to the back. I tie the cord on to the top of the ladder and tuck the other end around my belt. Then I climb up.

I can see the flat is completely bare — no carpets, even. I wait until I can hear a big truck coming down the highway and smash the window with the screwdriver, coat around my hand. The latch is not a lockable one but the sash has been nailed shut. I wait until the noise of the road is at its loudest and clear the glass from the lower panel. Then I carefully crawl in and pull the ladder up on the cord. Three out of ten for subtlety but I'm in and that's the important thing.

I go down and check the door. It's deadlocked. As I thought. No waiting in the hallway for Cadwell. I've tried those doors before and they take an age and some proper kit to get through.

Plan B. I'm about to get two out of ten on the "cat burglar who moves like a shadow" stakes. I use the screwdriver to take up some floorboards. There's not a heap of space between the joists but there's enough for someone who's been stuck in the mountains eating sand pie for weeks.

Four boards come up and then, for the second time in my life, I put my foot through a ceiling. The first was rewiring the house I used to share with Chloe and Rachel. Just thinking about them makes me well up. It's funny, you manage to hold on to your emotions through a tidal wave of grief that sweeps down on you and then you just think of your kid's face and it breaks you up.

I smash a good hole in the ceiling and try to get through. Can't do it with the body armour on, so I take that off and chuck it through the hole. Then I squeeze in myself. For a second I think I'm going to get stuck but then I swing on down off a joist. My arm is agony. Luckily for me, and unluckily for Cadwell, I come down right on top of his piano. It's an upright job and I stand on top of it before lowering myself to the floor. I've got a nice cut on my side where I've caught myself on a nail but apart from that I'm OK.

It's a typical, if not stereotypical, middle-class lounge though very messy: some sheet music by Bach on the piano, stripped boards, Afghan carpet, lots of books, various Afghani paintings on the wall, a big collection of vinyl records — classical music, natch — and a Bose stereo system. There's also a lot of empty whisky bottles about and the place is far from what I'd call top order. It hasn't been vacuumed in a while and there are books and papers all over the place. In the kitchen are discarded milk cartons, instant coffee granules spill out from an upended jar onto the work surface, and on the floor is a newspaper that's a month old. Cadwell's clearly a mucky pup, which is unusual for an ex-army guy.

I put the armour back on. If he's not alone I might need it. I check out the place. There's a comfortable office — Victorian-style with a big roll-top desk. I wonder how much it cost the taxpayer to fly that out here.

There are pictures all over the wall: Cadwell rowing at public school, at Durham University, in the army — Intelligence Corps — deer stalking with the bodies of three stags next to him. A bit greedy. He has a degree certificate on the wall. A first in modern languages. That's how a lot of people come to the intelligence services. Funny how "Bonjour, Monsieur Hulot" at age twelve can lead you to mass murder by the age of fifty.

332

Also, mounted on the wall opposite the door is a long Jezail Afghan rifle, inlaid with pearl. I inspect it. It's a hundred-year-old weapon but they're still in use in some parts of the country and, if well maintained, are deadly accurate. They're basically muskets but the barrels are rifled and in the right hands they'll knock an ant's dick off at five hundred paces, as any number of widows of the British Empire could tell you. It actually chills me to look at it, which is odd considering the number of considerably more deadly weapons I've seen. There's something organic about it, its strange curves, its slightly grotesque length.

There's also a weapons cabinet — open, keys nowhere in sight. This is careless and sloppy. I don't care if you are only nipping out to the café round the corner. He wants to get off the booze.

Inside are all sorts of goodies — grenades, a couple of AKs, an M4 assault rifle, an Armalite AR50 sniper rifle in its three pieces and a tear-gas gun with various boxes of ammo. There's also a snub-nosed pistol — an OTS 38 Stechkin. This is a special bit of kit — an integrally silenced five-shot pistol designed by the Russians. It produces next to no noise and no flash at all on firing. It's an assassin's weapon. I take it. It's going to come in useful.

I pocket the gun and two grenades and make sure none of the rifles have a loaded magazine in them. Then I shift everything I don't want into the bedroom. I don't want him to know where his stuff is, should he be thinking of making a grab for it. In the bedroom, which is a pigsty, is evidence of why Cadwell might not be on top of his game at the moment. On the bedside table are some pieces of burned foil with a sticky residue on them. Opium. He's been chasing the dragon. Might explain why he was easy to corrupt.

I go back into the office once more, glancing at that Jezail. You'd think that being around guns would rid them of their power to give you the creeps. That's true for me — most of them don't, not any more. Just that one. I take it down and check it's unloaded. It is. Better safe than sorry.

In the office is a safe. This bloke has to keep records. I'm not sure they'll be in a form that's readily understood by anyone — in fact, I'm sure they'd be encrypted in some way. But it won't be impossible to crack that. He'll have some sort of record of his transactions with Bulwark — beyond what John's turned up. That would be enough to send anyone normal down but I'm not sure it'll work with Cadwell. One thing's certain: he's giving me the contents of that safe before I leave.

There's also something quite interesting on the desk — a wireless earpiece, the sort you use with a phone — the sort that's Bluetooth enabled.

I got into the toilet. This too is filthy. He clearly lives on his own and is too mean or too secretive to employ a cleaner. That gives me an idea.

It's a fairly standard room, not fancy and, despite Cadwell's grime, not down at heel. White walls, intricate blue tiles around the bath. There's a few empty toilet roll tubes on the floor and a good crust of used toothpaste on the sink. The man's an animal. I open the bathroom cabinet. Painkillers, toothbrush, toothpaste for one. Good. I can use that and spend a few minutes fettling.

Then I go to the computer and use a knife from the kitchen to undo its cover. I have the hard disk out of it in no time. I'm not hopeful because I think he'll cover his tracks better than that, but it can't hurt.

I also case the joint for panic buttons. None that I can see. Good.

That done, I realise I'm starving. I help myself in the kitchen — Weetabix that the tosser has got from somewhere and some nice bread. There's a kettle and some Typhoo. I'd love a cuppa — but the noise of the kettle might alert him if he opens the door.

All I take from the Mowag is a pen and a clipboard. I'm going to need those. I also take a mobile off the seat. On impulse I flick it to bluetooth. St John; seems it was Anderson or one of his boys following me all along. Odd, you'd have thought I'd have noticed the military buzz cuts. I call the dutch guy and tell him to expect the team. He's as good as gold about it.

After that I sit and wait. I've got a quarter of an hour until he gets back. I call Beccy.

"Yes, sir?"

"Who are you calling Sir?"

"Nick? This is Cadwells phone. Have you . . ."

"No, he's not here yet. It was on the seat of the truck."

So Cadwell was St John. Right, well I suppose that makes sense.

"Jesus. How you doing?"

"Not bad. Pamir?"

"Not so good. He's with the Dutch doctor. Are you in?"

"Yeah, I'm in."

"Be careful, he's a slippery bastard."

"He's going to need to be. Bye."

"Bye."

There's a short corridor from the front door into the lounge so he won't immediately see how I've damaged his ceiling and piano. Even if he does, I don't think he'll immediately clock what's happened. It looks more like some building collapse through damp than it does a break-in.

I need to interpose myself between him and the door. If he has a guard with him that could cause problems. I don't want to have to kill him, so I'll have to subdue him. That won't be a problem because in the closet by the door there's all sorts of kit — including some handcuffs. I can't help noticing they're the same brand that was put on me up at the swimming pool. I take those, pleased I won't have to kill any guard. He won't have two, will he? Stop being paranoid. No one has two guards just to come home to a secure house. Now I'm imagining a platoon. Bollocks, relax, see what comes.

A key turns in the lock. I can smell the fags and alcohol on him as he opens the door. Coffee shop, my arse. He comes in, closes the door behind him, puts the chain across. No guard. Why would he have? This is a secure complex. He doesn't even disengage the alarm and, as I guessed, he hasn't bothered to turn it on. I could have saved myself the climb up the ladder and smashing through the floor.

He comes into the living room and slumps on the sofa, clearly a bit pissed. He has his eyes closed. Then he opens his eyes and clocks the ceiling.

"What the . . .?"

Then he sees me standing with my back to the wall nearest the front door.

"Hello, Mr Cadwell."

For a second I see the terror on his face as he sees the Stechkin in my hand. Then he composes himself.

"Nick, how are you?"

"Better than you right now, I should guess, sir."

"You're here to kill me?"

"That rather depends on you. Put your hands in clear view."

He extends his hands. "Do you mind if I get a drink?"

"Did Ben get a drink in that dump in Hammersmith?"

"No."

"Then that's your answer."

"I'd like to use the loo."

"I should just do it where you sit if I were you, sir, you're not getting up from that chair. Now take your clothes off and if I see you go for a weapon I will shoot you without thinking about it."

"Very civilised."

I feel my hackles rise. "I've been to Priand, Mr Cadwell. I know all about your idea of civilised behaviour."

He starts to strip off and I can see he's wearing a shoulder holster with a Glock in it. I level my pistol right at his forehead so he knows he will have no chance to use it. He doesn't try, just throws the holster aside. Soon he's naked, clearly unarmed. This has the bonus of making him feel vulnerable. The fact he knows the drill won't stop it having an effect on him.

"Priand was nothing to do with me."

"I think it was. And to that end, I just want answers to a couple of questions and then I'll let you go."

"I doubt that."

"No, I mean it. I'm interested in incriminating you. I've always fought for what I believe is a better way of doing things. Democracy, the rule of law. You know, the things that you've dumped all over for your own personal gain."

"You don't see the full picture."

"Clue me in."

"We're doing great work here. The Chinese are infiltrating in the valleys up there. You think we've got a problem with the Taliban, you wait and see what happens with communism."

"Horse shit."

He's drunk and not in control of himself, speaking too quickly, his eyes flicking up to the right to show he's inventing the story. But it's not that that tells me he's bullshitting; if you know your history, it's common sense.

"Throughout the 1980s that lot were fighting the communists as hard, if not harder, than they're fighting us," I tell him. "If you think I'm going to believe they've all suddenly started waving the red flag you must be more stupid than you look."

He smiles a tight smile.

Suddenly, in a moment of clarity, I see what's been going on. "Do you want me to tell you what I think went on there?"

"As it'll be prolonging my life, I think I'm going to have to say yes."

"I think the Chinese got a sniff of what was going on there and were threatening to come in with big money. I think they were after outbidding you. It isn't communism you're afraid of, it's capitalism. You'd done your little deal and you were afraid of getting pushed out. That's why you killed the Chinese blokes. You wanted to convince them this was hostile territory and not worth the trouble of trying to invest."

Again, the tight smile. I can tell I'm right.

"You could come out of this well yourself," he says.

"In what way?"

"I could use a man like you. Bulwark could. Sir John needs close protection. You'd be on yachts, in five-star hotels. His intimate parties are well worth attending. He has access to some extremely attractive women and he makes sure his friends are very well served by them."

"So you're suggesting I travel the world banging expensive whores paid for by the death of children. Pardon me if I refuse."

"Your friend took our money. Thirty grand of it."

"I don't believe you."

"Did you see his bank statement?"

It all makes even more sense now. "No, but you have. You planted that money there, didn't you? I don't know how but you hacked his bank account and made it look as though he'd been paid off."

"What makes you so sure?"

"Because Ben was a decent bloke. He wouldn't want your money."

Suddenly Cadwell gets impatient, the booze kicks in, or his bravery. I'll say this for him: he's not going to beg for his life.

"Oh, grow up," says Cadwell. "If you're so concerned then why are you sitting there sipping tea that's produced in conditions of total misery? Do you shop at cheap clothes stores? Have you any idea of the suffering that means you get a pair of cheap underpants? The interest that you get from your bank account is created by investing in firms like Bulwark. Western prosperity depends on the misery of others. All we're talking about is a matter of degree."

"Sorry. I've heard that argument before and it doesn't fly with me. I've spent my whole life standing up against bad people — murderers in Ireland, in Iraq, Serbia and now here with you. There's a big difference between buying a cheap pair of jeans in the high street and sending an animal like Anderson into a village armed with a fifty cal and supported by a bunch of murderous, impressionable, ill-disciplined kids armed with weapons they're only half trained to use. You've gone against everything you're supposed to stand for and killed innocent people to line your own pockets."

"Spare me the sentimental moralising."

"All right," I say, "how's this for sentimental? You open that safe or I'll gag you and kneecap you — for starters."

That shakes him, as well it might. I'm not going to do that because I'm not the sort of weakling who enjoys torturing people. But he doesn't know that, and I guess he thinks I've been through enough that I might just do it.

"The information in there is useless to you."

"I'll be the judge of that. Get up and go to the safe."

There's no way I'm opening it. Again, it may be paranoia but this guy is a spook and you never know what emergency measures he has in place. It's a long shot that he could give me a combination that would set off an explosion, so I'm being cautious.

He goes into the office. I'm right behind him with the gun in my hand. If he makes a false move he's dead.

He opens the safe. No explosions, no alarms. He takes out a memory stick and puts it on the desk. I lock the door of the office and make him stand back.

I point the gun at him and I run my hand around the inside of the safe.

Sure enough, stuck to the upper surface of the safe is another memory stick.

From the look on his face I can see I've hit pay dirt. But no, no! His eyes keep flicking to that rifle on the desk. The Jezail. He must know it's not loaded so what are his eyes telling me? It's a breech loader and I only checked the chamber, not the muzzle. I take a step back and pick up the rifle. I tip it forwards on to the desk. Nothing. Then I put my finger into the muzzle. Stuck inside about two inches down is another memory stick. I go to the other side of the desk, poke the memory stick free with a pencil and upend the gun to get it out — all the time with the pistol on him. If he wants to rush me he's going to have to come over the desk and I can see by his face he doesn't fancy it.

His face goes ashen. You can't fake that. However, he still hasn't attempted to bribe me directly — never mind CP work for Sir John Carlyle. If he was truly scared of exposure that would be his next move. He clearly thinks all this can be handled. It'll be difficult but he can get round it.

How?

He comes up with an idea.

"How about Chloe, Nick? What's going to happen to your little girl if you expose me? Do you think Sir John is a forgiving man? He knows your role in this, Nick, and it won't take long for him to work out the rest. If you don't kill me, I'll tell him. If you do kill me, he'll find out quickly enough. Your only chance of saving her is to walk away."

I look at him directly. This is the sort of stuff we used to come out with when assessing recruits to the SRR. You'd interrogate them and look for the chinks in their armour. "How long have you been away trying to get in this regiment? Two weeks. I bet your bird's banging every squaddie in Aldershot." He's seen my weakness and exploited it.

However, whatever I do now isn't going to make any difference to Chloe. They'll either come for her or they won't. He has a weakness of his own and it's a very straightforward one. He believes everyone, everywhere, can be jerked around. They can't and that means he can be jerked around back.

"I'll go," I say, "but on one condition. You tell me what happened to Ben. Don't bullshit because I know most of it."

"Can I trust you not to kill me if I tell you?"

"No, I'm going to kill you now. The only way you're going to live is by telling me something so incriminating it puts you in prison for the rest of your life."

I put up the gun and he starts talking quickly. He can see I'm serious. If I don't hear something that gives me evidence to put him inside then I will shoot him.

"We tried to reason with him. We set up a meeting for that purpose. He wouldn't see reason. We put an operative in a toilet cubicle. When your man went to the lavatory we shot him with a short-acting animal tranquilliser, took him back to the hotel and faked his suicide. I shot him."

"You?"

"Yes. Well, when you want a job done properly and all that. He didn't do as he was told and he needed to be punished for it. When I discovered you were investigating the case I put you under surveillance for a while. Then I realised you could be useful to me. Hence the smack in the mouth."

"What do you mean?"

"I knew you wouldn't back down after that. Macho pride. You sorts are all the same. We've got a file on you a foot thick. We know you better than you know yourself."

"Was this file in addition to the bullshit one you showed Beccy?"

Again, that tight, punchable smile.

"You're a funny little man," he says. "It was amusing watching you scoot about with your crippled mate in Hammersmith. I knew right then I'd got you where I wanted you."

"Yeah St John."

I take out the phone. I haven't examined that yet but I should guess it might have some pretty incriminating stuff on it.

"It's clean," he says, which makes me think that it's not.

"We'll see about that."

"I should have killed you where you sat on Swimming Pool Hill. You did too good a job of convincing me you were an ignorant squaddie."

"You were there?"

"Buzz buzz!" he says, miming applying electrodes.

"You ordered my death."

"Not me. That was Pratap, my man who does. My attitude was originally one of indifference. I'd thought you might be useful in clearing up a few little messes for us and then in clearing yourself up into prison. You got caught by our men and the sudden possibility that you were going to add to our problems rather than solve them came to mind. I ordered you brought back here so I didn't have to bother myself travelling in this shitty country to see you. I was actually all for letting you go once we'd established that you thought this was all about heroin. I wanted you to kill a few of the

344

Priand killers — it would have been an elegant solution — but if that failed, I was willing to go for an ugly one.

Is he trying to rile me? Yes. There's a desk between us and maybe he thinks his best chance is if I come round and hit him. It'll close the distance and he can get the gun. Stay focused.

"You didn't order the Priand massacre?"

"Of course I did. But at the moment Brad and his crew of Neanderthals finished shooting, they became a problem to me. As did your friend Ben, who so unfortunately stumbled across the killing."

I digest this information, trying to fight down my temper. Why would he tell me he'd killed Ben, why would he reveal he'd seen me tortured, maybe even taken part in it himself? Why would he tell me he's been playing me for a mug? Someone like Cadwell calculates his every move. Is he trying to convince me he's goading me into killing him because he has nothing left to live for if the information I have on him comes out? The logic is that I'll let him live to suffer it.

It's actually a tempting way of looking at things. He's clearly read my file, knows how I think. Or does he think that whatever is on the memory stick is so incriminating he may as well get it all off his chest now?

I come round the desk towards him pointing the gun at the centre of his chest. I think I am going to kill him. He swallows deeply.

"Of course, once you broke free without us having the chance to complete our interrogation, you were a marked man. That's why I ordered Beccy to kill you."

345

Should I kill him? Yes, he will probably walk free even if I have got evidence on him. Also, I'll never make it out of the country with him alive. I could drag him up to Swimming Pool Hill and leave him manacled there. I could . . .

There's the sound of keys in the doorway. The crafty bastard has triggered a silent alarm, hasn't he? Where was that?

"Inside the safe," he says, reading my thoughts. "Over to you," he says, with a shit-eating grin on his face that immediately suggests the only possible course of action.

I chin him, properly, give him a right hook using the butt of the pistol. It's a good shot, right from the boots. I hear his teeth crack. I meant that one. He goes straight down, flat out but I pick him back up again and lift his car keys. I've got the Stechkin in my pocket and I'm pulling him to his feet as best I can with my beat-up arm when the guards come into the room. There's two of them, some sort of emergency response team armed with pistols, though one has the weirdly shaped FNP90 submachine gun. A generation ago that sort of thing wouldn't go through body armour like I'm wearing. Tough luck for me he's got the latest model.

"He's having some sort of stroke," I say, "get him downstairs, I've called the ambulance."

I'm in Bulwark uniform, I'm exuding authority, they believe what I say and start to help me down the stairs. My ploy works. For about five seconds.

"Who are you?" says the one nearest to me.

"Michael Neumann," I say.

"You're not Michael!"

He goes to take his pistol out from his belt holster. I get my hand on to it to stop him and nut him. He wobbles a bit so I hip-throw him down the stairs into his mate who has just discovered the limitations of the SMG as a weapon when you're fighting in a space the size of a phone box, not to mention when your boss is spark out on the stairs behind the geezer you want to shoot.

The two crash into each other and for a breath I think about double-tapping them with the silenced gun. But I'm not a murderer. These guys are security men, not killers. I just level the pistol at them and they put their hands up. No choice, I pistol-whip both of them, knocking them cold, grab their weapons and head out into the street.

Five other guards are coming.

"In there, in there! Red Three down! Red Three down!" I shout and they stream past me. Cadwell's car is at the side of the building, a heavily armoured SUV. I open it up and get in, closing the doors as the first rounds spark off the side of the vehicle.

Fantastic, the fuel light's on. Twelve kilometres to empty, says the LED readout. I have a feeling that might be less at the speed I'm about to drive. It's almost exactly twelve clicks to the airport, so this one's going to be tight. The car's facing the wrong way so I slam it into reverse and L-turn it on the handbrake. Then it's into first and I'm banging towards the roadblock. The main roadblock is an arrangement of concrete barriers that make it impossible to get any

347

speed up approaching it the other way. From this side it's nothing more formidable than an old-fashioned railway crossing.

Two Bulwark guys with SMGs are in front of me. It's bulletproof glass and three rounds impact on it, starring the glass without penetrating. This car does 55 mph flat out so it's going to be interesting if they get mobile.

I hit the barrier hard and the whole car wobbles with the impact, knocking a good 20 mph off my speed but I'm through. It's designed to stop suicide bombers approaching the other way and the concrete bollards aren't really more than a chicane I have to weave through to get out.

Then I'm on the main A1 going the wrong way, back into town. I look in my mirror. Two Hummers and an armoured Land Rover. Luckily they don't have turrets or .50 cals or I'd be a dead man.

Given the size of our vehicles this isn't exactly going to be the fastest chase in history. I let them catch me, slowing to 30 mph. Then, fingers crossed, I handbrake turn it again. The SUV comes close to rolling but stays upright. The guy in the Land Rover tries to follow suit but he's going much quicker and just rolls it, the traffic careering around him.

"Careful, that's a British icon," I say as I look into the mirror. The other two are getting their act together and I can see the Hummers making big clumsy loops to get on my tail. Blue lights are flashing ahead and it's clear the police have been called in on the act. I open the glove box. There's a Sig Sauer P226 Blackwater Tactical pistol in there — twenty rounds. Add that to my Glock and I've got about forty. The silenced pistol isn't going to be any good in this sort of encounter.

There's also, interestingly, a spare button in the footwell, covered by a guard. I know what that is. Cadwell went on about hating 14 Company but he clearly doesn't mind borrowing some of its tricks. That's a flashbang trigger. There'll be a grenade dispenser at the back of the car designed for dispersing crowds or escaping roadblocks.

The Hummers are closing in on me. Luckily they can't shoot here because it's so built up and there are so many other cars on the road but that'll change soon.

My phone rings. I answer.

"Nick, what's wrong? We can hear firing." It's Beccy.

"It's all gone pear-shaped. I'm coming down the airport road but I'm not going to make it. I'm nearly out of gas."

Already the fuel gauge is down to eight kilometres from twelve and I haven't even gone two.

"We're coming to get you."

"Don't, get on the plane."

"What car are you in?"

"I'm not telling you."

The phone goes dead.

The Afghan police have got a couple of cars across the road but I swerve around them. As I pass I flick the guard off the pedal and press the button and momentarily look down to avoid catching the flash in the mirror.

I hear the bangs and look to see that one of the Humvees must have been temporarily blinded. He's gone straight into an ANP Toyota, nearly cutting it in two. The car in front is a Toyota. And underneath and behind in this case.

There's still one Hummer behind me.

The fuel light is winking like it's having a fit and I can see one kilometre come up on the "miles remaining" gauge. Well, game's up now so I might as well end it in control. Hoodies on council estates decamp every day and get away with it, so I don't see why I shouldn't. Except no one's shooting at the hoodies with military-issue SMGs. I let the Hummer get close. Then I press the switch to wind down my window, fire off the remaining flashbangs and put the car into a spin, bringing it about to face the Hummer. I always used to think it hilarious that Americans had to have "objects in the mirror are closer than they appear" written on their mirrors in cars but I wish I'd paid attention now.

The Hummer's right on top of me and goes crashing into the side of my car, pushing me down the street. I'm sitting no more than eight feet from its driver and I can see the passenger is leaning out of the window with a 416. I don't want to kill any of these boys even in self-defence and I'm not going to shoot him. I quickly get the window back up and dive flat on the seat while I press the switch.

Rounds go zinging through the interior of the car and then the glass stars up as it comes between me and the shooter. At this range it doesn't do a lot of good and a shower of glass lacerates the skin of my scalp.

350

I open the far door and jump across just as another burst comes in, smashing the glass on the far side. I'm on the opposite side of the car to the Hummer now but I can't make a run because I'll be a sitting target for matey boy with the SMG.

I put the pistol up over the bonnet and fire a few half-arsed shots over it at the ground just to discourage any heroes who want to come storming around the side. Then I put the gun to the floor and loose off a couple of rounds beneath the car, in case someone fancies doing it that way. Oh no, I'm hit, there's a big bloom of red on my shoulder and it feels like it's vibrating though there's no pain yet. No time to think about that. How the hell am I going to get out of here?

The ANP are arriving but they don't know what's happening either and I can hear their sirens stop a good fifty yards away. I don't know what they think would happen if I had an assault rifle. That said, bravery does seem to run in the Afghan blood.

I realise what's about to happen just a second before it happens. I scramble into the back of the SUV and lie flat on the floor behind as many structural pillars of the car, as much body armour, as I can. The Hummer boys have withdrawn, haven't they? The ANP and the Bulwark bunch open up on the car. The bodywork rattles and spits as the rounds come in. I duck down, hoping that, if a round does get through, it'll hit the Kevlar of my helmet, not the flesh and bone of the rest of me.

There's a series of soft pneumatic noises behind me, popping sounds and then a huge screech. I look up.

The Mowag is alongside me. Someone's at the wheel in a respirator, someone else at the open door dressed the same. Suddenly I can't see a thing. They've let off a serious amount of tear gas and I'm choking and retching. I feel hands on me, pulling me out of the car. I'm bundled into another vehicle and there's a sickening turn as it does a J-turn in reverse and hammers it out of there.

"It's a mile to the Dutch. Just a mile." It's Beccy's voice. She throws water in my face, gives me a cloth to wipe away the irritant from my eyes.

I can't see her but she says: "Keep still, I'm going to get some morphine into you."

"No! Not that!" I say. I need to keep my wits about me. I feel her hands on my shoulder, she's applying pressure on the wound. I'm coughing still, my nose and eyes streaming. Then I feel a jab. She's stuck me anyway. I'm suddenly floating away. I hear Dutch voices, I think of tulips, clogs, silly hats, that stag weekend in Amsterdam and then nothing.

When I regain my vision I'm in a large hangar with a helicopter in it.

"Welcome to Holland," says a voice.

CHAPTER
THIRTY-TWO

It's an hour before our flight. The Dutch guys are great. I don't have a passport and neither does Dave or Beccy but they're flying us to a military base in Amsterdam and say we can sort things out there.

Also, as this is a military flight too, they've sealed the perimeter of the airfield. No one's getting in while it's taking off and there's three eight-wheeled Boxers touring the wire.

No one's getting in here, least of all the ANP. It's not unknown for terrorists to work undercover in the Afghan police.

But where are the British military?

"We don't need to let them in," says the Dutch colonel, "this is our compound. Under international law we don't have to surrender you without an extradition warrant. And besides, Nick, there's an arrest warrant for you from back home."

"What for?"

"Stealing a car. An Audi TT. A John Kent from the Serious Organised Crime Agency sent it over. We have to hand you into their jurisdiction unless someone comes up with better paperwork in the next half an hour."

John — he's come through for me again.

"How about Dave and Beccy?"

"Names haven't been mentioned to me."

"Pamir?"

"Not so good."

"That's bad. He was a great bloke."

"Yes. But that allows us to hold your friends as witnesses if things get sticky. He died on Dutch soil."

He's going the extra mile for me. I have to wonder why.

"Why are you helping me like this?"

"I did some background on you when I found you at the prison. You're a former Royal Anglian?"

"That's right."

"We did a parachute jump on exercise at night about eight years ago and ended up in a canal. Two guys with me died but the Royal Anglian boys fished me out. I said I owed them."

Cadwell could be making phone calls to get me out of there but he knows I have his memory stick. We put it into the computer. It needs a password but I guess that it won't take John too long to get round that. If I was Cadwell I'd be using whatever dodgy contacts I had to get somewhere without an extradition treaty with the UK. North Korea's nice at this time of the year.

The medic sees to my arm. It's a bit rubbish and might require an operation but there's a doctor on the flight and he's happy for me to travel. I'll need a drip, antibiotics and I'll be self-prescribing a couple of stiff whiskies.

It's odd to be in the Dutch offices. It's like some sort of sanity again. Everyone's calm and nice and they fetch you coffee and give you cakes. Haven't tasted them in a while.

The hour seems to take for ever. I go up to the top of the building. It's only four storeys high but I get a good view. Shit, there are Bulwark vehicles at the gate — a lot of them. I count eight at least — Hummers and Eagles with a couple of Land Rovers. Two more Boxers have been rolled out to meet them and there's an almighty row going on. I can see Cadwell from where I am. He's holding his jaw, so I'm guessing I broke it. He's not letting it stop him argue, though. I'm going to do him, murder his reputation, send him to prison, and he needs to stop me getting on that plane.

He's got a bit more to worry about than that, as he well knows.

Beccy comes up to my side. "Don't worry, they won't let them through. They have orders not to."

"Are you sure?"

In my mind I can see phone calls to England, prime ministerial requests to the Netherlands, orders to hand us over.

"I'm sure. We're due on the plane in ten minutes."

I watch as Cadwell gets into a Land Rover and drives away. Good riddance.

I spend the time just holding her hand and looking out of the window. The mountains are beautiful, snow on the peaks, the afternoon sky a wonderful blue, with just a hint of smoke haze in the air. It's calm and lovely and I find myself thinking some stupid thoughts about wishing people didn't have to mess it up. I shelve them. I'm no good at deep stuff and, let's face it, people do bad things so there's no point wishing they didn't. You have to do something about it.

I won't be sorry to say goodbye to Afghanistan and I'm dying to see Chloe again. I'm not going to call her to say I'm OK until I get to Amsterdam. It's superstitious of me but we all have them.

For that reason I'm not going to think about the future with Beccy until I get there either. Do I love her? Yeah. Next question. Something about rugby, please.

"Nick, Beccy."

It's the Dutch commando colonel.

"Time to go."

We go down the stairs.

Dave is having a fag outside and walks with us as we cross the tarmac. I'm next to Beccy. We're all looking up at the plane, desperate to get away.

"Do they do beer on these flights?" Dave wonders.

"It's the Netherlands — they probably chuck in a spliff and a pancake halfway through," says Beccy.

Out of the corner of my eye I see one of the Boxers trundling around the perimeter. What towards? Shit, there's a Honda Prelude of all cars, parked up just behind the fence. I see the flash of the gun and hit the floor.

"Get down!" but Beccy's too slow reacting. The bullet takes her in the temple and she hits the ground hard. Then I'm running, I don't know why, but I'm charging the wire, unarmed, mad with rage. I see the long shape of a sniper rifle heaved to the ground as the shooter jumps into the car. I should have put the Armalite beyond use. Concentrating too much on revenge, not enough on cool thinking. The Prelude spins around and guns it out of there, leaving the lumbering Boxer way behind.

"Shoot him, shoot him!" I'm screaming.

But the Boxer just stops to look at the rifle.

I go back to Beccy. She's dead on the tarmac. She's been hit in the head and it's a mess. I check her pulse and shout for a medic but I've seen enough dead people to recognise another one. I rerun the scene in my head. I ducked. That bullet was meant for me. It should be me who's dead, not her.

Now the Dutch are everywhere. A couple of saloons race into town after the Prelude. They won't catch it. He'll be back on embassy land in ten minutes, less if he floors it.

I squeeze Beccy's hand but a commando is screaming at me. I'm looking at him. I can hear what he's saying and he's speaking perfect English but I can't understand what he's saying.

"Get on the plane, Nick, they want it out of here, not sitting on the runway while people are shooting."

Dave's pulling at my arm, dragging me up the steps. Then I'm on the plane, the doors are closed and we're taxiing, faster than I've ever taxied before.

We turn to the runway, the engines engage and the plane powers forward. Afghanistan is disappearing below me like a bad dream.

There's a bleep in my pocket. I haven't even turned off Cadwell's phone.

It's a hidden number.

I answer.

"Keep quiet or your kid gets the same."

I want to shout at him, to tell him to fuck himself, to call him a murdering bastard. But I don't. I just keep silent because I know two things. One is that I hit Cadwell hard enough to break his jaw. The second is that that's going to leave him with a pretty sore head so he'll need painkillers. When he goes back to get whatever he needs to get to wherever he's going he'll want to take them with him — he can hardly take his opium on the plane. I know where he keeps the ibuprofen because I saw them in his flat. I also know that, when he opens the bathroom cabinet, he's never going to have to worry about having a headache ever again.

CHAPTER
THIRTY-THREE

The Chinese delegation is escorted into the foyer of 30 St Mary Axe. This is the address of Norman Foster's triumph of glass and steel more commonly known as the Gherkin, owing to the shape it cuts in the London skyline with its forty floors. They're impressed by the structure, as they are meant to be. Bulwark wants its clients to be impressed, awed and intimidated by them, and the Gherkin certainly helps with that.

The Chinese note that it's different to Beijing, for sure. The business people are scruffier, many of them don't wear ties and their manner isn't always serious. Some are laughing and joking. Still, who cares about London? The business world is moving east and this place is just an outpost of the new empire of Chinese money, and can be bought and sold.

The young woman who leads them from their limousine is far from scruffy. She is tall, exotically so to the Chinese, and immaculately dressed in a Chanel suit. Again, she is designed to impress.

She chats to them in good Mandarin and asks them if they had a pleasant trip. They did. First-Class Virgin goes out of its way to take care of its passengers.

They go up in the lift to the thirty-fourth floor. Then they take what their guide describes as the "exclusive, prestige lift" to the thirty-ninth. That's as far as the lifts go. From there it's a marble staircase to the restaurant and bar. The effort of these last steps was thought worth it by the architect. He didn't want an ugly lift-winding room spoiling the lines of his cathedral to money on the top floor.

Very few people have the cash or the connections to hire the whole top floor for an evening but Sir John is one of them. He was once asked whether he considered himself old money or new money. It was a good question. His knighthood was hereditary, bestowed just after the Norman Conquest, but his family business was in poor shape by the time he inherited it at twenty-three years of age. Forty years later, it's the richest conglomerate on the planet, taking in defence contracting, arms contracting, mining, TV stations, newspapers and a good spread of green initiatives that it trumpets in its annual report. So Sir John's reply was revealing.

"Just money." He is not a man for small talk.

He greets them at the top of the stairs. He's an imposing figure, six foot three, tanned and white-haired, his body trim not from the gym but from his hobby of racing yachts. It's no accident he's met his guests in this way. Very little Sir John does is by accident. He is not only very bright — he's at least as well qualified as his top engineers — but he's shrewd, too.

The Chinese businessmen are short; he is tall. Coming up the stairs, he appears to them like a giant. So this is a little pantomime of dominance, his way of taking the upper hand.

But Sir John knows that a pantomime is all this is. The big guys, the boss men, the boys whose ball it is and who can take it home, are the ones who are coming up the stairs, not the one standing at the top.

He leads them out into the huge glass atrium, which extends in a shape somewhere between a cone and a dome twenty metres above them. London lies out around them, as if it's theirs to command.

They sit at the virgin white cloths — the four Chinese men side on, Sir John with his back to the window. Now they can't look at London without seeing him. Dry champagne is served, two-hundred-year-old from the house of Juglar — one of seventy bottles rescued from a Finnish shipwreck. In case the businessmen should mistake the anchor on the bottle for something as cheap as Veuve Clicquot, the wine waiter explains in Mandarin just how rare the drink is and that it is Sir John's favourite.

A toast is made to success and Sir John speaks. His voice is cultured and could be mistaken for lazy if it were not for the contrast with his eyes, which miss nothing.

"Thank you for coming here, gentlemen. It really does please me to be able to offer you this opportunity."

The businessmen thank him for inviting him. One of the businessmen speaks, and in good English. This is

Mr Zhang Yonghong, one of the most successful capitalists in the new China. His given name is a little ironic — it means "Forever Red".

He talks about his daughter and how she is Grade 8 violin at only ten years old. He speaks of his son, who he feels sure is ready to represent the People's Republic at skiing. He asks Sir John if Bentley can be regarded as a truly prestige automobile now that so many footballers drive them. He speaks about his plan to buy a major English Premier League club and asks Sir John if he knows much about rugby. The game fascinates him and he would like to become involved.

Dinner is served and pudding is on the table but still the conversation has not turned to business. In the end, Sir John feels he must come to the matter in hand.

"You received the prospectus we sent you on Afghanistan." It's a statement, not a question.

"Oh yes."

"And what did you think?"

"The situation on the ground is unstable," says Mr Zhang.

"Not so," says Sir John, "our relationships with the newly installed tribal leaders are first-class. They're on the payroll."

"Sir John, Sir John," says Mr Zhang, "do you think you are the only one with links to the intelligence community? We Chinese were spying on each other when you were still running around in animal skins."

Sir John suppresses the urge to note that Mrs Zhang seems to have quite a thing for animal skins, and rare ones too, but he says nothing.

Mr Zhang continues. "You have difficulty over there. It started with the death of your military intelligence man, Mr Cadwell. The one killed in the explosion in his apartment."

"Cadwell wasn't anything to do with us. We have other good men on the ground."

"Not so. Mr Cadwell was directly in your pay. And you have a surprise coming. There are documents that have been obtained by Military Intelligence. Your company's role is exposed. For you, everything has . . ." He fumbles for words and turns to the tall blonde woman who has been standing at a discreet distance throughout the meal. She comes forward and he speaks to her in Mandarin. She whispers in his ear.

"Gone to shit," says Mr Zhang.

"That is being handled. The people responsible for all that have been sacked and we will support their prosecutions, should the evidence prove conclusive, which is far from certain."

"Sir John, do you think I've been in business this long without recognising a bad deal when I see one?"

For the first time Sir John looks angry. "You were keen enough to get in on the action, I think. Your men made repeated approaches to people from whom we had obtained cast-iron commitments. Not on."

Now Mr Zhang's expression changes. "Nor was it on to leave those people fertilising the poppies. In about four hours' time a major offensive will take place in that area to, let us say, clarify the political situation on the ground. I have good contacts throughout the world and my friends in the US and British governments have accepted my case for urgent military action in that province. There is urgent need, no doubt. The lot you installed were worse than the Red Guard. You have nothing to sell, your firm is likely to be fined and its executives imprisoned. I have no doubt you will escape but I do not do business with people like that."

"So you had no intention of striking a deal?"

"None at all."

"So why did you come here?"

"I wanted to see what you look like in the flesh. I hear a lot about you, Sir John, and some of it would make Old Mao blush."

"That was the only reason you came?"

"Oh no," says Mr Zhang, "not at all. I heard about the champagne! Cheers!"

And all the businessmen laugh.

When they are gone, Sir John sits watching the dark fall, the lights of London spread out before him like a carpet of jewels. How did this all go wrong? Already the investigation has begun. He has no idea what caused the collapse of his Afghan operation but he is in the process of finding out and, when he does, heads will roll. Literally.

On the yacht off the Isle of Wight, Nick trims the sail and watches his daughter as she watches the sunset. Chloe is ten, funny and cheeky, just like she should be. For a second the wind catches the sail and Nick loses sight of her. The shining water flashes into view, the blood-red path that stretches to the sun. It makes him put his hand to his forehead to shield his eyes from the glare. Then the sail moves and Chloe comes back in to view.

"Can we have tea now, Dad? I'm getting cold."

"Sure, we're only ten minutes from land, how about you wait and we'll get chips on the island?"

"Great."

Nick lets the sail take the wind and the boat glides forward towards the dying sun.

Postscript

Use of private security contractors in Afghanistan has tripled since June 2009. Today there are roughly 30,000 staff working for 52 private companies in the country.

A congressional report into the activities of private security staff found rampant abuses. In one district alone researchers found that contractors delivering supplies to coalition bases had killed more than 30 innocent civilians between 2006 and 2009.

US military officials complain that efforts to create local support are consistently undermined by security contractors protecting NATO convoys who "regularly fire wildly into villages as they pass".

A Pentagon report estimates Afghanistan's mineral wealth, including Lithium, Gold, Mercury and Copper at $1 trillion.

Analysts fear:

- Mineral riches will worsen the war, inspiring the Taliban to push harder to gain territory.
- Endemic corruption means the find will benefit the country's oligarchs rather than ordinary Afghans. In 2009 Afghanistan's former minister of mines was

accused by American officials of accepting a $30 million bribe to award China the rights to develop its copper mine.

- Insecurity will make it impossible to fully exploit the resources-the mineral deposits are scattered throughout the country, including in the southern and eastern border regions, scene of some of the most intense combat of the war.
- The wealth will create conflict between central government and the provinces.
- With virtually no mining industry, infrastructure or environmental standards in place, it will take decades for Afghanistan to reap any rewards from the find.

Coalition forces are due to pull out of Afghanistan in 2014. The contractors — working for companies charged with developing Afghanistan's wealth — will remain.

Also available in ISIS Large Print:

Blitz

Ken Bruen

Detective Sergeant Brant is tough and uncompromising, as sleazy and ruthless as the villains he's out to get. His violent methods may be questionable, but he always gets results.

A psychopath has started a killing spree across London. Calling himsel "The Blitz", his weapon of choice is a workman's hammer. And his victims are all cops.

The police squad are desperate to catch the killer before he catches up with them. And Brant is top of his list . . .

ISBN 978-0-7531-8916-0 (hb)
ISBN 978-0-7531-8917-7 (pb)

Last Chance to Die

Noah Boyd

Forget life and death: this is a matter of international security. And Steve Vail is running out of time.

A Russian agent makes an offer the FBI can't refuse. He can identify traitors leaking government intelligence. All he wants is $250,000 a head, in cash. Assistant Director Kate Bannon needs former agent Vail to hunt down the leads. He's been fired twice, and considered out for good. But then the informant vanishes. The Russians have him, and once they get the names, they will show no mercy. Reaching the targets first will push Vail to breaking point. And once he finds them, it's going to get downright deadly . . .

ISBN 978-0-7531-8970-2 (hb)
ISBN 978-0-7531-8971-9 (pb)